What was Simon doing here?

Amanda's stomach tightened. There was no way Simon would fly this far to see her after the way they'd last parted. She'd almost convinced herself that she was mistaken—that it wasn't him standing over there. She'd even managed to quiet the instinctive, involuntary response that took over her body every time she'd seen him in the past ten years.

Then the man turned. It *was* him. His bright green eyes met hers as he scanned the crowd.

Amanda wanted to look away, but she was caught. He was the one person in the whole world guaranteed to make the soul-crushing pain she felt even worse.

He stopped a couple feet in front of her, reached a hand out to stroke her cheek. "Oh, sweetheart, look at you."

She stiffened. "What are you doing here?"

"I'm here to take you home."

"I'd rather take on an entire shiver of sharks than spend one second in your company."

"Well, then, I guess we're both in for a bumpy ride—because this time you aren't getting rid of me."

Dear Reader,

Every once in a while, an author gets the chance to write the book of her heart. For me, *From the Beginning* is that book. It's an idea that I've had for over four years, one that I had hoped would be my second Everlasting Love novel, and one I'm thrilled to finally be bringing to you as a Harlequin Superromance.

Early in my writing career, Amanda Jacobs took up residence in my head, and no matter what I did, she wouldn't leave. She was smart and sarcastic, strong and selfless, and she kept talking to me. So when my fabulous editor gave me the go-ahead to write this book, I was thrilled. Not much compares to telling the story of a character you've lived with for so long, and one you admire as much as I do Amanda.

Now, being me, I had to take Amanda on an emotional roller coaster. I tested her limits and wrenched every ounce of emotion from her. In doing so, I think I made her a better character and firmly believe I made myself a better writer. I hope you agree.

I love, particularly, that this book is coming out at the end of winter, just when things here in Texas, where I live, are starting to come back to life. Starting to bloom, as that rebirth is so important to both Amanda and Simon in this novel.

Thanks so much for giving *From the Beginning* a try. I hope you enjoy reading it as much as I enjoyed writing it. I love hearing from my readers, either at my email, tracy@tracywolff.blogspot.com, or at my blog, www.tracywolff.blogspot.com. If you get the chance, please stop by and say hello!

Happy reading!

Tracy Wolff

From the Beginning
Tracy Wolff

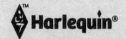

TORONTO NEW YORK LONDON
AMSTERDAM PARIS SYDNEY HAMBURG
STOCKHOLM ATHENS TOKYO MILAN MADRID
PRAGUE WARSAW BUDAPEST AUCKLAND

Recycling programs
for this product may
not exist in your area.

ISBN-13: 978-0-373-71760-6

FROM THE BEGINNING

ABOUT THE AUTHOR

Tracy Wolff collects books, English degrees and lipsticks, and has been known to forget where—and sometimes who—she is when immersed in a great novel. At six she wrote her first short story—something with a rainbow and a prince—and at seven she ventured into the wonderful world of girls' lit with her first Judy Blume novel. By ten she'd read everything in the young adult and classics sections of her local bookstore, so in desperation her mom started her on romance novels. And from the first page of the first book, Tracy knew she'd found her life-long love. Tracy lives in Texas with her husband and three sons, where she pens romance novels and teaches writing at her local community college.

Books by Tracy Wolff

HARLEQUIN SUPERROMANCE

1529—A CHRISTMAS WEDDING
1568—FROM FRIEND TO FATHER
1607—THE CHRISTMAS PRESENT
1649—BEGINNING WITH THEIR BABY
1676—UNGUARDED
1703—DESERVING OF LUKE

Other titles by this author available in ebook format

To Beverly Sotolov and Wanda Ottewell,
for giving me a chance to tell this story and
for making me a writer worthy of telling it

Acknowledgments:

As always, to my amazing agent,
Emily Sylvan Kim, who is as fabulous a person as
she is an agent. Thanks for always being there.

To Wanda Ottewell, who is never afraid to tell me
when I've gone too far—or not far enough. Having
you as an editor has made me a better writer.

And to my three boys, who put up with a
not-so-great summer as I was writing this book.
Thanks for understanding and for being such
amazing people. I love you very much.

CHAPTER ONE

Somalia, 2011

HE WAS GOING TO DIE and there was nothing she could do to stop it.

Five presses, one breath.

Even knowing that it was over, she continued the chest compressions on his frail and bloated body.

Five presses, one breath.

All around her the nurses shook their heads, their expressions sad but accepting.

Five presses, one breath.

His mother looked on with hopeless eyes.

Five presses, one breath.

Outside, the howling wind stopped as if the very desert itself was holding its breath as it sensed him slipping away.

Five presses, one breath.

But she couldn't let him go. His eyes had implored her when he first came into the clinic so many hours ago. She couldn't just let him die of the ache in his belly. Not when everything inside her raged at the unfairness of allowing a six-year-old child to slip away, when all of her training taught her to fight harder and longer. After all, malnutrition could be countered, as could starvation and most of the diseases found here.

But it was too late for Mabulu. Too late for high-protein drinks from the States, too late for peanut-butter sandwiches or fresh bananas. Too late for the vitamins and shots that could so easily have saved him a few weeks before.

Sometimes it felt as if everything she did in this god-forsaken country was too little, too late.

Five presses, one breath.

It was time to stop. Her intellect knew it, but her heart was already so cracked that she feared one more loss might shatter it forever. So she continued pressing down on his small chest, long past the time her medical experience told her to stop.

Sweat ran down her face, and her arms trembled from the strain.

Five presses, one breath.

Tears blurred her eyes—an appalling lack of professionalism she could do nothing about.

Hundreds of thousands of deaths she could do nothing about.

She railed at the unfairness of it, at the complete and utter hopelessness of this battle she had been fighting for eleven years now. What good was a medical degree if she couldn't save *anyone?*

Five presses, one breath.

"Time of death—11:42 a.m." The deep voice boomed across the impromptu operating room, and Amanda Jacobs glanced up, startled, into the face of Jack Alexander—head doctor of this particular clinic and a close personal friend since they'd done their first year of medical school together fifteen years before.

"He's my patient," she said, continuing CPR. "I say when he's dead."

"How long has he been down?"

She bit her lip, knowing that the answer would damn Mabulu—and herself. "Twenty-seven minutes."

Jack's eyes cut to hers, narrowed in disbelief. "Stop the CPR—*now,*" he roared when she ignored him.

Her hands trembled and her shoulders slumped as she slowly let her arms drop away from her patient. He had been a beautiful little boy, even with his belly bloated and his bones all but sticking through his skin. His eyes had been bright, inquisitive, and his ongoing stoicism made her own sudden emotional instability even more humiliating.

Sobs choked her and she could barely stop the scalding tears from falling.

"Call it," Jack ordered.

Her gaze met his. "You already—"

"Call it." His voice was implacable, his look compassionate as he stared her down. "As you said, he was your patient."

She glanced at the clock, then cleared away the lump in her throat. "Time of death—11:44." Her breath hitched and she felt—actually felt—her heart break wide open. She'd been right. Mabulu's death had been one too many, Somalia one country too many in a list so long she'd learned years ago to stop counting.

"I want to speak with you in my office," Jack said, his voice uncompromising.

"My patient—" Their eyes locked in a battle of wills she didn't have the strength to win—at least not today.

"Nola will take care of him." He nodded toward the head nurse, then turned, without waiting to see if Amanda would follow, confident of his power and leadership even here, in this hospital composed of a series of olive-green tents and overstressed generators in the middle of the desert.

Amanda followed slowly, trying to steady herself for the confrontation she knew was coming. Her behavior was growing more and more erratic, her inability to let Mabulu go just the latest in a series of bad judgment calls. She was exhausted, overemotional, burned out. She knew the symptoms well, had witnessed them in others time and again in the past decade.

She'd simply never expected it to happen to her. Then again, she could say that about so many of the things in her life lately.

"What exactly *was* that?" Jack asked, closing the curtain on his makeshift office.

Her spine stiffened at his strident tone. "That was me trying to save my patient's life."

"That was you completely out of control, Amanda, and we both know it."

"That's not true," she protested, but her voice wasn't as solid as she would have liked.

"Yes, it is. I've worked with you off and on for fifteen years and I've never seen anything like that from you."

"It was a rough one." She tried—and failed—to shrug off the incident. "I'll be okay."

He studied her, and she knew his blue eyes were

taking in the strain around her mouth and the cloudiness of her usually clear gray eyes. Telltale signs she'd noticed herself. "I'm not so sure about that."

She stiffened. "What's that supposed to mean?"

Sighing, he gestured to one of the two chairs in the room. "Sit down, Mandy."

"Are you firing me, Jack?" If so, she would prefer to stand.

"Of course not," he snorted. "You know more about practicing medicine in these conditions than most of my staff put together. But I do want to examine you." He put his stethoscope in his ears and motioned her to sit.

"Absolutely not!"

"I'm not arguing with you about this. Before you go back on duty, I'm going to make damn sure you're all right."

She started to protest more vehemently, to tell him her health was none of his business. But she had enough self-preservation to realize that doing so would only reinforce his beliefs about her fitness for the job.

Plus, for the first time in her life, she just couldn't summon up the effort to fight.

"I told you I'm fine," she said as she sank into the chair reluctantly, but she could hear the shakiness in her voice.

"Which is obviously a falsehood." He put the stethoscope to her chest. "Take a deep breath."

"Jack—"

"Do it."

Amanda sucked in air as loudly as possible, before letting it out slowly. "I'm just tired. We all are."

"But we're not all in tears when one of our patients dies."

"Sometimes it gets to me. You know what it's like."

He reached for her wrist to check her pulse. "Sometimes it does," he agreed. "But *this* isn't you, Mandy. Tired or not."

"Well, who is it, then?" She laughed bitterly. "Please, tell me. If this isn't my life, whose hellish existence is it? Believe me, I'd love to give it back to her."

Jack didn't respond and she regretted the words as soon as they were spoken. "I didn't mean that the way it sounded."

"I think you did." He checked her reflexes and she took a childish delight at the involuntary kick that landed in the middle of his shin. "You need a break."

"Not now."

"Yes, *now*. You've been going hell-for-leather for eighteen months straight—more if you count everything that happened before you came back here. Is it any wonder that you're burned out? You need to get away from here for a while and remember that there's more to life than suffering."

"I can't." She stood and walked over to the crude window near his desk. "We're understaffed as it is."

"We'll manage. We always do."

"I'm overtired. A couple of nights' sleep and I'll be fine."

His smile was sad. "Not this time. You need to step back for a while, go home, live a normal life for at least a year."

"A *year?*" She whirled to face him. "You can't be serious."

"I'm very serious. You're the best doctor I've got, one of the best I've ever worked with, but even you can't keep going at this pace indefinitely. You're strung out, stressed-out and you're going to make yourself sick."

He paused, stared at her for a long minute as if debating with himself. Finally he quietly commented, "You can't hide from what happened to Gabrielle, Amanda. And you can't bring her back."

The words hit her like an out-of-control freight train, had her fists clenching and her blood pounding even as they flattened her completely. "You think I don't know that?" she demanded, unable to look at him. "You think I don't wake up every morning, wishing that my daughter was alive?"

"I think you do." His tone was compassionate, his voice matter-of-fact. "Which is part of the problem. It's been a year and a half, and you haven't even begun to deal with what happened."

"I deal with it every day."

"No, you *hide* from it every day. Here, and in Uganda. In Mozambique. You've been running from the truth since the funeral, and all it's gotten you is one step away from a nervous breakdown."

"Is that your professional opinion, *Doctor?*" She sounded like a sulky four-year-old, but couldn't help herself. If he kept pushing, the emptiness yawning inside of her would completely overwhelm her.

"It is." He sighed, then reached out to cover her hand with his. "I know what I'm asking of you, Amanda."

Her laugh was bitter. "You couldn't possibly know, Jack. If you did, you wouldn't have the nerve to ask."

He squeezed her hand, letting the silence build until her eyes—once again—met his. "You can't save her. No matter how many children you help, no matter how much you punish yourself, you still can't bring her back."

"It's my job to save these children." She yanked her hand away, then ran it carelessly through her short, dark hair. Her fingers snagged in one of the many curls, but she barely felt the pain. These days, she rarely allowed herself to feel anything at all. "They became my responsibility the day I signed up to come here."

"I know." His voice was soothing.

"This has nothing to do with Gabrielle," she insisted. But her voice broke and Amanda rubbed the heels of her hands over her eyes as the tears began to flow. "It's about there never being enough. Enough food, enough medicine, enough doctors. Enough time. Nowhere on this whole damned continent is there enough of anything."

She gave a watery, sarcastic laugh, then corrected herself. "Except the bad stuff. There's plenty of that. Corruption. Famine, drought, poverty."

Glancing out the screened-in window, she watched a trio of vultures circle above the camp, impatient to get their claws into Mabulu's frail, bloated body. She wouldn't let that happen.

"And death. There's always enough death." Her voice cracked, and the sobs she'd been trying to hold in for months finally broke free.

"Oh, Mandy." Jack sighed, then pulled her into his oversize embrace. "That's it, honey. Have a good cry."

She tried to stop the meltdown—she really did—but

she was too exhausted, and her emotions overcame her iron will. A small part of her stood back, untouched, watching in horror as her professional demeanor crumbled like clay left too long in the vicious African sun.

This wasn't what they'd taught her in medical school. This wasn't who she was. The Amanda Jacobs she knew was cool, professional, in control at all times. That Amanda Jacobs had graduated top of her class at twenty-four, had worked eleven years in the world's battle zones with barely a grimace. She'd sat by her daughter's bedside, dry-eyed and composed, doing everything she could to comfort Gabrielle as she suffered a slow and painful death from cancer.

That Amanda hadn't shed so much as one tear at the funeral.

Where was that woman now? she wondered hysterically. She wanted her back. Living like this, her emotions an open, aching wound, was too hard.

Jack continued to rub her back soothingly as she sought to pull herself together. It took a few minutes, but when she'd finally managed it, he drew back and asked quietly, "Do you feel any better?"

Was he kidding? Her head throbbed, her eyes burned and her mouth felt as if something had crawled inside it and died. How could she possibly be feeling better when she'd never felt worse? But she nodded as she reached across his desk for a tissue. There was only so much humiliation a woman could stand in one day.

He watched silently as she wiped her face and blew her nose, struggling for the composure that was still a little out of reach. Finally he said, "You know I'm right.

If one of your patients came in like this, you'd tell her the same things I'm telling you."

"I can't, Jack."

"You mean, you won't. But this time, you don't have a choice. I run this place and I say you go."

She studied him with narrowed eyes for a minute, then shrugged even as unease crawled up her spine. "There are other clinics."

"And you won't get a job at any of them. Not with this organization or any other."

"You can't do that!"

"You'd be surprised what I can do." He took a deep breath, then let it out slowly. "You're on the edge, Amanda. No reputable clinic will take on a doctor who is so obviously going to blow. And I won't give you a recommendation—not right now."

"Why are you doing this?"

"Because I care about you." He ignored her snort of derision. "Because you've been here too long."

She folded her arms over her chest and glared at him accusingly. "You've been here as long as I have."

"Yes," he agreed. "But I know when to draw the line—for myself and others. You don't. You never have. It's what makes you such an incredible doctor, but it's also what brought you to this point. You're used up, Mandy."

The hell of it was that he was right. She knew it, had recognized the signs for a while now but had ignored them. Because to admit to them meant she'd have to go home. She'd have to face what she'd been running from since Gabrielle's pediatrician had delivered her death sentence.

She didn't know if she was strong enough to do it.

"Do I have a choice, Dr. Alexander?" Her voice was stilted, her hands ice-cold.

"Mandy." He sighed. "It doesn't have to be like this."

She eyed him steadily. "Oh, I think it does."

He stared at her for long moments, before shaking his head sadly. "Then no, you don't have a choice. The supply truck comes in four days. You can ride back to town with Josh and catch a flight from there."

CHAPTER TWO

"FOUR DAYS?" HER WORLD imploded, even as she told herself that there had to be a mistake. No way could Jack find someone to replace her on such short notice. "You expect me to be ready to leave Africa in *four* days?"

"Yes." His tone was implacable.

"That's not enough time."

"To pack one suitcase of clothes?"

"To deal with my patients. To find another—"

"The patients aren't your problem anymore—and neither is my staffing shortage. In fact, I'm taking you off rotation, effective immediately."

"Jack! You can't."

He crossed the room, scribbled something on the schedule that was always hanging by the door. "It's already done."

"Who will take care of my patients? You can't do everything—"

"That's no longer your problem."

It was as if he'd slapped her, her entire body recoiling with pain and betrayal. "We've been friends too long for you to treat me like this. How can you do it?"

"Because we are friends." He crossed the room and took her hand in his own, ignoring her sudden stiffness. "Because I want to work with you for another fifteen years, at least." He reached up and tucked a wayward strand of hair behind her left ear. "This isn't forever, kid. Only until you get yourself rested and back in fighting form. I can't hold the fort indefinitely, you know."

But that was exactly what she was afraid of—that he would have to hold the fort alone, forever. It was why she'd worked her way past exhaustion, beyond burnout. Because she feared if she ever left this place, she would never come back. Not just here, to Somalia, but Haiti or Cambodia. Bosnia or Sierra Leone. Chechnya, Afghanistan, Lebanon, Palestine. So many places. So much pain.

"Well, that's it, then." Anger and fear came through in her voice, despite her struggle to regain her professionalism. Amanda didn't mind if Jack saw her anger, but she would be humiliated if he knew how afraid she was to return to the easy, civilized life most people took for granted.

"For now. Go back to your room and lie down. Get some rest and I'll check on you later." He paused, shot her a guilty look. "Three days ago, I emailed—"

She didn't wait for him to finish. Didn't want to hear him admit that he'd ratted her out to the administrators of the program. Instead, she turned and left, walking briskly through the clinic, despite the calls of nurses and patients. They weren't her responsibility anymore.

The thought cut like a knife.

So, what happened now? she wondered, dazed. What on earth was she supposed to do?

It was crazy, really, how completely unprepared she was for life away from here. How could an intelligent woman of thirty-five be so frightened of living a normal life? And how was she supposed to get past the gut-clenching, palm-dampening fear?

She headed outside, toward the tents pitched to the left of the clinic. She'd lived in them for almost a year, never leaving this stretch of desert since she'd arrived, fresh from Mozambique, ten months before.

She'd run here, one more stop in the headlong flight that kept her from thinking about—

Amanda shut the thought down before it could form. She wasn't ready to go there yet. She wasn't strong enough to examine her feelings about Gabby. She'd buried them for one year, six months and twenty-three days. She could bury them for a few more days or weeks or months—whatever it took for her to feel strong enough to deal with them.

But even as she mentally repeated the too-familiar sentiment, she knew it was a lie. She would never be strong enough to accept Gabby's death. She'd failed her daughter, and that was not something she could get over.

Shaking again, Amanda paused for a moment and looked around the camp and surrounding desert that were as familiar to her as her own face. It was hot, the sun high in the sky as it roasted this part of East Africa. Drought and famine, AIDS and Ebola, tuberculosis and cholera, more diseases than she could count had taken their toll, year after year, until some weeks bodies actually piled up in the villages, waiting to be buried or burned.

But despite everything that had happened here in the past three decades, Africa was beautiful. The landscape was empty, barren, but there was an elegance in its stark simplicity. Endless miles of dirt and sand and desert brush as far as the eye could see, the sun reflecting brightly off the hard, arid ground. It appealed to something primitive inside of her, this country with its harsh truths and frightening realities.

There was beauty in its complete and utter devastation.

At a loss for what else to do—knowing only that she couldn't go back to her tent and stare at the four canvas walls without losing what was left of her control—she began to walk. Without her patients, without her job, it wasn't as if there was anything else to do out here but wander for a while, saying goodbye to this continent that had such a huge impact on her life. If things went as she was afraid they would, then it didn't matter what Jack said. She was done here.

She walked for a long time—through the village and beyond, oblivious to the heat that was so much a part of Somalia. It was harvest time for the meager crops that this poverty- and drought-stricken nation could produce, and the men were few. Between the wars, the famine and the harvest, the village was almost a ghost town during the day. Many of the children were in the fields with their mothers; the others were in the hospital or at the government-run school that was built on the east side of the village. It was here that they learned math and history and how to read and speak English—at least until they had to give up their education to help feed the family.

She shook her head. Somalia had so many languages. Somali and Arabic were the two main ones, but each village in the line sweeping through the nation's interior had a variation of its own. Her village, Massalu, spoke Chimbalazi, but most of the children who lived here were almost illiterate in the language of their parents. The language of their blood.

Her fatigue—a soul-deep weariness—caught up with her, and Amanda slumped onto a large rock. Her thinking rock. She'd used it so much in the past ten months that she could swear she'd worn a flat spot on it. Or maybe she wasn't the only one who came to this desolate stretch of land to brood. God knew, there was more than enough to think about...

The sound of a faraway engine caught her attention and she looked up in time to see a Learjet coming into view. She watched it for a few minutes, until it passed over her, but she grew alarmed when the plane slowed as it approached the village.

Who could it be? Only the top government "officials"—Samatru and his crew—had access to planes like that. But even they usually arrived by car. Fuel and airplanes were hard to come by and saved for very special occasions.

The plane coasted in for a landing on the dusty road that ran about a thousand yards in front of the hospital, and though it was officially no longer her business, she couldn't help worrying. Nor could she stop herself from running toward it as she tried to figure out what new threat the clinic was in for.

Despite the famine ravaging the country, it had been almost impossible for their organization, For the Children, to gain access to Somalia—the government frowned on outside interference. Even reporters and tourists had very restricted access to the small besieged nation—which made running a clinic here that much more difficult.

Add in the fact that the government had decided the doctors were ripe for exploitation, and it was a miracle that the hospital managed to hold on to any supplies to treat their patients.

As she ran, Amanda wondered what official had gotten a sudden "concern" about their presence here? And how much money it would take for his "attack of conscience" to be mollified.

How many people had to die so that he could wear his expensive suits and fly in his little plane? How many children had to starve?

Concern whipped through her, making her run faster despite the heat and the exhaustion. Making her incautious, when her life and the lives of the other doctors and patients at the clinic often depended on keeping a delicate balance with the current administration.

But what did she have to live for?

Gabby was gone.

Simon, the only man she had ever loved, had disappeared from her life, for good this time.

She had shut out everyone who cared about her until she was alone, isolated.

And now that Jack had stripped her of the only reason she had to get up in the morning, maybe she was better off dead.

Despair swamped her—black and overwhelming—but her long strides didn't falter. Jack was a good doctor and a hell of an administrator, but even after ten years in these war-ravaged conditions, he had no tolerance for the way the country—and its corrupt officials—worked. If he lost his temper, he could bring everything they'd accomplished down around their heads.

Not that she blamed him. Every dollar he paid the rulers was one less to buy medicine and food for the people who desperately needed it. All the money he'd paid through the years meant days and weeks off the lives of Mabulu and all the other boys and girls like him.

But as Amanda approached and got a glimpse through the small crowd that had gathered when the plane landed, she realized that this was no government official. Dressed in jeans and a clean, white Aerosmith T-shirt, the newcomer stuck out like a sore thumb among the impoverished villagers who had come to observe the landing.

The sun glinted off too-long wheat-blond hair, but it wasn't until she caught sight of the worn leather backpack over the visitor's shoulder that the truth occurred to her.

She stopped breathing, shock holding her lungs and rib cage immobile.

Still, she told herself that she was wrong. It couldn't be him.

He was in Haiti, putting together a documentary about earthquake victims.

In Colombia, investigating the cartels and their negative influence on the indigenous population.

In Cambodia, uncovering shady CIA deals. Anywhere and everywhere but here, where she'd been safe from thinking about him, insulated against her past by the immediacy of the present.

But the build was right—tall and rangy with a lean, long-legged frame that was deceptively strong. The shaggy blond hair worn too long—more from carelessness than fashion. Even the T-shirt advertised his favorite band.

Her breath caught in her throat, but her brain refused to accept what her eyes were seeing. That Simon was here—*here*—when years ago he'd decided that he'd had enough of Africa's endless suffering.

But if it was him, what was he doing here? There had been no coup, no newly reported human-rights violations, no recent massacres. Only the ongoing famine that was neither glamorous nor seedy enough to attract the Western press here.

To attract *Simon* here.

For a moment, Jack's guilty expression flashed into her mind, his warning that he had contacted someone. She'd ignored him at the time, but now, as her stomach constricted, she wished she'd let him have his say. At least then she would have been prepared.

Even as the idea formed in her mind, she told herself that she was being paranoid. There was no way Simon would fly this far to see her after the way they'd parted. She'd completely ignored his existence—and his pleas—in the days after they'd buried their daughter.

The argument was a good one and she'd almost convinced herself that she was mistaken, that her mind was playing tricks on her. She'd even managed to suppress the instinctive, involuntary response that took over her body as it had every single time she'd seen him in the past ten years.

Then the man turned and everything within her stilled. It *was* him. She was sure of it, especially when his bright green eyes met hers as he scanned the crowd, looking for something. Looking for *someone*. At first, he looked right past her, but then he froze. His gaze returned to her. Clung.

Amanda wanted to look away, but she was caught. Ensnared. A rabbit in a trap. And she'd do anything to escape. Because he was the one person she didn't want to see her like this, the one person in the whole damn world guaranteed to make the soul-crushing pain she felt even worse.

She looked like hell. Jack hadn't been exaggerating when he'd emailed three days before. Even from this distance, Simon could see that she was much too thin. Tall and naturally slender, Amanda always lost weight when she was on location, refusing to take time to eat when so many people needed her help. Refusing to take any more of the essential supplies than she absolutely needed to stay alive.

"I can eat when I'm home," she used to tell him. "I'll curl up on the couch with a loaded pizza and a gallon of ice cream and eat it all."

"But you never go home," he would answer. "It's been two years."

She'd smile at him, her smoky eyes twinkling silver in the moonlight. "Soon," she'd promise. "I just need to do a few more things here."

It hadn't taken him long to realize that *soon* almost never came. There was always one more country, one more disaster, one more person who needed her. In that, she was very much like him—except, Amanda had spent the past decade of her life getting her hands dirty, while he'd done exactly the opposite.

But he couldn't do that anymore, couldn't hide behind his camera lens and maintain his objectivity. Not with her. Not when she so obviously needed him. For a man who'd built a career around making sure no one got too close—even his lovers or, God forgive him, his daughter—it was a frightening state of affairs.

But what else could he have done? He hadn't been able to walk away, not after reading those few heart-stopping lines.

Close to a breakdown, Jack had written. *Strung out. Making herself sick.*

He had been in an open-air market in the middle of the Andes when he'd gotten the message. Jack wasn't prone to exaggeration, so Simon had literally forgotten everything but Amanda, had dropped his story and his deadline without a qualm, to get here before it was too late.

In the end, it had taken him three hellish days of travel by everything from donkey cart to airplane to reach this small, secluded village. But looking at Amanda now, almost as frail and sick as the patients who waited in a long line outside the clinic's canvas doors, he couldn't help thinking that he was already way too late.

Weaving his way through the curious onlookers, he walked toward her—his gaze still glued to hers. But the closer he got, the more concerned he became. Her beautiful eyes—usually so filled with life—were bruised and sunken. Her cheekbones were razor sharp, her skin pale and waxy despite the strong African sun. And whatever small amount of color she'd had in her face had drained the moment she realized he was here for her.

She looked like hell. Anger began to churn inside him. How had she gotten herself into such a state? And why had Jack waited so long to tell him about it?

He stopped a couple of feet in front of her, reached a hand out to stroke her cheek and maybe push one of her short corkscrew curls out of her face. But she flinched away before he could touch her, freezing him in mid-motion.

So, she hadn't forgiven him. But then, why should she, Simon asked himself viciously, when he hadn't even begun to forgive himself? Most days, he brushed his teeth in the shower because he couldn't stand the sight of his own reflection in the bathroom mirror.

Doubts assailed him for the first time since he'd gotten Jack's missive, and he let his hand drop to his side. Maybe he shouldn't have come, no matter what the surgeon had said. Maybe he was destined to make things worse for her.

But as he stood there, his eyes locked on her red-rimmed ones, the truth was a no-holds-barred punch to the gut. She had been crying. Amanda, who had never shed a tear in the twelve years he'd known her, had cried hard enough—and recently enough—to make her eyes bleary and bloodshot.

"Oh, sweetheart, look at you." The words tangled up on his tongue and he could barely get them out. "What have you done to yourself?"

She stiffened even more. "What are you doing here?"

"I was just passing through…" He recited the old cliché in the hopes that she would call him on it—which she did.

"Yeah, right. You hate Africa."

"No. I hate the suffering here, when I'm so ill-equipped to do anything about it. That's a totally different thing."

"Is it?" If possible, she looked even more disgusted, and he felt the familiar shame start to creep up his spine.

"Absolutely. Besides, I'm not here for a story."

She didn't move, didn't betray her emotions by so much as an eyelash flicker, yet her entire being somehow, impossibly, grew even more wary. "So, once again, *why* are you here?"

"I think you already know the answer to that, Amanda, or you wouldn't be looking so upset." He watched her steadily. "I'm here to take you home."

The look she gave him was a mixture of disbelief and dare—with enough repugnance thrown in to let him know she ranked him in the same category as pond scum. "Are you, now?"

"I am. Amanda, you can't—"

"Oh, no." Her voice sliced like a whip. "You don't get to tell me what I can or cannot do. You've never wanted that right and you don't suddenly get to change the rules just because you don't like the final score. Besides, I would rather swim back to the States under my own power than go *anywhere* with you."

He grinned. "It's a big ocean, baby—and filled with sharks."

"That's rather telling, then, isn't it? That I'd rather

take on an entire shiver of sharks than spend one second longer than I have to in your company."

"Well, then, I guess we're both in for a bumpy ride—because this time you aren't getting rid of me."

"Since when have I ever had to get rid of you?" Her smile was as sharp as her cheekbones. "I'll just wait five minutes until a better opportunity comes along. You'll be in the air before I even get my suitcase packed."

CHAPTER THREE

WITH THAT PARTING SHOT, Amanda turned away and headed toward the sleeping tents. And though every instinct he had demanded he follow her, Simon chose instead to stay where he was and simply watch her walk away. He'd known her long enough to recognize when she needed some time alone.

But the hollow feeling that had haunted him for the past eighteen months grew stronger with each step she took in the opposite direction.

Was this how she'd felt, he wondered, all those times when he'd been the one to walk away? When he'd chosen a story over her—and over their daughter? If so, he had even more to feel guilty about than he'd imagined.

He watched her until she disappeared inside one of the small tents set aside for the doctors, then watched some more—waiting, he supposed, to see if she was going to come back out and finish their discussion. It wasn't likely, of course, but hope hung around—for a little while, anyway.

Right when he'd decided that he was going to have to go after her, he felt a large hand clap him on the shoulder. He turned to see the man who had started them down this path so many years before—and who was also responsible for this latest detour—standing in front of him with a definite scowl on his face.

"I had decided you weren't going to come," Jack said as he shook his head. "If I'd known you were due in today, I might have gone a little easier on Amanda earlier."

Simon thought of Amanda's red-rimmed eyes and felt every muscle in his body tighten. Jack was one of his closest friends, as well, but no one had the right to turn Amanda inside out like that. "What did you say to her?"

Jack eyed his clenched fists with interest, and Simon could feel himself flush. There was nothing quite like laying all your cards on the table for the world to see.

"I told her the same thing I told you. That she was exhausted and had to go home for a while."

"She's not going to want to go. That house—" His throat started to close up, so he stopped and took a few deep breaths. "That house is filled with memories of Gabby."

"Hence the reason I didn't sideline her sooner. She needs a reason to get up in the morning, and without her work, I don't think she has one anymore. That's why I emailed you."

Simon wanted to think that Jack was exaggerating, but he couldn't now that he'd seen Amanda himself. "I'm not that reason, never have been. Besides, it's pretty obvious she can't stand the sight of me."

"Yeah, well, you're going to have to find a way around that."

Simon snorted. "I'm sorry. Have you met Dr.

Amanda Jacobs? She's not exactly the easiest person to get—"

"Listen to me, Simon. I know what I'm talking about. She can't be on her own right now. If she goes back to the States by herself and rents some small apartment somewhere because she can't deal with the memories, I don't think she's going to make it."

Everything inside of him went cold at Jack's assessment—so cold that he actually shivered, despite the harsh rays of the sun beating down on him. "You think—" Simon's voice broke for the second time in as many minutes and he had to clear his throat a few times before he could force any words through. "You really think she's suicidal?"

Jack paused, looked past him to the barren desert that surrounded them. "I'm not sure how to answer that."

"It isn't that difficult. Either you think she'll try to kill herself or you don't."

"It's not that simple. Do I think Amanda will actively try to kill herself? No. But—" he continued, before Simon could relax "—I don't think she wants to live, either. I think she's gotten to the point where she's too apathetic to do anything about it, one way or the other."

Simon tried to read between the lines. "So what are you saying? You don't think she cares enough to kill herself? Is that even possible?"

"I'm not a psychiatrist, Simon. I'm not sure what's possible or what isn't in this case. I'm just telling you what I think, what I've observed over the past few months. Amanda gave up caring about what happens to herself a long time ago. That's why I let her stay here this long, even though I've known almost since she got here that she was eventually going to break.

"I tried to get through to her, tried to keep her busy. Let her work almost exclusively with the children—the only thing that brings her around is when she's working toward healing a child." He shook his head. "But it's not enough. Things are dire here and getting worse every day. She lost a patient today—the third this week—and she didn't handle it well."

"What does that mean?"

"It means she almost had a nervous breakdown in the middle of the O.R. And I believe, really believe, that if she could have crawled onto that gurney with Mabulu and died alongside him, she would have. I've never seen her like that before, not in all the years we've known each other, and it scared me—so much that I relieved her of her duties and told her I'd block any application she made to work with another clinic. At least for a while."

Simon was having a hard time getting his mind around what Jack was saying. The picture the other man was painting was of a woman so far removed from the Amanda he knew that she was almost unrecognizable. Amanda was the one everyone turned to in a crisis— she was the one who never fell apart, who always knew what to do.

That had obviously changed, and he was suddenly at as much of a loss as Jack was. How the hell was he sup-posed to fix a woman who'd never been broken before, especially when she couldn't stand the sight of him?

What was he supposed to do?

He hadn't been aware that he said the last aloud,

until Jack grimly responded, "My best advice? You get her out of here—tonight. You get her home, get her to a doctor and to a counselor. And then you wait."

"For how long?" Waiting wasn't exactly Simon's strong suit.

"For as long as it takes. It took her at least a year and a half to get into this state. She isn't going to come out of it overnight."

Simon thought, briefly, of the stories he had lined up. Of the exclusive access he'd managed to finagle behind the Israeli wall after six years of pulling in favors.

Of the upcoming Middle East peace talks in Europe that he was supposed to cover.

Of the story he had started investigating in South America, and of the documentary he had already gotten footage for in Afghanistan. He'd been putting that story together, off and on, for months now, and it had Edward R. Murrow Award written all over it. He could almost taste the award and so could his director.

He closed his eyes and with a sigh let them all go. For more than a decade, Amanda had taken second and third and sometimes even two hundredth place to his work. This time, everything else was going to have to wait.

DESPITE HIS BEST INTENTIONS, the sun was setting before Simon finally caught up to Amanda again. Wanting to give her some space, he'd spent part of the afternoon shadowing Jack in the clinic. But by the time he went to the tents to find her, she'd been long gone and he'd spent much of the early evening searching the clinic and village for her—and cursing himself for letting her out of his sight. Especially after what Jack had told him.

In the end, he'd had to ask the other doctor where Amanda might have wandered off to—which had grated, since every time he opened his mouth it felt as if the other man was condemning him for his callous treatment of her through the years.

Then again, maybe it was his own conscience doing all the condemning.

The surgeon had pointed him toward the desert, and Simon had followed his directions until he'd happened upon her, about a mile and a half away—in the middle of an empty stretch of dry, cracked sand.

She was sitting on a large, flat rock, her knees drawn up so that she could rest her chin on them, and she looked so young, so vulnerable, that it was hard for him to imagine it had been so many years since he'd first met her.

Five years since he'd last held her, loved her.

And before today, eighteen months since he'd so much as laid eyes on her.

Part of him wanted to rush up to her, to wrap her in his arms and pretend that everything was the same. That they were still lovers, still friends.

Still parents.

But another part, the one that was buried under guilt and pain and his own anger, couldn't help wondering how much more rejection he could stand.

At Gabrielle's funeral, Amanda had frozen him out so completely that he still hadn't thawed a year and a half later. It had been a defense mechanism, a way to bury her own pain—but knowing that hadn't made it hurt any less.

They'd stopped being lovers not long after Gabrielle was born. Amanda had feared that what they'd had together wasn't stable enough to raise a child and he'd gone along because he hadn't wanted a relationship that would tie him down. But they'd remained friends, right up until their daughter had died.

Then Amanda had excised him from her life with such brutal efficiency he swore he could still feel the blade.

But this wasn't about him, he reminded himself fiercely as he struggled for something to say. This was about Amanda, about getting her well again.

"If you're going to spend all evening skulking in the shadows, don't be surprised if someone mistakes you for a rebel and shoots you." Her words were cool and collected, a marked difference from their earlier meeting.

"I didn't want to disturb you—I figured you might shoot me yourself if I did."

"I'm not the bloodthirsty type." She still hadn't bothered to look at him. "I would have thought you'd know that by now."

"Yeah, well, people change."

"More like circumstances change them."

There was an underlying bitterness to her tone that had him moving forward and sinking down beside her on the rock. She didn't protest as he expected her to. Instead, she scooted over to make more room for him. He wanted to think of it as progress, but Jack's words haunted him—especially when he got his first glimpse

of her blank face. It was as if the Amanda he'd known
had simply disappeared, leaving only this shell of a
woman behind.

She didn't say anything else, and for the longest
time, neither did he. He was too caught up in how
strange it felt to be near her again, yet how eerily familiar, as well. She smelled the same as she always
had—like lavender and peaches and cool spring eve-
nings— despite the heat and dust of the surrounding
desert. Strange how nothing could change that, not even
years in this drought- and famine-stricken land.

Yet she felt different sitting next to him—skinnier,
frailer, more delicate than he had ever seen her. As different from the warrior he once knew as Somalia was
from the cozy home she'd made for herself and their
daughter in Boston after Gabrielle had gotten sick.

The silence stretched between them, fraught with everything they didn't want to say. No, that wasn't quite
right. It wasn't that he didn't want to say it—it was that
he didn't know how.

How did you apologize for all the mistakes you'd
made, when some of them stretched back over a decade?

How did you tell the mother of your child that you
still cared about her even though she'd cut you out of
her life?

How did you reach past the cool reserve to tell her
that you wanted another chance? That, this time, you
weren't going to disappear?

In the end, he didn't have to say anything, because
she broke first. "I'm not leaving with you, Simon."

"Jack says he's put you on sick leave. That you have to go."

"Yeah, well, it's a big world out there. There's no reason our paths should have to cross again."

"They've been intersecting for over twelve years now, Amanda. Do you really think it's possible to keep that from happening again?"

She shrugged. "I don't see why not. The world's on fire—as usual. I'm sure there are a million places you could be right now, taking pictures. Reporting the news. America—with its stable government and abundant resources—isn't exactly your speed."

"Is that where you're planning on going?" he demanded. "To America? Back home to Boston?"

She didn't answer, but then he hadn't really expected her to. At a complete loss as to what to say—or how to reach her—he dug into his backpack and came up with the last Twix bar. "You want half?" he asked as he broke open the wrapper. It was her favorite candy.

She glanced to see what he was offering her and stiffened, the blood draining from her face and her body turning to granite. When she spoke, it was in a rush and he had to struggle to understand. "I don't want that!"

He pushed himself up, staring at her in bewilderment. "What's wrong? I thought you liked these." But even as the question formed in the air between them, the answer came to him and he wondered how he could have been so stupid. Again.

Twix had been Gabrielle's favorite candy bar, too. She and Amanda had shared one at least once or twice a week—even when Amanda had been on assignment.

She'd always carried a bunch of them with her, to help
Gabrielle settle as they moved from one clinic—and
country—to the next.

Shit, how could he have forgotten that?

He dropped the candy into his backpack. "I'm sorry.
I didn't think."

"Like that's a surprise," she said as she got to her
feet. Her voice was level, but her hands were squeezed
into fists so tight that her knuckles were white. "Go
away, Simon. Go back to wherever you came from. I
don't need or want you to take care of me."

"Yeah, well, have you looked in a mirror lately? Because you may not want to be taken care of, but you
definitely need to be. And, no offense, but it looks like
I'm the only candidate for the job."

She whirled on him. "Why are you here? Why are
you doing this to me? Can't you see that I don't want
anything to do with you?"

He could see it—and it was killing him. "Look, I'm
not suggesting we jump into bed together—"

"Glad to hear it, because that part of our lives is long
over."

He ignored her, and the pinprick of hurt her words
caused. It wasn't as though he hadn't been expecting
them, after all. "I just want to make sure you're all
right."

"Why?"

"Excuse me?"

"Why do you suddenly feel responsible for me?" she
demanded, her silver eyes steady on his. "You never
have before."

He started to deny it, to tell her that he'd always

wanted to take care of her, but it would be a lie and they would both know it. One of the things that had originally attracted him to Amanda was how self-sufficient she was. How she could take care of herself and whatever came along. How she had never needed a man— never needed him—to lean on.

Diabolically, that same self-sufficiency was what had caused their relationship to end—just when he'd wanted most for it to continue. But then, he'd always had a gift for impossible relationships.

They stood there for long seconds, staring at each other as he tried to figure out what he was supposed to say. In the end, he did what he usually did—told the truth, even if it was guaranteed to get him into trouble. "Because for the first time since I met you, you need me."

SIMON'S WORDS, DELIVERED IN the crisp British accent that had once sent shivers down her spine, worked their way through Amanda and she had to fight not to show her incredulity. There was so much wrong with what he'd said that she wasn't sure which part to take exception to first—his assumption that she'd never needed him, or his idea that she suddenly did?

Could he really believe what he was saying? she wondered incredulously. Could he really think that in all the time they'd been together she'd never needed him before? That she'd done everything alone because she'd liked it that way?

She'd managed by herself because she'd never been able to count on him to do anything for her. For that, he would have had to be around for more than a few days at a time. He would have had to show an interest in something besides sex and that damn camera of his.

Part of her wanted to say something, to throw his words back in his face. But doing that would mean admitting that he'd had the power to hurt her, and she couldn't see letting herself in for that. Not now, when simply standing here looking at him was taking more strength than she had. Besides, what they'd had—whatever it was— had been over long before Gabby had gotten sick. Her funeral had been the final death knell for a relationship that never should have happened.

"Simon—" She cleared her throat. Tried again. "I don't need you to feel guilty about me. I'll go home and get some rest. I'll be fine in a few weeks."

But even as she said the words, she knew he wouldn't believe them. After eighteen years as a journalist, Simon's bullshit meter was finely tuned.

Sure enough, one of his eyebrows shot up the way it always did when he was about to call her on a fib. "Really? You think rattling around in that house by yourself is what you need right now?"

"I don't have the house anymore. It sold a few months after..." She cleared her throat again. "After."

His eyes darkened until they were the color of the storm-tossed Atlantic. "I wish you hadn't done that."

Sometimes so did she. The house held so many memories of Gabby, good and bad. That was why she had sold it to begin with—she hadn't been able to contemplate the idea of ever crossing the threshold, knowing that it was where her child had died.

But now, a year and a half later, she would give anything to walk through the halls and remember what it had felt like when her daughter had been alive. Even the pain that came with the memories would be better than this yawning emptiness that threatened to swallow her whole.

"Yeah, well, it seemed stupid to hold on to it, when I would only be in town every once in a blue moon."

"Stupid?" he demanded. "That was your home. Our home."

Anger sparked. "Just because I let you stay there when you passed through town didn't make it your home, Simon. To be that, you need some kind of emotional investment in the place."

"I had an emotional investment, Amanda. Not in the house, but in you. In Gabby."

His words hit like blows and she trembled under the onslaught. But she caught herself, fought back. "The only thing you've ever been emotionally invested in is the story. You, of all people, should know that trying to rewrite history doesn't work—not if there's someone still around who remembers how things actually happened."

He clenched his teeth so tightly that she worried he would crack a molar—or five. She waited for him to swallow the bait, to explode and walk away, as was his modus operandi. But sometime in the past year and a half, he must have learned self-control, because he didn't defend himself. Didn't say anything at all.

Instead, he looked out across the sand, his eyes focusing on some distant point, while his jaw worked furiously. Long seconds passed in hostile silence until, in a voice that sounded a lot more reasonable than he looked, he said, "Since you sold the house, where are you planning to stay?"

"Why?"

"Why do you think? I want to pull in a few favors, have your place firebombed."

"It wouldn't be the first time," she said, remembering one of the reports Simon had done about Chechnya when she'd been there—a report that had ended with her clinic being attacked by the government. She'd barely gotten Gabby out in time, which was one of the main reasons she'd decided to end the romantic part of their relationship once and for all.

"That wasn't my fault," he answered with an amused resignation that hadn't been there a few moments before.

"It never is." She grinned at him for a second, before remembering that he was the enemy. No, she corrected herself firmly. Simon wasn't the enemy. She refused to give him that much importance in her life.

He scooted closer, cupped her face in his palms. She forced herself not to flinch this time, when all she really wanted to do was flee. "I didn't have any nefarious intentions in asking, Amanda. I just wanted to know where we were going to settle."

His thumb stroked gently across her cheek, and despite everything—despite her anger at him, despite her resentment and her despair—she found herself melting into his touch. Simon felt safe, even though she knew he was anything but. And she was so tired that it didn't matter.

Tired of fighting.

Tired of talking.

Tired of living.

But then he moved, shifting a little closer until his body brushed hers. It was all she needed to shove him away, once and for all.

"Jack might have contacted you a few days ago, but I just got my walking papers today. I haven't exactly had time to decide where I want to end up."

"Come with me," he urged. "We can decide together."

She shook her head, backed away some more—not even caring that it looked as if she was in full retreat. "I'm not getting on that plane with you."

"Well, then, you and I have a problem."

"Not from where I'm standing." She gave him her most obnoxious smirk. "Get on your little puddle jumper and go back to whatever it was you were doing before Jack interrupted you."

"Yeah, well, that's not going to happen. I came a long way to find you, Amanda, and I'm not leaving here without you. Not this time. One way or another, you're getting on that plane with me. Tonight."

CHAPTER FOUR

"HEY, JACK. WAIT UP." Simon ran to catch up with the doctor as he crossed from the clinic to his small tent.

"Where's Amanda?" Jack asked, looking behind Simon. "I thought you were getting ready to leave."

"I am, but she's dug in her heels. She refuses to come with me, says she's going to hitch a ride into the city with the transport driver."

Jack sighed, shook his head. "That sounds like Mandy."

"We can't let her do that."

"I'm not sure how we can stop her."

Simon cast around for the best way to say what was on his mind. He knew what he wanted to do was extreme and was certain that Jack would object to it, but he was also convinced it was the only way to get Amanda on the very beginning steps to recovery.

"She'll disappear, Jack. If she gets into the city, gets to the major airport, she could go anywhere, do anything, and I'll have a hell of a time finding her."

Jack nodded. "That's why I contacted you to begin with. But at the same time, if she really won't have anything to do with you, I'm not sure how I can help. Do you want me to talk to her?"

"I want you to drug her."

The words hung between them for long seconds as

Jack's eyes widened. He took a step back and then another, shaking his head. "I can't do that. She's a grown woman—she's allowed to make decisions for herself."

"I know that. Believe me, I know that." Amanda was the most independent woman he had ever met. "But at the same time, she's not thinking rationally right now. She may say she's given up, that she's going to go home and rest, but you know as well as I do that she's not built like that. She's hurting and she's going to keep running from the pain until she kills herself. I can't stand by and watch her do that."

"But to drug her? Simon, she'll never forgive you for taking the choice away from her. She'll never forgive either of us."

Simon swallowed back the unfamiliar thickness in his throat, forcing himself to talk through the fear Jack's words—which only echoed his own thoughts—engendered.

"Do you have a better suggestion? Please, if you do, tell me. I've been racking my brain for hours trying to figure out how to do this another way. But she's so angry, so hurt—"

"It'll only be worse if you do this."

"I know. Believe me, I know. But I need her to live. I need to get her someplace where she can recover, where she can remember that there are good things in life. You know how dire the situation is—you wouldn't have emailed me if you didn't. If we can't get her somewhere safe, we both know that the next time we meet, it will be at her funeral. I can't—" He turned away, terrified. He'd already lost his daughter. How could he ever survive losing Amanda, too?

"I know where you're coming from, but I still don't think it's a good idea. I mean, it's a huge betrayal." Jack sighed heavily. "Look, let me talk to her one more time. Try to change her mind."

"It won't work."

"Maybe not, but before I ruin a fifteen-year friendship, I'm damn well going to try."

Simon's whole being sagged with relief. "So you'll do it."

"I'm going to talk—"

"I know, I know. But if you can't convince her, if she insists on doing this completely on her own so she can disappear the second we turn our backs, you'll help me?"

"Yeah." Jack nodded, but he didn't look happy. "If that's really what's going on, then I'll find a way to help you."

"Thank you."

He snorted. "Don't thank me yet. If I drug her, I'll be hundreds of miles away when she wakes up. But you'll be right there. Good luck with that."

AMANDA LOOKED AROUND the tent she had called home for the better part of a year. It seemed even more barren than usual.

Her belongings, except for the outfit she planned to wear the next day, were all packed in one large suitcase and the worn green backpack that had traveled around the world with her. It was old and on its last legs, but she knew she wouldn't part with it, even after she got to a place where replacing it was simply a matter of driving a few blocks to the nearest shopping mall.

She could still see Gabby smiling and tugging the backpack off the rack all those years ago. At the time, it was bigger than she was, but she'd insisted on getting it down herself. Just as she'd insisted that this was the one her mother had to buy. It was the same color as Dada's eyes, after all.

Blocking out thoughts of Simon—and his ridiculous ultimatum—Amanda stowed the last of her toiletries and wondered where she'd be when she finally unpacked them again. Jack wanted her to go home, back to America, but there was no way she was going to do that. She couldn't face everything she'd lost there. Maybe she couldn't work with For the Children, but the world was full of countries—here in Africa and elsewhere—that needed a skilled doctor willing to work for almost nothing. Surely it wouldn't be that hard to find another position.

She zipped the backpack closed, then pulled the only picture of Gabby she had allowed herself to bring to Africa out of the front pocket. The others were all in storage in Boston. Locked away like so many of her emotions.

The photo was ragged and well-worn, the edges crumbling a little from her daily handling. Her baby looked so beautiful, so vibrant and happy and alive.

So very alive.

She was dressed in a pair of jean shorts with embroidered peppermint candies around the waist and hem and a bright pink T-shirt covered in pictures of lollipops and gumdrops. Her black hair was swept up into two ponytails and she was wearing her favorite pair of jeweled tennis shoes—she had talked Amanda into letting her decorate them with the BeDazzler herself. There wasn't a square inch on the shoes that wasn't covered in sequins or jewels or beads.

They were terrifically gaudy and eye-catching, and Gabby had loved them. She'd worn them every single day for months, until she'd gotten so sick that she didn't need shoes and all she could do was lie in bed all day. Even then, they'd sat on the nightstand, waiting for her to get better. Waiting for her to need them again.

She never had.

The familiar pain welled up inside of Amanda, but she fought it, just like she always did.

Fought against the fist squeezing her heart and the hollowness invading her stomach with every strangled breath she took.

Fought against the razor blades slicing along every nerve ending in her body.

It was a little bit harder this time than the last. That's the way it always was. Just a fleeting thought of her beautiful, precocious daughter almost brought her to her knees.

Outside the tent, someone cleared his throat, which was as close to a knock as you could get here. She ignored it, ignored him. There was no one she wanted to talk to right now, anyway. Especially of the male gender.

But whoever it was wasn't put off by her silence. Instead, he called her name softly before flipping the tent flap aside without waiting for an invitation. That alone told her it was Jack.

"What do you want?" She didn't even try to sound

gracious, but then, why should she? He had completely
sold her out.

"To say goodbye."

"Oh, right." She turned her back on him. "Goodbye."

"I didn't have a choice, Amanda. You're—"

"It's fine. I get it."

"Do you?" He reached out, put what she figured he
thought was a comforting hand on her shoulder. But all
it did was make her want to scream. She shrugged him
off, pressing her lips together. If she started to scream
now, she'd never stop.

"Don't worry about it. I'm not your problem anymore. I'll catch a ride into the city with the next transport. There's one scheduled to come tomorrow, isn't
there?"

"I thought you were going back with Simon."

Her laugh was harsh and hurt her throat. "I don't
know what gave you that idea."

For long seconds, he didn't answer. Then he finally said, "You *are* going back, though. To America.
Right?"

"Where else would I go?"

"That's not an answer."

"You made it pretty clear that you're not my boss
anymore. I don't have to tell you anything."

"Don't do something stupid, Amanda. This is a dangerous place for anyone, let alone a woman without pro-
tection."

"Look, I'm not your problem any longer. And I'm
sure as hell not Simon's problem—I don't even know
why you called him."

"He's your—"

"He's my nothing. Not anymore. In case you haven't noticed, the only connection we had is long gone. Besides, this whole discussion is moot. You wanted me gone. Fine. I'm leaving. What I do after that is none of your damn business."

She finally faced him, fixed him with the most intimidating doctor look she had. It didn't really work—his scowl was a hell of a lot better than hers and always had been—but he did have the grace to look ashamed. Good. They'd been friends forever, and a friend wasn't supposed to throw her to the wolves when she was at her most vulnerable.

Even worse, he'd thrown her to one particular wolf.

"You need someone to take care of you."

"I can take care of myself."

"Yeah, because you've done such a bang-up job of it so far. And I've let you get away with it because I was afraid of hurting you more. That's on me. But why take the transport truck when you have Simon, and an airplane, ready to take you to the States with no hassle? The situation here is escalating. If you have an option other than the transport truck, it makes sense that you take it. Besides, you and Simon need some time to work things out."

"There's nothing to work out, Jack. I keep telling you that. Whatever Simon and I once had is long over. And now that Gabby's gone, there's nothing between us at all. I don't have a clue why he came, but I do know that I will not be leaving with him."

"Yeah, because wandering around Africa, purposeless, is such a good idea."

"It's better than wandering around Boston alone."

"So go somewhere else. Go to California or Hawaii. Jamaica. Lie on the beach somewhere. Eat, sleep. Recuperate."

"Sure. Why not? My daughter's dead. Why the hell shouldn't I take a tropical vacation? If I'm really lucky, maybe they'll let me keep the little umbrellas from my drinks."

"You'd rather punish yourself forever?" he demanded. "Work yourself to death? What's that going to do? You still won't bring her back."

"No, but if I'm dead, at least I won't feel the pain anymore."

Jack blanched and she knew, right away, that she'd said the worst thing she possibly could have. She hadn't really meant it, at least not the way Jack was taking it. She wasn't suicidal, had always been too much of a fighter to consider that, even now, when everything was so messed up. But the oblivion provided by working twenty-hour days, week after week, month after month, was welcome. If she was tired enough, maybe she'd finally be able to stop thinking. To stop remembering.

"Don't hate me, Mandy," he said gently, moving closer to her.

Some sixth sense kicked in, warned her of danger. But it was too little too late. She felt a prick on her upper arm. Watched in shock as Jack emptied a syringe into her biceps.

"What are you..." Her mouth and tongue wouldn't cooperate enough to form words. The world around her went fuzzy, and she reached a hand out, trying to keep her balance. Jack tried to steady her, but she stumbled. Would have fallen if he hadn't caught her. And then everything went black.

SIMON WAITED THE ALLOTTED fifteen minutes, then entered the tent in time to see Jack cradling Amanda in his arms. Even though he knew the two of them were only friends and Jack was following through on the plan—at Simon's request—something ugly welled up inside him at the sight of Amanda held so intimately by another man.

His reaction caught him by surprise. It had been years since they'd been a couple and he thought he'd sublimated any lingering romantic feelings he'd had for her. After all, the last thing he wanted to do was give her a chance to dump him again. The first time had hurt more than enough.

Besides, he should be thanking Jack instead of contemplating the best way to rip out his throat. God knew, it had been hard enough to convince him to go along with this plan to get Amanda on the plane.

"I'll take her from here," Simon said, slipping his hands under the woman he had loved for almost half his life. "Can you get her bags?"

"Sure." Jack checked her vitals then pulled away completely, and the first thing Simon felt was shock. He'd carried Amanda numerous times through the years—usually in circumstances a lot more pleasant than this—and never had she felt so…insubstantial. As if she would float away any second. Or worse, as if she really wasn't there at all.

What the hell had she been doing to herself for the past eighteen months?

And why hadn't he known how bad off she was? Why had it taken Jack to get him to check on her? Simon had known she wasn't okay after the funeral. He'd known that accepting Gabby's death was going to be the hardest thing she'd ever done, especially considering how valiantly she'd fought to save their daughter.

So why hadn't he said to hell with the story—with all of the stories? Why hadn't he come to get her long before this?

As he berated himself, Simon strode quickly through the darkness, his boots finding easy purchase despite his unfamiliarity with the terrain. He hadn't been to Africa in longer than he cared to admit, but his body remembered the land as though he'd last been here yesterday. Jack walked beside him, grimly silent as he carried Amanda's backpack and suitcase.

When they got to the plane, Simon made quick work of getting Amanda buckled in. Who knew how long the sedative Jack had given her would last? He had said it would be effective long enough for Simon to get her out of the country, but Amanda was incredibly strong-willed. If anyone could pull herself out of a stupor, it was Amanda.

After making sure she was safely settled, he walked to the plane's open door and took her backpack from Jack while the pilot stowed her suitcase down below. Then he shook the other man's hand.

"Thank you for calling me." He kept his voice steady through sheer will alone. "I should have been here."

"Don't push her too hard, Simon. She's more delicate than either of us ever suspected."

Though that part of him that had been jealous earlier

reared its ugly head a second time—who was Jack to tell him how to treat Amanda?—Simon pushed it down. Again. He wasn't so far gone that he didn't realize how right the doctor was.

"I'll take care of her."

Jack nodded, then clapped him on the back before leaving. Simon stowed Amanda's backpack before walking up the aisle and settling himself next to her.

In the next few minutes, the pilot finished with the pre-takeoff maneuvers. Before Simon had even registered the time passing, they were cruising down the makeshift runway, their only guide two men waving flashlights in the direction they were supposed to go.

Looking away, he pretended that risk didn't drive the control freak inside of him completely bat-shit crazy. Hands clenched on the armrests, he glanced at Amanda as the plane finally became airborne seconds before the dirt road turned to sand. And wondered how angry she was going to be when she finally did wake up.

Angry enough to make his life a living hell for the next few days, or weeks, he figured. She knew how to hold a mean grudge, after all. Which wouldn't matter if he was certain that he'd done the right thing so far. He only hoped his deviousness didn't end up leaving her more damaged than she already was.

In a perfect world, he would have stuck around the camp and tried to convince her to see things his way, but their situation was far from perfect. To begin with, he was doubtful Amanda would ever trust him again. Not after what he'd done…and, more important, what he hadn't.

And even more than that, he didn't have the luxury

of time. He'd pulled a bunch of strings and used up all his clout at the cable news agency he worked for in order to get this plane. But he hadn't been able to swing it for more than four days. They needed to be in Atlanta two days from now—the network execs had a board meeting planned somewhere exotic and the plane could not be MIA when it came time for them to leave.

He might have run the risk of taking regular planes home—probably four at least—if he wasn't absolutely convinced that Amanda would slip away from him in one of the airports while waiting for a connecting flight.

Admittedly, he'd thought they were going to Boston when he'd first commandeered the plane, but now that she'd sold the house, there was nothing for her there.

Pain kicked him in the stomach, hard, at the thought of someone else living in the house he had once shared with Amanda and Gabby, but he ignored it as he always did. He focused, instead, on the problem at hand. She had no friends left in Boston, really. And there was no family for either of them. Which meant they were going to Atlanta. To the apartment he'd moved into after taking the job at the network a year ago.

It wasn't an ideal solution—his apartment was a one-bedroom, so small that twenty-five paces would take a person from one end to the other. It was perfect for him, given the amount of time he spent at home, but it would definitely be cramped with two of them.

Maybe he could talk to his landlord about switching to something a little bigger. Though he wouldn't mind staying with a one-bedroom. There was a part of him that found the idea of sleeping next to Amanda again, after so long, very appealing.

That is, if she didn't maim him, which he wouldn't put past her after the various stunts he'd pulled through the years. He'd behaved bad enough when Gabby was alive, shirking responsibility and chasing after stories as far from home as he could get because he couldn't deal with the fact that he was losing his little girl. But now he'd gone and kidnapped Amanda.

Sitting next to her on the plane, he was forced to acknowledge that perhaps this wasn't the best-thought-out plan. Despite the fact that she looked like a stiff wind would knock her over and shatter her into a thousand pieces, Amanda was tough. The toughest woman he'd ever met.

He'd be lucky if she didn't call the police as soon as they were back in the States. Still, if he could get her to his apartment, get her rested and fed and stabilized emotionally, everything would be worth it. Even spending a night in jail.

It hurt him to see her like this. The vibrancy that had been such a big part of her for as long as he'd known her was damn near extinguished. The fact that he was partly responsible... He shook his head, ran a hand over his face. The fact that he'd had a part in it made him want to kick his own ass. Or at least bend over, a target painted on the body part in question, as Amanda did it for him.

But he'd had to do something. Benign neglect certainly hadn't worked.

Reaching over, he brushed his knuckles down Amanda's hollowed cheeks. And wished for a forgiveness he didn't think he deserved.

CHAPTER FIVE

As AMANDA STRUGGLED slowly toward consciousness, her first thought was that she had contracted something from one of her patients. Her head was pounding, her body ached and her stomach was trying to turn itself inside out.

She groped for the small trash can she kept a few feet from her bed, but her hand met only air. Eyes flying open, she was struck by several new realities.

First, she wasn't in her tent.

Second, wherever she was, Simon was sitting next to her, his green eyes both wary and urgent.

Third, her seat was vibrating.

And finally—though it was probably the most urgent of her realizations—she was going to throw up.

"I need—" She started to bolt out of her chair, only to be yanked back by the belt fastened low over her hips. She wasted precious seconds trying to figure out what was happening, even as her fingers fumbled frantically with the buckle.

"Whoa, Amanda, take it easy, sweetheart." Simon's voice, low and soothing, barely registered as panic overwhelmed her.

She was on an airplane.

She was going to puke.

She was on an airplane.

She was going to puke.

She was on an airplane.

She was going to— The clasp finally gave way and she leaped to her feet, made a mad dash up the aisle toward…she didn't know what. A trash can. Some privacy. Anything.

She careened into something hard—another seat maybe—and got knocked backward. Reaching a hand out to steady herself, again she grabbed only air. The next thing she knew, she was on the ground, Simon pounding up the aisle after her. But it was too late. Her stomach revolted.

Thank God there was nothing in it.

Still, Simon shoved a paper bag in front of her, then squatted beside her as she dry heaved, again and again, her entire body shuddering with the force of her convulsions. When they finally stopped after what felt like hours, she pushed the bag away and let her forehead rest against the muted gray carpet. Inhaling long, shaky breaths, she tried to figure out what the hell was happening.

It didn't take long. Perhaps the only good thing to come out of her nausea was that it cleared her head of the cobwebs that had taken up residence there and let her think clearly.

Obviously, she was on an airplane. Obviously, she hadn't put herself there—she would remember making the decision to accompany Simon back to the States. In fact, the last thing she did remember was her conversation with Jack, and then the prick to her arm followed by a sudden onset of dizziness. All of which added up to the realization that she'd been drugged. She'd never responded well to sedatives, which explained her sickness.

As the last of the sluggishness cleared, she became aware of Simon crouched over her, his hand rubbing soothing circles on her back. She jolted upright, shrugged off his hand.

"What the hell did you do to me?" she demanded, her voice sounding shrill to her own ears. Not that she gave a damn. Being kidnapped pretty much granted her the right to be as shrill as she wanted to be.

Simon drew back, his eyes wary as he scanned her face. Before he could say anything, the plane shook and shimmied as it hit a pocket of turbulence. "Let's go back to our seats and talk this out. I don't want you to get hurt." He stood and offered her his hand.

She didn't take it. Instead, she grabbed on to the nearest chair and pulled herself up, despite the continued weakness in her legs. "It's a little late for that sentiment, isn't it?" she asked. "Considering what you've done?"

The plane hit another pocket of turbulence, and the pilot's voice came from the overhead speaker, asking them to fasten their seat belts. Furious—with Simon, Mother Nature, the hapless pilot and perhaps the entire world—Amanda flounced to where she and Simon had been sitting.

Strike that. To where Simon had been sitting and she'd been lying, unconscious. The bastard.

Refusing to sit next to him for one second longer— no matter how juvenile that made her—she plopped herself into the single seat on the other side of the aisle. As she did, she realized that the plane was quite luxurious. This wasn't some little charter jet from Africa—this plane spoke of money and executives and power. It didn't seem like Simon's normal style, but then, she reminded herself abruptly, a lot of things could happen in eighteen months. She wasn't the same woman she'd been a year and a half ago. Why should Simon not have changed?

The thought made her uncomfortable, particularly since she had plans to be coldly furious with the old Simon for the next five decades or so. She didn't want to imagine Gabby's death as having affected him. She didn't want to have any sympathy for him at all.

Of course, he wasn't too different from the old Simon. Otherwise he never would have dragged her out of Somalia without her permission. Although, if she was going to be technical, Jack had been the one to drug her. At Simon's behest, obviously, but her oldest friend had betrayed her as surely as her ex-lover had. The next time she saw Jack, she'd have something to say to him and it wasn't going to be pretty.

"Amanda, please." Simon had settled himself across the aisle from her. "Can we talk about this?"

She very deliberately turned her head away from him. Nothing good would come from talking to him right now. The way she was feeling, she was as likely to hit him as she was to tell him to go to hell. And while she didn't mind the latter, she'd never been a violent person and didn't relish the thought of becoming one, even with these extenuating circumstances.

Of course, looking out the window only made her angrier. It had been night when she and Jack were talking in her tent and now it was full daylight outside.

Which meant a lot of time had passed, especially considering the fact that they were traveling west. If only a few hours had passed, it would still be pitch-black.

The thought galvanized her, made her speak when she'd sworn to herself that she wasn't going to say another word. "Where are we?"

He cleared his throat, shifted uncomfortably. "A few hours out of Atlanta."

"*Atlanta?*" she demanded incredulously. "How long have I been out?"

"About sixteen hours."

"Sixteen— What the hell did you give me? Ketamine? You could have killed me!"

"I called Jack when we stopped to refuel. He had me check your vitals, and they were fine. He said the sedative was probably hitting you so hard because of how run-down you are."

"I'm overwhelmed by both of your concern." Sarcasm dripped from every syllable as she turned back around to face the window. Looking at the clouds was a lot easier than looking at Simon right now.

"Don't do that," he said suddenly. "Don't pretend I'm not here—I used to hate when you did that."

"What you like and don't like is high on my priority list right now." She refused to give him the satisfaction of facing him.

"I hate how you always retreat behind that stony wall of silence. I know you're mad at me—you have the right to be. But can we talk it out like adults instead of sulking like a couple of children who've lost their ball on the playground?"

The words were clipped, crisp, and she realized it

had been years since his accent sounded so heavy. He really was as upset by this whole thing as she was. Good. He deserved it. If that made her bitter and un-feeling, so be it. But at least she wasn't a criminal—transporting another person from one continent to another without her permission.

"What do you want me to say, Simon?" The words were wrenched from her. "That it's okay that you did this? It isn't. Not at all. I've been making my own deci-sions since I was seventeen years old. I don't appreci-ate one of this magnitude being taken out of my hands. And Atlanta? What the hell is in Atlanta?"

"My apartment. A little over a year ago, I took a job at a cable network based out of Atlanta."

Despite herself, she glanced around at the very lush interior of the plane. "I think you mean you took a job at *the* cable network based in Atlanta, don't you?"

He flushed a little. "Pretty much."

She didn't say anything else. She didn't know what to say, not when she was so shocked at the changes in Simon. A couple of years ago, there was no way he'd have tied himself to anyone. He'd relished being one of the top freelance journalists in the world, free to follow whatever story caught his fancy.

"I still travel a lot, though. I'm one of the people they send out when all hell breaks loose somewhere in the world."

And there it was. That sounded like the Simon she knew. An inexplicable sense of relief filled her.

When she still didn't respond, he cleared his throat. "Are we going to talk about this?" he asked. "About what happened in Africa and about…how you ended up here?" His voice trailed off lamely.

"Do you want me to wrap my hands around your throat and squeeze until your eyes bug out of your head?" she asked, sugar-sweet. "No? Then we probably shouldn't talk quite yet. I'm still a little raw."

He sighed heavily. "I'm sorry, Amanda. I really am."

"You're not the least bit sorry. Don't insult me by pretending that you are."

"You were killing yourself."

"I was working. It's what I do." She forced herself to lower her voice, to swallow the words and insults and pain that wanted to spill out. Wanted to spill all over him. Taking a deep breath, she said as civilly as she could, "I was leaving, anyway. I was already packed."

"You wouldn't have come to the States—wouldn't have gotten the rest you need."

"That's not your problem. *I'm* not your problem."

"I can't stand by and watch you do that to yourself."

"Nobody asked you to. You could have gone on your merry way. God knows, you're good at that."

"Damn it, Amanda. I want to help you!" His voice was raw, impassioned. "When are you going to see that? When are you going to let me in?"

"Damn it, Simon," she mimicked him, but her voice was as devoid of feeling as his was overwrought. "I don't want your help. When are you going to figure that out? When are you going to leave me alone?"

It was his turn to lock his jaw. His turn to face the window and the seemingly infinite sky.

She knew he was angry. Knew that, even more, he was hurt by his inability to reach her. For a brief second, she tried to care. She'd never been one to take pleasure in someone else's pain. But when she reached down inside of herself, tried to find some remnant of the feelings she'd once had for him, there was nothing left. Only a terrible numbness.

She went back to looking out the window herself. Started counting clouds. It was going to be a long few hours until they landed in Georgia.

SIMON UNFASTENED HIS SEAT BELT with combined feelings of relief and unease. Relief because they were finally in Atlanta after what had been one of the most emotionally uncomfortable flights of his life, with the exception of the one after Amanda had called to inform him that Gabby was dead.

He was uneasy, though, because these past few hours of silence between them had been colder than the temperatures he'd endured in Antarctica covering a story on climate change. The emotional chill and Amanda's total and complete introspection made him wonder what she had planned. Because if he knew anything, it was that Amanda Jacobs was not the type to accept her fate—especially if that fate had anything to do with him.

Crossing to the rear of the plane, Simon retrieved her backpack from where he'd stashed it. She accepted it without a word, then walked toward the front and waited patiently for the door to be opened. Simon grabbed his bag and followed her.

In only a couple of minutes, they'd collected her suitcase and then headed toward customs. More than once, he tried to start a conversation, but she shut him down every time with her absolute refusal to speak. He might have thought her voice box had suffered some terrible calamity if she hadn't spoken clearly and politely, if a little woodenly, to the customs officer who questioned her.

After checking out her American passport and welcoming her home, he let her enter. She walked through and then it was Simon's turn to hand his documentation to the man. After answering questions about the stories that had taken him to four continents in three weeks, he, too, was allowed in.

Amanda wasn't waiting for him on the other side of the gate. Instead, she'd taken off, using the extra time he'd spent dealing with the customs agent to put some distance between them.

Swearing bitterly, he set off running. It was evening, so the terminal wasn't as crowded as it could have been, but it was still busy enough that he had trouble finding her, dressed as she was in simple baggy jeans and a black tank top.

When he got to the exit doors with still no sign of her, he paused, looked around wildly. Had he overreacted, jumped to conclusions? Maybe she'd had to use the restroom? But that didn't make sense. She would have told him if that was the case. Wouldn't she?

Walking slowly back the way he'd come, he scanned the exiting masses carefully. If he lost Amanda here, in Atlanta, he might never find her again. No cell phone, no address to go on, nothing at all. And while he'd spent the past eighteen months without her, he'd always known where she was. The idea of never finding her again was a sucker punch to the chest. Besides, how was he supposed to put his plans into action if he didn't know where she was?

It was on his third scan of the area that his gaze fell on a sign that read Ground Transportation, Taxis. His heart kicked up its rhythm as he took off in the direction of the arrow. Why hadn't he thought of it right away? Of course she would try to get a taxi.

As he burst into the steamy Atlanta night, he prayed he wasn't too late. Not that he didn't deserve to be left behind after his total and complete stupidity. But still, he couldn't help hoping—

There. There she was. Thank God for the delay at the taxi stand. Amanda was still five people away from getting a cab.

Weaving through the crowd, he came up on her left side. "Thanks for getting in line," he told her nonchalantly, as he cupped her elbow with his hand.

She whirled to face him, lips tight and eyes completely blank. The blankness frightened him. He'd always been able to tell where he stood, where Amanda was emotionally, by looking into her eyes. She'd never been one to hide her emotions away, so whatever she felt—happiness, anger, sorrow, confusion—shone brightly in the varying shades of gray.

Now there was nothing. He didn't know if it was because she'd finally found a way to lock her emotions down deep inside her or if it was because she really didn't feel anything. Either way, it didn't bode well for her or the tattered remnants of the relationship he'd been hoping to salvage.

"I would suggest going to the back of the line," she

told him woodenly. "Because you are *not* sharing a cab with me."

"Of course I am. How else are you going to find my apartment?"

A flash of surprise in those glorious eyes. Finally. "Why exactly would I need to know where your apartment is?"

"Because you'll be staying with me."

As they talked, the people in front of them slowly filed into cabs until, too soon, it was their turn. Simon slipped his hand from her elbow to her upper arm, tightening his fingers almost imperceptibly as he did so. Definitely not enough to hurt her, just enough that he'd have some warning if she decided to jerk away. He really didn't relish the idea of explaining this whole scenario to airport police.

"How many riders?" the taxi regulator asked.

"One," Amanda answered at the same time Simon said, "Two."

The tired-looking woman glanced between them, no alarm on her face but a definite perking up of her ears. "What's it going to be?" she asked.

"Two," Simon said firmly, guiding Amanda toward the waiting car.

"I am not going to your apartment," she insisted. "And I suggest you let go of my arm or I'm going to scream to the whole world how you managed to get me here."

"Get in the cab, Amanda."

It was the wrong thing to say, and the wrong tone to use. Every muscle in her body tightened with what he was sure was a painful intensity, and she said, very quietly, "Go to hell, Simon."

"I'm not going to let you wander around downtown Atlanta on your own, especially not at night."

"I am not your problem and haven't been for a very long time."

"In case you haven't noticed, I've made you my problem."

"Well, that's too bad for you, isn't it?"

Simon gritted his teeth, shoveling a hand through his hair in frustration as the taxi driver came around to get Amanda's suitcase. "Is there a problem?" the round little man asked in heavily accented English.

"No problem," Simon said. "We're going downtown. I'm about—"

"We are not going anywhere. *I* am going to a hotel." It was the most forceful Simon had heard her sound, and he was so relieved to see any expression of emotion from her that he conceded defeat. At least temporarily.

"Take us to the Loews." He turned to Amanda. "Okay? I'll get you settled for tonight and be back tomorrow so we can talk.'

She shook her head, a twisted smile on her lips. "I've been to a lot of places more dangerous than downtown Atlanta, Simon. I think I can handle this on my own."

He didn't like it, but short of kidnapping her again— something he didn't think would fly a second time— he didn't see that he had a choice. He felt the click of a sudden shift in the power dynamic between them and nearly choked as he firmly repeated, "The Loews," to both her and the cabdriver. Maybe if he didn't acknowledge his loss of control over the situation, no one else would notice.

"Fine. The Loews," she agreed.

He stepped back, angry and confused and more than a little worried, as Amanda settled herself into the back of the taxi. As it eased from the curb, he rushed to the first of the three cars that had pulled up behind hers.

"Follow that cab," he told the driver, feeling like a total idiot. "They should be going to the Loews, but I want to make sure she gets there safely."

Point of fact, he wanted to ensure that Amanda didn't change her mind halfway to the hotel and decide to go somewhere else. Or worse, back to the airport to catch a flight to God only knew where. After years of living in areas where it was almost impossible for her to spend her salary, she had the cash to disappear if that's what she wanted to do.

But much to his relief, her cab didn't stop until it deposited her outside the hotel. And still he made his driver wait outside the huge glass doors as he watched her walk through the lobby, toward the registration desk. Only after she was engaged in conversation with one of the desk clerks did he return to his own taxi.

He'd give her some space tonight. God knew, she deserved it. But by tomorrow, all bets were off. One way or the other, Amanda was going to learn that, though their daughter was dead, she was still very much alive.

CHAPTER SIX

AMANDA DROPPED HER SUITCASE by the door and then spent a minute studying her hotel room as if she'd never seen one before. It was large and luxurious, as rooms at the Loews usually were, and the bed was as big as a lake. Part of her longed to curl up on it and sleep. Sleep and sleep and sleep. It had been eighteen months since she'd slept in a real bed, longer if you counted the fact that she'd spent much of the six months before Gabby's death sleeping in a chair beside her daughter's bed—at the hospital and at home.

Images of Gabby from those last days—frail, emaciated, but still smiling—flipped through her mind and she knew she wasn't going to sleep. Not now, despite the bone-deep weariness that dogged her every step.

Walking farther into the room, she laid her backpack on the dresser and crossed to the huge picture windows that looked out over downtown Atlanta. Business hours had ended long ago, so the city was relatively quiet—or at least as quiet as a place this size could get. It was still too loud, too bright, too crowded for her. But then, she always felt that way after a stint in Africa, as if the world she had been born into was too vibrant for her. As if she'd never really belonged here.

She knew she didn't belong in this hotel in Atlanta. She'd been born and raised in Massachussetts, had gone to medical school at Harvard. Had established her own home there as an adult, as well. Her home and Gabby's.

The smart thing to do, she told herself as she walked into the bathroom to take a shower, would be to catch a flight to Boston. She knew the city and her stuff was there, even if her life no longer was. It would be so much easier to start over in Boston than Atlanta, a place that felt more foreign to her than Africa ever had.

But just the thought of returning to Boston without Gabby had her hands shaking and the blessed detachment that had enveloped her for the past few hours threatening to wear off. Anger cracked through her—at Jack, at Simon, but mostly at herself for being so stupid. For not anticipating that they would come up with drugging her to get her on that plane.

She hadn't planned on returning to the States, not now when the past was still so alive to her. When Jack had issued his ultimatum, she'd figured she would drift around Europe for a while. Find some low-income clinic to help out in until her friend decided to lift his ban. Not once had it occurred to her to come back here and face the cataclysm of agony that seemed to wait for her around every lamppost and street corner.

Caught up in her thoughts, she stepped into the shower without testing it and was hit with a blast of near-boiling water. It should have burned, especially considering the fact that in Somalia she'd been making due with water heated by the sun.

But instead of burning her, it felt good, the warmth seeping through her skin and into all the hollow spaces deep inside of her. She could feel her resolve melting, feel thoughts of Mabulu and Gabby and Simon all creeping in as the numbness finally began to thaw.

Panicked, she reached over and flipped the lever all the way to cold. Yet even as the frigid water bombarded her, she knew it was too late. She couldn't refreeze her emotions, couldn't put everything that had happened in the past two years back into the neat compartment it had once fit into.

Pain washed over her in waves, swamping her, nearly dragging her under, and Amanda started to cry. She turned, shoved her face into the shower spray so she wouldn't feel the tears rolling down her face—after all, she'd learned in the past eighteen months that if she didn't feel them, they weren't real—but it was too little, too late. Sobs decimated her, harsh, painful convulsions that wracked her whole body and ripped into fears and sorrows and memories she would much rather have kept buried.

She didn't know how long she stood there, crying, under the ice-cold water. Long enough for her teeth to chatter and her body to ache. Long enough for her stomach to burn with regret. More than long enough for exhaustion to swamp her and make her legs tremble beneath her.

Eventually the tears stopped, leaving her with a low-grade headache and eyes that felt as if she'd polished them with sandpaper. After making quick work of washing her hair and body, she wrapped a towel from the shower around her hair and then stepped out onto the bath mat. As she reached for a second towel, she got a full-body glimpse of herself.

It wasn't a pretty sight.

Amanda froze in front of the full-length mirror attached to the bathroom door and simply stared. In Africa, there wasn't much privacy and no full-length mirrors, so she hadn't had a chance to look at herself, really look at herself, in months. Now that she did, she realized why Jack, and even Simon, had been so concerned.

She looked *exactly* how she felt. Like hell. As if everything important to her in the world, everything that made her who she was, had been yanked out of her and all that was left was this sick, empty shell.

She closed her eyes, wanting to turn away. Wanting to hide from this newest realization as she had done all the others. But this time, the doctor in her wouldn't accept her cowardice. Her medical training forced her to stand there and catalog all the damage she'd done to herself since Gabby had died.

There was a lot of it.

Not sure what else to do, she finally decided to start at the top and work her way down. It was as good a method as any other, she figured.

Her hair was dull, lifeless, its usual glossy sheen almost completely gone, its curls limp. She ran a hand through it and realized it was thinner than it usually was. Vaguely she remembered it falling out in clumps for a few months right after she got to Africa. At the time she hadn't paid any attention, but now...now it seemed that she should have.

Her face didn't look any better, the skin sallow despite the tan that came from months of working under the African sun. The circles under her eyes were so dark that she looked as if she'd been punched, and there were deep grooves around her mouth that hadn't been there two years before.

She dropped her gaze, continued to carefully consider the damage she'd done to herself. She'd always been on the thin side—often too busy working to eat—but now she looked downright emaciated. Her collarbone stuck out in stark relief and each of her ribs showed prominently beneath her skin. Even her elbows, knees, the knobs on her wrists were starkly outlined—as if every ounce of fat and muscle had somehow vanished and the skin now lay directly on top of her skeleton.

And even her skin was in bad shape. Dry, lackluster, it was cracked in numerous places.

She was a mess. An utter, absolute, unmitigated disaster. And she had no one to blame but herself.

Not enough nutrition. Not enough care. For too long, she had been so wrapped up in her inner torment that she had neglected her physical body. Now she was paying the price.

She remembered thinking, more than once, that her clothes had somehow gotten bigger. She wore baggy scrubs so much of the time that it was easy to forget the way her jeans had once fit. But this almost skeletal image staring back at her wasn't her imagination. It was real and unhealthy, and if she didn't do something about it, very soon she would be in real trouble. Shocked and more than a little appalled, she ran her hands over her too-narrow hips. Even at her skinniest, she'd always had a little bit of padding there, a little bit of roundness. All that was gone now. She could actually trace the bones of her pelvis through the fragile skin.

Forcing herself to look away from the macabre image, she reached for a towel. Dried herself quickly without looking in the mirror again and then went into the bedroom. She opened her suitcase, pulled out a pair of sweats and a T-shirt and tried to ignore how big they felt when she pulled them on.

The last thing she was interested in was food, but she crossed to the phone, ordered an omelet with toast, fruit salad and a large glass of milk. It might take her most of the night to finish everything, but she was determined to do it.

She might have longed to die in Gabby's place, longed to die after her daughter had been taken from her. But she hadn't. Which meant that unless she planned to actually neglect herself to death, she had to start taking better care of herself.

And since she'd never been able to stand the idea of failure, starving to death was not really an option, no matter what she'd told Jack last night in her tent.

With at least half an hour to kill before her food arrived, Amanda pulled out her laptop and logged on to the internet. The first thing she did was check her bank balance. Thanks to her job, the small inheritance from her parents, the money from the sale of her house and Simon's child-support payments through the years— which she had socked away in a college fund Gabby would now never need—it was very healthy. Certainly healthy enough for her to do whatever she wanted for the next couple of years without having to worry about how she was going to support herself.

The only problem, then, was that she had no idea *what* she wanted to do. No place that she wanted to be besides back in the trenches, which she knew was out of the question.

So what *was* she going to do? Was she going to stay here, in Atlanta? There was nothing for her here but Simon, and now that they no longer shared a child, they had no bond. Yes, she had loved him desperately once, but that love was long gone. And even if it wasn't, it wouldn't matter. After what he'd done, there was no way she would risk letting him get close to her again.

At the same time, there was nothing for her anywhere else. She'd grown up in Boston and loved it, but she wasn't sure she could ever live there again. She and Gabby had spent a lot of time traveling the world together with For the Children, but once Gabby was diagnosed with cancer, they'd settled in Boston. If she went back there now, her little girl would be in every park Amanda walked by, in every corner ice-cream parlor and art store.

No, Boston was out of the question. And though she had no idea if Atlanta was where she wanted to be in the long term, for now it was as good a place as any, she supposed. Besides, she was here, and she didn't have the energy to go anywhere else.

So what exactly was she going to do here? she wondered as she hit on a visitor site for Atlanta. Maybe it was time for her to figure out not just what she should do, but what she *wanted* to do.

If there was such a thing.

And if there wasn't, well, she needed to know that, too. Because with all the uncertainties in her world, there was only one thing she was absolutely sure of. If she kept going on the path she was on, she would die.

She would simply dry up and float away, until there was nothing left of her.

And much as a part of her might wish for that very thing, for the cessation of pain that came with death, she couldn't just give in to it.

Her whole life, she'd been an overachiever. When Gabby got sick, Amanda had hunkered down for the fight of her life, a fight she swore that she wouldn't lose. Only, she had, and nothing had made sense since. Her whole world had gone spinning wildly off the rails. If she gave in to the misery inside of her, it would be just one more thing in her life that she'd failed at. And that wasn't an option.

So she would spend the night learning about Atlanta, looking for she didn't know what. At any rate, it was better than lying in bed and staring at the ceiling as she pretended to sleep.

Anything was.

SIMON SPENT AN ANXIOUS NIGHT worrying about Amanda. Was she okay? Was she sleeping or was she pacing the carpet at the Loews much as he was doing here? Was she even still at the hotel?

More than once, he tried to sleep, but ended up tossing the covers back and climbing out of bed in frustration. Finally, around 3:00 a.m., he gave up. Acknowledged that there would be no sleep for him that night, no matter how jet-lagged he felt.

He spent the time working instead. During the three weeks he'd spent in Asia last month, he hadn't gotten all the info he wanted on the lives of orphaned and badly injured children in war-torn Afghanistan, but he had enough to make a hell of a story. While he'd been on-site, one of the orphanages had been firebombed. He'd been there when it happened and the coverage he and his team had gotten—the individual horror stories he'd been able to tell—was more powerful than he could have imagined.

Which was a good thing, since he had no intention of leaving Atlanta anytime soon, story or no story. Amanda deserved better, and though he was years too late, he was determined not to leave her while she needed him. Not now. Not this time.

The minutes crept by, until he finally deemed it late enough to call Amanda. It was seven-forty, and though he was afraid of waking her when she so desperately needed to sleep, the need to check on her was more overwhelming.

But when the desk clerk put him through to her room, there was no answer. Maybe she was still sleeping, he told himself despite the uneasy feeling in his gut. Or in the shower. Or maybe she'd gotten hungry and gone downstairs for something to eat.

His thoughts were meant to convince him that there was nothing to worry about, but they didn't exactly do the job. Instead, by the time eight o'clock had rolled around and he'd called her room twice more to no avail, he was totally stressed-out.

Screw it, he decided. Even if she hadn't checked out of the hotel, that didn't mean she wasn't in trouble. With visions of Amanda lying injured on the bathroom floor, he slammed out of his apartment, barely remembering to yank on a pair of jeans before he went charging down to the parking garage and the car he rarely used but refused to give up.

By the time he got to the hotel, the nervousness had ratchetted up a few notches to alarm, despite the reassurances he kept giving himself. Amanda was fine. She was still asleep. She was ignoring him because she was angry with him. Believing that was a lot better than believing she'd done something stupid because she couldn't face life without Gabby.

He called her room from the hotel lobby and still got no answer. He checked out the restaurants and coffee bar, all to no avail. There was nothing to say that she hadn't left the hotel for breakfast at one of the nearby restaurants, but he doubted it. Still, it was worth a shot, so he settled on a bench near the elevators. He couldn't miss her if she came back.

At the same time, he continued to call her hotel room at ten-minute intervals, his concern growing. Part of him felt completely stupid for being this upset— Amanda was the most competent woman he'd ever met. She was fine, just angry at him for everything that had happened between them.

He might have believed all of the assurances he was giving himself if he hadn't seen her with his own eyes. But he had and he was worried—she had worked herself so close to exhaustion that an accident wasn't out of the realm of possibility.

He gave her another half hour and two more phone calls before he headed to the front desk. He might not know what room she was in, but he was going to find out.

After explaining the situation to a clearly skeptical

hotel manager, who at once refused to do anything to help him, Simon got desperate and did something he'd always sworn he wouldn't do.

"Look, maybe we should start over," he told the manager, an uptight little man in an expensive suit and constricting tie. He held a hand out to shake. "I'm Simon Hart." He named the news network he worked for, then said, "I'm one of their foreign correspondents. Maybe you've seen one of my special reports…"

The man's eyes widened as he realized who Simon was—which was exactly what he'd been counting on. "Anyway," he continued, "I know that Loews is one of the top hotels in Atlanta because of the individual care and attention that each guest receives. I can't imagine how awful the publicity would be if it came to the public's attention that one of your guests was lying injured in her room and you did nothing to help, despite being made aware of the situation."

The man's eyes narrowed and he turned an unattractive shade of puce that made Simon feel dirty. He hated using his journalistic credentials to threaten the guy, but at this point, he didn't know what else to do. Amanda's safety came first, and if the manager wasn't going to give him her room number, the least he could do was go check on her.

"Don't threaten me, Mr. Hart." The manager's voice had gone from understanding but firm to downright icy. "I am certain the Loews can withstand any dirt you might choose to throw at us." His sniff told Simon exactly what he thought of him.

"Please—"

"However, I will go upstairs and check on Ms. Jacobs myself. Will that satisfy you?"

"Yes. Absolutely. Thank you." Simon was shocked to realize he was shaking, sweating. He had managed to keep his cool under fire, both in battle and on some of the most dangerous streets in the world, yet he was now one small step from losing it completely.

Pulling back, he shoved his hands in his pockets and tried to get his too-fast heartbeat under control. But panic was a rampaging beast inside of him and he knew that he wouldn't be able to calm down until he was certain Amanda was all right. If she had listened to him the night before, if she had let him take care of her, none of this would be happening.

The manager started across the lobby and Simon followed him. But as soon as the man stopped at the elevators, he turned to Simon with a steely look in his eyes. "You don't actually expect to come upstairs with me, do you?"

Simon started to argue, again, but in the end figured it would be more expedient to wait in the lobby. He didn't want to waste any more time, even if every instinct he had screamed at him to beat the bastard's head against the wall until he began to see things Simon's way.

The ten minutes the man was out of his sight were some of the longest of his life. Guilt rose up, nearly suffocated him. What had he been thinking to let Amanda come here alone? Why hadn't he argued with her more? Why hadn't he forced her to listen to reason?

Sure, he hadn't wanted to upset her further, not when she looked so exhausted she could barely stand. But that hadn't been the only reason, he admitted to himself now. He hadn't wanted to fight with her because he'd been tired, worn-down, more than a little vulnerable himself. He'd wanted to be alone for a little while to lick his wounds, to regain his perspective, to shore up the wall he kept between himself and so much of the world. His sense of control had been precarious at best and he'd been afraid that spending much more time with Amanda would shatter it completely. He couldn't have dealt with that, not when she was so obviously out for his blood.

Now his worries and objections seemed petty. Ridiculous. If something had happened to her, if she was lying up there, hurt or worse—he wouldn't let himself even consider the possibility.

He resumed pacing his little corner of the lobby, his eyes on the elevators. And when he saw the manager striding quickly out of a car, he was across the cavernous room in a flash.

"Is she all right?" he demanded. "Did you talk to her?"

The man's expression had gone from icy to downright hostile. "Ms. Jacobs is, as I told you at the beginning of our conversation, *not* in her room. There is no sign of illness or foul play," he continued before Simon could ask. "It appears she has simply gone out to enjoy the many attractions Atlanta has to offer."

He shot Simon a fulminating glare. "May I suggest that you do the same?"

Simon bristled a little at the man's tone, but in the end, all he said was, "Thank you for checking." He had been the asshole who'd completely overreacted, after all.

Still, knowing she wasn't in her room freaked him out.

Where was she?

He highly doubted Amanda was doing the tourist thing. Not as jet-lagged and worn-down as she was. So where had she gone? He glanced at his watch for the thousandth time. It was already past noon—he'd been waiting for her for well over three hours.

A flash of purple caught his eye as he was walking to the sofa he had pretty much taken up residence in, and he turned his head abruptly, trying to find it again. That shade of purple was Amanda's favorite color.

Sure enough, she was striding through the hotel lobby, a shopping bag in each of her hands. Completely unaware of the havoc her little shopping jaunt had caused.

He was across the lobby in a shot, climbing onto her elevator car before she even realized he was behind her. *Play it cool,* he told himself. *Don't come on too strong or she'll shut down completely.* So much better to act as though her disappearance hadn't taken fifteen years off his life.

Almost convinced he could follow his own advice, Simon had turned to face her, when Amanda asked, all hostility and annoyance, "What are *you* doing here?"

"Where have you been?" he demanded, his good intentions flying out the window like so much confetti. "I've been here for three hours, waiting on you."

"No one asked you to do that." As she spoke, she raised one imperious eyebrow, and for a moment she looked so much like the Amanda he used to know, so much like the woman she was before life had beaten her down, that he felt himself respond instinctively to her. Felt his body come to life in the way it only ever did for her—heart racing, senses heightened, breathing quickened.

In the old days, when they'd been together, she had accused him of being an adrenaline junkie. He'd denied it, but even as he did, he'd known she was right. He did his job because he believed people deserved to know the truth, but he also did it because there was nothing else in the world that made him feel as alive as pitting himself against unfavorable odds.

Nothing, that was, except being near Amanda. Holding her, making love to her—

He slammed the brakes on his thoughts *and* his libido. Though he was grateful it was back after months of being MIA, he also knew this was not exactly the time to have any feelings for Amanda, good or bad, come raring back to life.

"I've been worried," he told her through clenched teeth as the elevator stopped on the seventeenth floor and they both stepped out. "I thought—"

"What?" she demanded as he trailed her down the hall like a puppy begging for attention. Which grated. A lot.

"I thought you'd—" He had enough sense to stop before he blurted out the ugly suspicion that had grown in his mind with every unanswered ring of her telephone.

But it was too late. The damage had already been done. "Committed suicide?" she asked, her voice low and furious now. "Twelve years and that's what you think of me? Do you even know me at all?"

She dropped her packages next to the door as she fished her key card out of her purse.

"It wasn't like that," he told her, wondering when he had lost control of the situation. This was *not* their normal dynamic—he was usually the one rushing off and *she* was the one trying to get his attention, the one worrying about *his* safety.

Not that he expected things to be the same between them, after all that had happened, but it would be nice if something felt familiar. Because right now, he had the shaky sensation of trying to find steady ground in quicksand.

"I wanted to make sure you were okay. Between the sedative and how frail you are, I thought something could have happened."

As soon as the words were out of his mouth, Simon knew he'd said the wrong thing. Again. And yet he didn't regret it, because for the first time since he'd found her in Somalia, Amanda's eyes blazed with life, with passion. The fact that it was anger driving her didn't matter, not when the dead, haunted look was finally gone.

"If you were so worried about me, perhaps you shouldn't have drugged me to begin with." She pushed the door open, thrust her packages inside and then walked in. The dismissive set of her shoulders told him that she was done with him. Conversation over.

As anger began working its way through his own system, replacing the bewilderment, it was only his quick reflexes that kept him from having the door slammed in his face. Bracing his foot against it, he shoved the door gently but inexorably, forcing Amanda to let him in.

For a second, he thought she was going to wrestle with him, but eventually she sighed and stepped farther into the room. "I did what I had to do," he told her. "You weren't going to come back to America on your own."

"It wasn't your decision."

"Bullshit. Just because we aren't together anymore doesn't mean that I don't still care about you. I couldn't leave you there. Not like that. If I hadn't come, what would you have done? Where would you have gone?"

Her eyes widened incredulously. "Are you even listening to yourself? Do you really think I need you? After everything that's happened, after all the things you've done, do you really believe that I will *ever* let myself depend on you again, *for anything?*"

She might have been down, but she wasn't out, and as usual, Amanda's words cut straight to the heart of everything he didn't want to discuss. Everything he didn't want to deal with.

Still, he couldn't walk away. Not now. "You can push me away all you want, Amanda, but it's not going to work. This time, I'm going to stick."

"Yeah, until the next story comes along. Isn't that your modus operandi?"

"Not this time. I'll be here for as long as you need me."

"Need you?" she repeated with a laugh that was anything but humorous. "You'll be here for as long as I need you? Don't you think you have that backward?"

"What's that supposed to mean?" he asked, starting to sweat. "I'm not the one on the verge of a nervous breakdown here."

"No. You're just the one hell-bent on atoning for his sins any way he can. You weren't there for Gabby when she died, weren't there for me after she was gone, and now you want to make up for it.

"You want to help me because it assuages your conscience, not because you give a damn about what really happens to me. You've never given a damn what happened to me, Simon. Never given a damn about anyone who wasn't involved in one of your precious stories.

"Need you? I'll never need you. I'll never *let* myself need you. Not ever again." She gestured to the door. "Now get out."

Her words slammed into him like bullets, each one causing more damage than the one before. He gaped at her in shock. Was that how she saw him? Was that really what she thought he was doing? Trying to make up for his mistakes?

As if that was even possible.

He wanted to help her, because she needed help, because he cared about her, because she'd been the mother of his child and he couldn't forget that any more than he could forget their long history. He wasn't under any illusion that she would ever exonerate him from what he'd done.

"I'm not looking for forgiveness," he told her. "I want to make sure you're okay."

"Bullshit." She threw the expletive back at him. "For once in your life, be honest, Simon. If not with me, then with yourself."

"What does that even mean?" None of this was going the way he'd planned it.

She shook her head, the expression on her face almost pitying. "You're more in need of redemption than anyone I've ever met. You're desperate for it—why else would you have come to Africa? Why else would we even be having this conversation?

"But I'm no one's redemption. I won't take that on, not even for you. *Especially* not for you. I have enough problems making it through the day without adding your guilt to the mix."

His head was whirling as he tried to comprehend all the accusations she'd hurled at him, and in desperation, he latched on to the last thing she'd said. "You think that's all I feel for you? Guilt?"

"What else is left?" she asked with a toss of her head. "It's not like we ever had anything real between us, anyway."

Nothing real? It took every ounce of willpower he had not to physically stumble away from her. Was that what she really believed? That his relationships with her, with their daughter, were nothing but shams? They were the only real things he'd ever had in his entire life. To think that she thought so little of him—so little of *them*—cut like the sharpest of knives.

Enraged, hurting, desperate to convince her—and himself—that her words were a lie, he grabbed on to her arms above the elbows and hauled her toward him.

"What are you doing?" she demanded, and he noted for the first time that her voice contained something other than anger.

Instead of answering, he lowered his mouth to hers.

CHAPTER SEVEN

EVEN AFTER ALL THESE YEARS, he tasted exactly as she remembered. Like coffee and cinnamon and sweet, ripe oranges. Despite her best intentions, and the little voice in the back of her head telling her that this was a really bad idea, Amanda allowed Simon to coax her lips apart.

To nibble on her bottom lip for long, leisurely seconds.

To slip his tongue inside her mouth and explore the hidden recesses.

Her hands came up to his shoulders—to push him away, she told herself. To stop this madness. And it was madness—painful, out-of-control insanity that was going to stop right now.

But her hands didn't work the way she wanted them to. Instead of pushing him away, they ended up tangling in the soft cotton of his T-shirt.

This was wrong, Amanda told herself, even as she tilted her head to give Simon better access. Wrong, wrong, wrong. Even if Gabby's death wasn't between them, there was still too much history. Too much pain and anger and confusion to ever make this a good idea.

Despite knowing all that, she couldn't find the strength to pull away. Not when the memories, good as well as bad, were swamping her. Not when she felt her body—really felt it—for the first time in longer than she could remember.

His hand crept up to cup the back of her head, his fingers tangling in her hair the way they'd done so many times before. It felt so good, so familiar, that she allowed herself to relax into him, allowed her body to rest lightly against his as she slid her own hands up to his shoulders.

He was as lean and hard as she remembered, his body bordering on skinny except for the rangy muscles that covered every inch of him. Muscles that came from lugging packs full of camera equipment in some of the most remote areas of the world rather than regular workouts at the gym.

She flexed her fingers, dug them into the muscles of his upper back, and he groaned. His hands tightened in her hair as he walked her across the room until her back was pressed against the wall. Then he leaned into her, and he felt so good, so hot, that she gasped. His body heat worked its way deep inside of her, soaked all the way through her until the core of ice at the center of her being began to melt. A core that the searing heat of Africa hadn't come close to touching.

She wanted the kiss to go on forever, wanted to hold on to this delicious warmth inside her for as long as possible. If she could stay here, right here, with her body alive and her thoughts wrapped up in something other than Gabby, she would be okay.

Simon started to pull away and she whimpered, tried to hold his mouth against hers for just a few more seconds. She wasn't ready to lose this connection, this heat, wasn't ready to start thinking again. He must have understood—and felt the same way—because his touch suddenly became a million times more aggressive. His hands slipped down her arms to her sides and then up to cup her breasts as he pressed himself firmly against her.

She gasped at the feel of him, hard and fully aroused, and for a moment she wanted nothing more than to touch him. To let him touch her. To take the sudden inferno blazing between them all the way.

But then, when she least expected it, he wrenched his mouth from hers. As he did, whatever spell had woven itself between them was broken. Shocked, and more than a little horrified at her behavior, Amanda shoved Simon away from her, stumbling along the wall in an effort to get away from him.

What was she doing?

What was she letting him do?

And more important, why?

At Gabby's funeral, she'd promised herself she was done. Sworn to herself that this would never happen again. And yet here she was, letting him do whatever he wanted to her. Letting him use her all over again.

Bitterly disappointed in herself, she crossed the room, went to look out at the city below. Today, it was bustling with traffic and people and noise and light, the view as different from the one she'd observed last night as she was from the woman she'd once been.

"Did that feel like guilt to you?" Simon asked, and he was still breathing heavily. Of course, so was she.

Without turning, she answered truthfully, "It felt like desperation."

A soft curse was his only answer. His footsteps whispered across the carpet and she braced herself for the feel of his hand on her shoulder again. She wouldn't react this time, she promised herself. She wouldn't let him get to her.

Except, his touch never came. Instead, there was only the soft click of the door as he let himself out.

Still, she refused to turn. To stare after him like a lovesick girl who didn't know any better. Though her body ached for him, she didn't turn. Instead, she stood by the window and tried to pretend the past few minutes hadn't happened.

She'd never been one for self-delusion, but this time it was a matter of self-preservation. If she had any hopes of putting the broken pieces of her life back together, she had to stay away from Simon. Because every instinct she had told her that letting him back in wouldn't just break her this time. It would destroy her completely.

SIMON STOOD IN the parking garage and stared around the space with unseeing eyes. He knew he needed to find his car and get out of there, but at that moment he couldn't do anything but relive the past few minutes in Amanda's room. Not the kiss, which had been as explosive as he remembered, but what had happened afterward.

A kiss that had meant so much to him, that had brought him back to a place where he was loved and wanted and desired, had done nothing for her. Oh, she'd reacted physically, but that was no big deal. The chemistry between them had always been explosive.

But the coldness she'd shown afterward, the wall

she'd thrown up between them without saying a word, had hurt him more than he'd believed possible. He'd thought they were connecting for the first time in a long time, while Amanda had just felt as if he was tearing her apart.

He didn't know what to think about that, or how to feel.

Forcing himself to put one foot in front of the other, he finally found his car and climbed in. A glance at the dashboard clock told him that it was after two. He'd wasted most of the day waiting around for Amanda and had nothing to show for it except the uneasiness still churning in his gut.

Not sure what else to do, he did what he always did when he was confused—headed into work. He'd come back early from Afghanistan, and the network was going to expect the special he'd promised them right on time.

When he'd flipped the news on after getting home last night, he'd seen the promo spot for his special at least three times. Which meant he needed to get his ass in the box and piece the whole thing together, including the voice-over work. He'd played around with it a little when he couldn't sleep last night, but now it was time to get serious.

Besides, dealing with the horrors of Afghanistan was a hell of a lot easier than dealing with the mess he'd made of his own life.

When he got to the studio, he really wanted nothing more than to do just that. Maybe then he could forget the churning in his gut, not to mention the confusion that had put it there.

But his back-to-back trips to Afghanistan and then South America had kept him out of the office for a few weeks and everyone seemed to want to check in with him. To check on him, since news of his unexpected trip to Africa had spread through the office like wildfire. Even those who didn't want to poke and pry—and when it came to journalists, they were few and far between—were happy to sit around and chat until he was nearly out of his mind.

By the time he finally made it into one of the editing rooms, he was close to snarling. He'd never been a huge talker at the best of times, and today it had felt as if every conversation, every word, was a slice across his already raw flesh.

Sinking into the nearest chair, he closed his eyes for a moment. Just sat there in the dark, resting, and tried to get out of his own head. This special was his baby, after all, and one he'd bugged the network for months to let him do. He needed to hit a home run with it. To begin with, a lot of time, money and effort had gone into the documentary, all of which demonstrated the higher-ups' faith in him, even though he hadn't worked for the network for a full year yet.

More important, the story he had to tell—the story of the children of Afghanistan—was one that needed to be told. The atrocities they suffered as the war ripped through their country had to be made public.

But every time he closed his eyes, he didn't see the footage he and his cameraman had so painstakingly shot. He didn't see the people he'd interviewed, the stories he'd recorded.

Instead, he saw Amanda. Fragile, dry-eyed, devastated as she faced him down. He saw Gabby, listless, miserable, in more pain than any child should have to bear.

He saw himself, running away, because that's what he did in situations he couldn't control.

Unable to deal with the guilt ripping through him yet again, he opened his eyes, shook it off, refusing to get bogged down in the memories of his daughter. He'd been running from the way he'd failed her for over eighteen months now. Seeing Amanda brought it all back, but that didn't mean he had to dwell on it.

Didn't mean he had to focus on what had been instead of what was.

Shaking his head to clear it, he shoved the emotion, the baggage, down where it belonged. And got started doing what he did best.

He worked for about an hour and a half editing the story, piecing bits of film together for the cleanest look and the biggest emotional payoff. He knew the feeling he was going for, knew the stories—the people— he wanted to use to best illustrate what was going on over there, but still, there was so much footage to go through. So much pain to document. So many incredible sound bytes that it was much harder to narrow them down than usual.

When Mark Douglas, his cameraman and friend, walked in, Simon was deep in the middle of footage of Tarek, a fourteen-year-old boy he had met in Afghanistan. The kid was blind in one eye, scarred on the left side of his face from being shot when he was eleven and not receiving the proper medical care. Like so many of the Afghan children, he was orphaned, having lost both his parents to violence in the past eleven years.

"I remember that kid," Mark said, tapping the screen. "He was a fighter."

Simon nodded, not bothering to look up until he'd inserted the interview piece he wanted into the beginning of his documentary. When he finally got it right, he turned to Mark with his first genuine smile of the day.

"Glad to see you made it back in one piece," he told the other man.

"I thought that was my line. You're the one who had to fly in and out of Somalia. How'd that go, anyway?"

Simon thought of Amanda, strung out and exhausted, and of the fight they'd had that afternoon. But all he said was, "It went good. Everything's fine."

"Glad to hear it." Mark clapped him on the back to emphasize his point. "I've never seen you like that before."

"Like what?"

"Freaked out. I mean, you're always so cool, no matter what's going on. It's one of the reasons the others are jealous that I get to go into the field with you."

Simon shook his head. "I watch this station every day. The other field reporters are just as good as I am."

Mark shook his head. "Some of them are, some of them aren't. But none of them is as good at keeping their head when things go to shit around them. You always manage to detach from what's happening, to stand aside from it and figure out what to do, no matter how chaotic or screwed up things get. Which, as some-

one who has benefited from that on more than one oc-
casion, I appreciate."

Simon wasn't sure how to respond to that—wasn't
sure his supposed detachment was a compliment. The
uncertainty must have shown on his face because Mark
clapped him on the back again and said, "I mean, that's
a good thing. It's an awesome trait to have when you're
a reporter."

Yeah, but maybe not such an awesome one to have as
a human being. Simon almost said as much, but bit his
tongue at the last minute. It wasn't Mark's fault Simon
was such an utter bastard. Wasn't anyone's fault but his
own.

As if sensing that he'd gone too far, Mark cleared his
throat and nodded at the screen. "Can I see what you've
done?"

"Sure." Simon cued the footage and it started at the
beginning. He had only about twenty-eight minutes of
the forty-seven-minute documentary laid down, and
about five of those weren't yet set in stone. But as he
watched the scenes play out in front of him, he couldn't
help nodding. Already the voice-over parts were weaving themselves together in his head. His crew had done
a good job.

He glanced at Mark, intending to congratulate him,
but saw that his cameraman had tears in his eyes as he
watched the screen. Of course, Mark caught him looking and flushed a little. He was obviously embarrassed,
but he didn't say anything. Neither did Simon. The stuff
they were watching was tough, some of it almost impossible to imagine despite the fact that they had been
there.

That was the whole point of the special, to bring the reality of life over there into people's living rooms. To touch them, to make them think. To help them understand.

He should be proud of what he'd done, proud of what they'd all done. He could see that Mark was. And Simon supposed that he was, as well. But that satisfaction was cushioned by the detachment he always felt, by the buffer he kept between himself and the people he reported on.

If he was honest, he would admit that it was the same buffer he'd kept between himself and Amanda all these years. The same buffer he'd kept between himself and Gabby, though she was his daughter and he had loved her very much. He hadn't allowed himself to show that love, at least not in the way that other fathers did.

Oh, he'd brought her things from all over the world, had taken her to amusement parks and movies and even on vacation to Hawaii, though she'd been too young to appreciate the beauty of the island. But he'd never been very demonstrative, never been one to hug her unless she hugged him first and expected it in return. Never been one to think about her when he was away from her.

Not like Amanda, who had let so much of her life revolve around their little girl. When Gabby was a baby, Amanda had turned her whole life around to stay in the States and work until Gabby was a year old and able to go with her to Jamaica and Mexico and Haiti.

And when Gabby had gotten sick, Amanda had turned into a tiger mom. She'd rushed their daughter back to the States, called in every favor she could from the best oncologists in the country, all in an effort to make Gabby well. She'd put her whole career, her whole life, on hold for their daughter.

Unlike him. Simon had rushed in with toys and sympathy, but had never managed to stick around for the hard stuff. For the aftermath of the chemo appointments, the bone-marrow transplant that didn't take, the last weeks and days as Gabby faded quietly away.

It had hurt him when his daughter had died. But he hadn't let it devastate him or even slow him down. He hadn't allowed his heart to break. Not the way Amanda's had.

God, he really was an utter failure as a human being, so concerned with being in control that he never really let himself feel.

With that knowledge in the forefront of his mind, Simon worked long into the night, long after Mark had taken off to be with his own wife and daughter.

As he loaded more footage, he had to stop several times when images of those last few months with Gabby kept slipping into his mind. He'd never let himself dwell on them at the time, or take them out and examine them after she had died.

Images of her wasting away to nothing, unable to eat because of the chemo-induced nausea.

Gabby crying from the pain. Sitting on her mother's lap, holding on to her for all she was worth as Amanda did everything she could to keep the nightmares—and the Grim Reaper—at bay.

Picture after picture after picture came to him as he tried to bury himself once again in work. The images weren't all sad, and maybe that was worse, because seeing her healthy and happy was somehow even harder.

Hours passed as he tried to work, battling back the emotions he'd suppressed for so long. When he couldn't take it anymore, when he thought he might actually go insane if he stayed in that editing room for one more second, he burst out into the main studio to find the offices all but abandoned. Only the skeleton crew that worked overnight was left.

He traversed the building quickly, striding onto the sidewalk just as dawn burst across the sky in a multi-hued spectacle. He paused for a moment, stared at the red-orange-and-purple-streaked sky, and very nearly broke down for the first time in his adult life.

Deliberately turning away from the dazzling beauty of the sunrise, he walked in the opposite direction. Not really caring where he was going, just wanting to be somewhere else. Wanting to be *someone* else, if only for a little while.

He walked for well over an hour, wandering the streets as Atlanta slowly came to life.

The narrow boulevards of downtown began to fill with cars and people. Traffic in and out of the skyscrapers that lined the sidewalks increased exponentially. Lights came on in restaurants and he found himself stopping at a coffee shop on the same block as the Loews, buying two huge cups of coffee and a couple of muffins.

Then, unsure of his reception but knowing there was nowhere else he'd rather be, he headed up the street to the hotel. To Amanda.

CHAPTER EIGHT

AMANDA CRAWLED OUT OF BED at the first knock, stumbling to the door on unsteady legs. She was exhausted, after having spent another sleepless night in her too-plush bed, trying to avoid her failures as a mother and a doctor.

She hesitated with her hand on the lock, unsure if she really wanted to open the door. She knew who was on the other side—who else would it be?—and she did *not* want to deal with Simon right now. Not if it meant they were going to fight. She was tired and more than a little shaky. Certainly not up to holding her own with him, at least not right now.

But she also couldn't leave him out in the hall. He wouldn't give up and it was still early enough that people in the neighboring rooms would be annoyed. Besides, she didn't want a repeat of yesterday, anyway. Finally, she turned the knob, prepared to tell him to get lost.

But the second she caught sight of him, the words clogged her throat. For the first time since he'd shown up in Somalia, he looked as tired and worn-down as she felt. And when he held up a cup of coffee and a pastry bag, she saw a hint of vulnerability in his eyes that he didn't try to hide.

It was that look, more than anything else, that had

her pushing the door wide and stepping aside so that he could come in. She thought about going into the bathroom and slipping on one of the hotel robes to cover the shorts and tank top she normally slept in, but in the end decided it wasn't worth it. It wasn't as if he hadn't already seen everything she had, more times than she could possibly count.

"I think I got it right," Simon said as he handed the coffee to her. "Lots of milk and one packet of sugar?"

She nodded. "That's perfect. Thanks." She took a sip and again felt that curious warmth deep inside of her. For a moment, she wondered if it was the coffee or Simon, then let the thought go. It didn't matter, because the only thing in the room coming close to her mouth today was the coffee.

Whatever had happened between them the day before had been an aberration and she was so *not* going to repeat her mistake. Not now and not ever.

Silence reigned for long minutes as they simply stood at opposite ends of the room and quietly sipped their coffee. Tension stretched taut between them and she had a difficult time keeping herself from doing something she *never* did—nervously chattering to fill up the disquiet. Mindless chitchat was so not her bag, but the tension was making her long for a distraction. Any distraction.

Simon must have felt the same because he broke first. Holding up the bag, he mumbled, "I brought muffins."

"Oh." Her uneasy stomach almost revolted at the thought of the rich pastry. "Well, thank you."

"Chocolate and blueberry. I mean, one of each, not together. I didn't know what you wanted. I mean—"

He seemed to forcibly stop himself, and as she stared into dazed green eyes, Amanda realized he was as shocked by his inane outburst as she was. Simon was a lot of things, but a rambler was not one of them, and there was something oddly endearing about watching him bumble around. Maybe because it meant he was even more nervous than she was.

Concern bloomed inside of her, along with a hint of affection that made her head hurt all over again. She tried to nip both emotions in the bud, not wanting to feel anything for him after the debacle of yesterday afternoon. But it was nearly impossible. Not when she suddenly remembered all of his good points and the warm feelings she'd once had for him. Feelings that she'd thought had been totally eclipsed by what he'd done eighteen months before. Now, however, she wasn't so sure, and while that uncertainty made her very nervous, she also felt more compassion toward Simon than she had in a long time.

"Blueberry," she told him.

"What?" he asked, staring at her blankly. She almost laughed. It was as if his mouth had been totally disconnected from his brain.

"The muffin. I'll take blueberry." But only because she remembered that he had a liking for all things chocolate. "You want to sit down?"

"Yeah. I'd like that." He handed her a bag, before sinking gratefully into the chair near the window, while she perched on the bed.

She stared at the pastry for long seconds, trying to

decide if her stomach could handle the sugar and fat it was sure to be loaded with. Before she could make up her mind, he whispered, "I'm sorry, Amanda."

The words were so unexpected that at first she couldn't process them. But as they sank in, she found herself stiffening, her fingers forming fists of their own volition.

"For what?" she asked, the words coming automatically. But as she waited for him to answer, she realized they were completely apropos. Not because she didn't think he had anything to apologize for, but because he'd done so many things wrong, she wanted to be clear what it was he was sorry for.

He looked her straight in the eye. "For drugging you, for bringing you here against your will. For—"

She forgot how to breathe, waiting for the words she'd spent the past eighteen months anticipating, but never really thinking she'd hear. Still, when they came, she was completely unprepared.

"For Gabby. I'm so sorry for not being there, when she died. I should have listened to you. I should have—" He crossed to the window, but not before Amanda saw the tears sliding down his face.

She wanted to be hard-hearted. Wanted to let him suffer, as she had for so long. But now that the moment she'd thought she wanted was finally here, she couldn't do it. She had loved this man once, enough to want to marry him. Enough to have his child. And no matter how satisfying she'd thought it would be to see him humbled, she was in no way ready for the reality of it.

Crossing the room quickly and quietly, she slipped her arms around his waist. Rested her cheek against the rigid muscles of his shoulders. He stiffened even more, jerked as though an electric current had hit him. But he didn't pull away and neither did she.

"She asked for you. At the end. She wanted to see you." She didn't say the words to hurt him, but because they needed to be said. For months now, she'd held them inside and nursed her bitterness. Nursed her anger and disappointment at him.

That's not why she told him, though. She told him because she could hear his heart beating unsteadily beneath her ear, feel the same anguish coming off him that she'd always felt. And it made her understand in a way she never had before.

He needed to know that he'd mattered. For too much of his life, he hadn't. To anyone. If she could give him the gift of knowing how much his daughter loved him, then the pain—for both of them—would be well worth it.

Her words made Simon jerk again, harder this time, and he let out a low moan that she felt all the way to her bones. "I'm sorry I wasn't there. Sorry I didn't understand. I didn't want to understand, didn't want to believe that she was really that close to the end."

"I know," she whispered.

"I was stupid. A child. I thought if I wasn't there, it wouldn't happen. She wouldn't die. She couldn't." Tears thickened his voice and he sucked in a deep breath, talked through them, though the effort obviously cost him. "But then she did. And I didn't know what to do. I got that phone call from you and I wanted to die. Wanted to curl up in a ball and die, right along with her."

He was sobbing now, deep, harsh cries that shook his whole body and were oh, so painful to listen to.

"She knew you loved her," she told him, because it was the truth and because she wanted desperately to stop his pain. She'd lived with that kind of agony for eighteen months—she wouldn't wish it on anyone, not even Simon. No matter how much she'd once thought he deserved it.

"Did she?" he demanded bitterly. "Did she really?"

"Oh, Simon—"

She didn't get a chance to finish, because he turned, wrapped his arms around her and squeezed so tightly she could barely breathe. His breath came in shaky gasps as he buried his face in the curve of her neck. "Our baby died and I wasn't there, Amanda. She died and I was in Europe, following up on yet another bombing. She *died* and I was off, listening to other people talk about their own pain, about losing their own children."

He took a deep, shuddering breath. "She died and I wasn't there. I wasn't there. I wasn't there."

She couldn't hold out any longer, against Simon or the pain that seemed to flow from his body and into hers on an invisible current. Though she had shed copious tears the night before, it turned out there were more inside of her. So many more that she feared she'd drown if she didn't get them out.

So she did, standing there, clutching Simon to her as if he was the only other survivor in a shipwreck. And maybe he was—the only survivor in their own personal disaster.

For long minutes, he cried along with her, his

hot tears mingling with hers—on their cheeks, their necks—as they mourned their daughter, together, for the first time since the funeral she'd been too numb to pay attention to.

As she stood there, holding Simon, Amanda felt the anger she had carried with her for so long slowly begin to drain away. The hard kernel of resentment that had resided in her stomach for two years now slowly dissolved until only sorrow remained.

Sorrow and guilt and more regret than she imagined one body could hold.

Eventually Simon pulled away. Strode into the bathroom and returned with a box of tissues that he offered to her. She took a couple, wiped her face and blew her nose. Waited as he did the same.

His eyes, when he looked at her, were red-rimmed and filled with the regret she, too, felt. "I wish—"

She shook her head and pressed trembling fingers to his lips. "Wishes don't get the job done," she murmured, repeating one of Gabby's favorite phrases.

He winced, but nodded. Then he didn't say or do anything else for a long time. When he did talk, it was in a whisper so low she had to strain to hear. "I'm tired. I'm so tired, Amanda."

She knew exactly what he meant.

Without giving herself time to second-guess her motives, she led Simon to the big bed she'd had such a hard time crawling into on her own. Somehow it wasn't so difficult when he was there with her—a fact she was *not* going to examine too deeply.

"Sleep," she told him softly as she stretched out beside him.

He reached one big hand up between them, cupped her face in his palm. "Stay. Please."

"I will." She stroked the too-long strands of his damp hair away from his face. Watched his swollen eyes close and his face relax as he drifted into sleep, quick and quiet as a baby.

She hadn't planned on sleeping, hadn't thought she'd be able to with the numbness obliterated and emotions running riot inside of her, but as she lay there on the comfortable bed, her body pressed tightly against the familiar warmth of his, Amanda felt herself begin to relax for the first time in a long while.

Closing her eyes, she let the dreamy lassitude take over and drifted, slowly, into the first restful sleep she'd had since Gabby was diagnosed with cancer.

SIMON AWOKE WITH GRITTY EYES and a pounding in his head that was so bad he feared it was the result of a weeklong bender. But as he opened his eyes, squinting against the early-afternoon sunlight that was drifting through the window, he remembered everything that had happened. Not sure how he felt about his loss of control—and subsequent vulnerability—he started to stretch. Then stiffened when he realized that Amanda was curled against him like a cat.

"What's wrong?" she murmured in sleepy protest.

"Nothing," he whispered, brushing his mouth against her jasmine-scented hair. "Go back to sleep."

She shook her head, then it was her turn to stretch a little. "What time is it?"

"I'm not sure." He craned his neck around to get

a glimpse of the clock on the nightstand behind him. "Almost two."

"Wow. We slept the whole day away."

"Yeah." He tried to pull her close again, but Amanda pressed against his chest, rolling until she was sitting cross-legged on the edge of the bed. She was facing away from him and he didn't like it. Not after everything that had passed between them that morning.

He pushed himself onto an elbow, ran a gentle finger down her back. "Thanks."

"For what?" The eyes she turned to him were dark and stormy, the way he'd always liked them.

"For not kicking me out. For listening. For not hating me. Take your pick."

"I'd rather take a shower," she said, climbing off the bed and heading toward the bathroom. "I won't be long and then it's all yours."

He watched, perplexed, as she closed the bathroom door firmly behind her. What had happened here? He'd tried to start a real, meaningful conversation and she was the one who had ducked out? After years of telling him that they needed to communicate more?

It was another role reversal, another change he wasn't sure how to deal with. Still, he wouldn't try to force her to talk to him. Not when he was still feeling so raw and exposed himself.

Maybe they'd done enough soul-searching for one day.

His stomach grumbled, loudly, and he reached for the room-service menu. After a cursory glance, he ordered both of them a steak, complete with baked potato, salad and dessert. Amanda wasn't a huge meat eater,

but she was going to have to suck it up for a while. She
needed to put some weight on, needed to get herself
healthy, and a bunch of vegetables weren't going to cut
it on their own.

The shower was still running, so he stood and
stretched. What he wouldn't give to be standing under
the hot spray right now, letting the water wash away all
the kinks and knots that seemed to have taken up permanent residence along his spine.

What he didn't relish was the thought of getting back
into the same clothes when he was done. He'd been
wearing them for over thirty-six hours, and while it
wasn't the first time he'd slept in his clothes—doing so
was practically Journalism 101—he'd never enjoyed it.

As he glanced around the room, his gaze fell on
Amanda's suitcase and he wondered if she had any
scrubs in there. Whatever she had was guaranteed to
be utilitarian and baggy and might fit him. The pants
would be a little short and snug, but if it meant not
having to put these clothes back on, he could live with
his ankles showing for a little while.

He felt more than a little guilty rummaging through
her suitcase, but it took only a minute for him to find
something he thought might fit—scrubs that were a
size large despite her extra-small frame. Either he was
right and they completely dwarfed her or she'd packed
a pair of Jack's scrubs by mistake.

The thought had every muscle in his body tightening as he imagined how she might have ended up with
the other doctor's clothes. None of the scenarios—and
if he was honest, there was really only one—were re-
assuring and he found himself wondering if there was

more between Jack and Amanda than he had thought to look for. They'd been friends for ages, but had that changed into something else, something more, during this last trip?

Not that it should matter if it had, he told himself viciously. He and Amanda hadn't been together for years. Whom she chose to spend time with was absolutely none of his business.

Of course, that didn't mean he didn't want to rip Jack limb from limb, because he did. Very much. It was bad enough that the other man had been there for Amanda when Simon wasn't able to face the pain of losing their daughter. The idea that Jack had also made love to her when she was at her most vulnerable was almost more than Simon could bear.

Failed romantic relationship or not, a part of him still thought of Amanda as his. A feeling that had been reinforced by the fact that he'd never seen her with another man. Not in that way.

Which only made this whole thing with Jack more concerning. He didn't know exactly how he felt about Amanda yet, but he knew he didn't want to lose her. Not to a man he'd considered a good friend for well over a decade now.

Determined to get his mind off thoughts of Amanda and Jack together, Simon glanced around the room. And in doing so, realized how little Amanda had let herself relax there. Her bag was still neatly packed and there was nothing personal anywhere else in the room, except for the gray sweater draped across the table. There wasn't even a water bottle—the only clutter the still-full coffee cups he'd brought with him that morning.

It didn't take a genius to figure out that she had no long-term plans to stay here. Which made him nervous—the last thing he needed was for her to bolt. Or maybe she simply wasn't comfortable here. Which meant he might be able to talk her into moving into his apartment, for a whil, anyway.

He hadn't pushed Amanda about choosing to stay at a hotel instead of with him because she had seemed determined to be on her own. Plus, he'd needed time to assimilate their situation on his own, to wrap his head around the changes—in her and in his life.

And he hadn't wanted her to think it was a lascivious thing. Sure, he wanted her—sometimes he thought he'd go to his grave wanting her—despite the fact that she looked as if she'd been ridden hard and put away wet. But his desire for her wasn't a factor in why he wanted her to come stay with him. He wouldn't let it be, not now, when she had so much healing to do.

Besides, she couldn't stay in this hotel forever, he told himself as he folded the sweater and shoved it into the suitcase. It was too expensive, too impersonal, too empty. She needed to come home with him, where he could take care of her.

The shower finally turned off. Convinced he'd be able to persuade her to move to his apartment, Simon waited impatiently for the bathroom door to open. Of course, when it did, he found himself face-to-face with an Amanda he hadn't seen in a long time. Wet, wildly curling hair, dark, sexy eyes, a skimpy towel wrapped around her slender body but still showing plenty of skin.

Desire hit him with the power of a freight train and it was as if all those years without her had never existed. He was taken right back to the beginning, when he had first seen her and would have done anything to have her.

Still, just because he'd shot back in time didn't mean she had, and he tried to tear his gaze away from her. Find something other than the soft, creamy expanse of her thighs to focus on.

But even as he told himself to look away, he couldn't do it.

Instead, he skimmed his eyes over her, lingering at the slight curves of her breasts where they pushed against the towel before moving on to her long, long, *long* legs. While they were skinnier than he remembered, they were still killer. Beautiful and strong. He couldn't help remembering what it had felt like to have them wrapped around his waist as he moved inside her.

"Sorry. I forgot my clothes." Her voice sounded strained as she brushed past him. The tension he heard there snapped him out of the flashback, and he turned in time to see her duck her head, cheeks flushed.

Her obvious embarrassment made him feel like a total lech. He cleared his throat. "No big deal. I'll just look...somewhere else." He crossed to the window.

"Thanks." A pause, while he heard her rummaging in her suitcase. Yeah, real smooth. He probably should have thought about her getting dressed before he packed her up.

"Hey, did you mess with my bag?" she asked, her

voice more vulnerable than he had heard it in a very long time. "Or am I losing my mind?"

"No, it was me. I wanted to help get you ready." He glanced at her over his shoulder, felt his whole body go on red alert as one side of her towel dipped precariously to reveal a glimpse of a perfect, rose-tipped breast.

She clutched at the towel, and he looked away quickly, but not before he hardened painfully. He told himself to chill out, that sex was the last thing Amanda was interested in right now, but it didn't work. His body didn't seem to care. But then it never did when he was around Amanda. He'd wanted her from the first time he'd set eyes on her, and though their relationship had evolved through the years, that desire had never gone away.

"Get ready for what?" she asked, heading toward the bathroom.

"You can't stay in a hotel forever," he told her. "I figured, after everything that happened earlier, you'd be okay with coming home with me."

A stunned silence was his only answer as the bathroom door closed firmly behind her.

As he waited for her, he cursed himself and his rampaging libido. He hadn't planned on bringing the subject up quite so abruptly, but he'd gone stupid at the first sight of her. Could he have been a bigger idiot?

What he should have said was that he'd been looking for a pair of scrubs to fit him, not that he'd packed up her errant possessions as if he expected her to follow him wherever he went. As if he was a jealous idiot who thought he had the right to control every aspect of her life.

He shook his head, slumped down on the bed. Nothing quite like taking one step forward and seven back. Of course, that was the story of his life with Amanda.

She emerged from the bathroom a couple of minutes later, fully dressed and with a look of total disbelief on her face. "We have one conversation that doesn't end in a fight and you think that means I'm ready to move in with you?"

"I know, I'm sorry. I handled that badly."

She snorted. "So you're not sorry for thinking I'd drop everything and move in with you. You're just sorry about the way you handled it?"

Well, yeah. Pretty much. But thank God his brain started working before he could blurt that out. "I wasn't trying to push you into anything you weren't ready for—"

"Right. Because you never do that."

He narrowed his eyes. "Sarcasm is not becoming on you."

"What a shame since I'm so fond of it."

It was his turn to snort, this time with laughter. It took only a few seconds before she joined in.

When they'd sobered, she said quietly, "You know there's not a chance I'm going to move in with you, right?"

His levity fled. "Why not?" He put his arms out, gestured around the hotel room. "Come on, Amanda, this is no place for you. You deserve better."

"Better than one of the best hotels in Atlanta? You *are* the one who sent me here, if you remember correctly?"

"That's not what I meant, and you know it. You're not taking proper care of yourself—"

"And what? You're going to change all that?"

"Why not?"

"In case you've forgotten, you have trouble keeping a goldfish alive, let alone a person."

He ground his teeth in frustration. "I want to help you, Amanda. What's wrong with that?"

"Nothing, except I don't need your help." She crossed to him, laid a gentle hand on his forearm. It felt so good that he closed his eyes for a moment, just soaked the sensation in. Soaked her in.

"I'm a grown woman, Simon. I've traveled all over the world—in places a lot more primitive and dangerous than downtown Atlanta. I'm pretty sure I can take care of myself."

He sighed, thrust a hand through his hair. "We've already had this fight."

"And we're going to keep having it until you get it through your thick skull that I don't need to be your do-it-yourself renovation project. I can handle things on my own. I swear."

"Usually, I'd agree with you. But, no offense, lately you've done a pretty crappy job of taking care of yourself. I understand why, but still, you're in bad shape, Amanda. Let me take care of you."

He expected her to tell him to go to hell, to reiterate all the things she could do on her own. Instead, she tossed her head and asked scornfully, "You don't actually think I'd let myself depend on you, do you? I've been there and I still have the skid marks on my back."

CHAPTER NINE

SIMON STARED AT AMANDA stonily. Her response to his plea had cut him off at the knees. He was reeling, shocked by the attack after the compassion she'd demonstrated the night before, but the last thing he wanted was for her to know how bad she could hurt him. With the way she felt about him, giving her that kind of control would be disastrous.

For long seconds, he didn't know what to say to her. After all, he hadn't expected her forgiveness for not being there when Gabby died—not when he couldn't forgive himself—but he'd hoped for a little understanding. Obviously, he'd been dreaming.

"We're never going to be able to get past that, are we?" he finally asked, dully.

Amanda bit her lip, and her gray eyes were sad, but she didn't retreat. "I wasn't talking about Gabby. I was talking about all the years before that, when you flitted in and out of my life at whim."

"I was *working*."

"You're always working, Simon. There's always another story to tell, always something happening, somewhere, that's more important than I am. That isn't going to change now."

"I'm a reporter, Amanda. I go where the news is. Besides, I never complained about you 'flitting off' to country after country doing your doctor thing. I never said a word when you dragged Gabby through five countries in four years."

"Why would you have? It made your life infinitely easier not to have me waiting at home for you, wondering where you were. I couldn't complain about your absence if I wasn't home, either."

"Are you saying you'd give it up? That you wouldn't work with For the Children anymore?"

"I think you're forgetting, I did give it up. Twice."

"That doesn't count. You always knew you'd go back."

"You really think that's what I did? That I weighed my options when Gabby got sick? You think I said to myself, 'Oh, well, I'll give it a year and by then she'll be dead and I can go back to doing what I really want to do?'"

"You're putting words in my mouth."

"Yeah, well, you sure as hell implied it."

"Don't change the subject. I may not have always been there, but I was committed to you. You're the one who walked out on me."

"Because I couldn't handle never knowing where you were or who you were with—"

"I *never* cheated on you."

"It doesn't matter." She waved his words away as if they were inconsequential, which only angered him more.

"Really? I thought the fact that I loved you—wanted to build a life with you—did matter. My mistake."

"You didn't want to build a life," she flung at him. "You wanted a drive-through relationship, one where you could show up for a few days, have great sex and then get the hell out of Dodge before anything got serious."

The words hit hard, took all the righteous indignation right out of him. "That isn't true," he whispered.

Amanda sighed as she crossed the room, put a gentle hand on his arm. "It doesn't matter," she told him softly. "That period in our lives is over."

"What if I don't want it to be over?"

"Come on, Simon. Gabby's dead. There's nothing connecting us anymore."

"Gabby wasn't the only thing we had between us, Amanda." He grabbed her hand, tugged her closer. Nearly groaned at the feel of her body against his own. Even when they were angry at each other, they responded to one another physically. "I never found what I had with you with anyone else," he told her. "I've never wanted it with anyone else."

The words were so honest, so raw, that they hurt coming out. As did the instinctive rejection he saw in her eyes.

Wanting to delay that rejection, wanting to pretend that things were going to be okay, if only for a little while, he bent his head, pressed his lips gently to hers.

And there it was, the fire that never seemed to dampen between them. The second their mouths touched, it blazed hot and wild. For a moment, it felt as if she was going to pull away, but he slipped his arms around her waist, pulled her closer, and the moment dissolved.

Instead, her lips opened under his like a flower, and he groaned, low in his throat. He told himself to take it slow, not to spook her, but she tasted so good and he'd waited so long to have her again, to really have her, that he dived right in.

He nibbled on her lips, pulled her lower lip between his teeth and nipped a little—the way he knew she liked. She shuddered against him, her hands clutching at his shirt, and he nearly howled in triumph.

He managed to control himself, though, just barely, and focused instead on tasting her. On bringing her as much pleasure as he could. On reminding her of how good things had been between them before they'd gone bad.

Sliding his hands down, he cupped her ass and lifted her against him, so that the softness of her sex was pressed directly over his own hardness. She gasped a little and he took advantage, delving his tongue deep into her mouth and exploring her hidden recesses.

She tasted exactly like he remembered—of strawberries and the deep, dark chocolate he had a weakness for. He pulled her closer, opened his mouth wider. He wanted to bury himself in Amanda, to immerse himself inside of her until she acknowledged how crazy she was being. Until she admitted that they belonged together, that he *could* take care of her, despite the mistakes he'd made in the past.

The kiss went on and on and on, long minutes of touching and tasting and exploring that drove him out of his mind. He wanted to caress all of her, wanted to reacquaint himself with every inch of her body. Wanted to claim her so completely that she'd never try to leave him again.

Driven nearly mad by his need for her, he walked

them slowly across the room until they were at the bed. Then he lowered her to the mattress, careful not to break the kiss. And when he dropped onto the floor between her spread thighs, she moaned—a wild, tortured exclamation that shot deep inside of him and brought him right to the edge of his control.

Wrenching his mouth from hers, Simon pressed against Amanda's shoulders until she sank gracefully back onto the bed. And then he looked at her for long seconds, taking in her dazed eyes, swollen mouth, open thighs.

Lust beat deep inside of him, a need to take her, to make her his, to silence her objections once and for all. He wanted to fall on her, to devour her, to kiss and suck and bite every inch of her until she was as wrapped up in him as he had always been in her.

The only thing stopping him was the tenderness he felt toward her, a softness that tempered the wild claws of desire and slowed him down like nothing else could. She looked beautiful and amazing and sexy and yet so delicate that he was almost afraid he would break her.

Leaning forward, he forced himself to be gentle, to go slow, as he slid his lips over her jaw and down the slender column of her throat. She gasped, pressed her head to the side to give him better access as her fingers trailed over the nape of his neck.

They were the signs he'd been waiting for, the acceptance he had craved deep inside himself. And still, he made himself ask. She was so vulnerable right now he didn't want to do anything to hurt her.

"Let me love you, Amanda," he whispered against the hollow of her throat. "Let me make you feel good."

"Yes," she gasped as she slipped her fingers under his shirt and started to shove at the well-worn fabric. "Please, Simon."

Her voice was almost a wail, and a flash of desire shot through him so quickly that he feared he would be burned alive if he didn't get inside her soon. Levering himself away from her, he ignored her moan of disappointment as he ripped his shirt over his head, then pulled her up and did the same to hers.

She wasn't wearing a bra and his eyes nearly crossed as he got his first glimpse of her breasts. She was smaller than before, but she was still beautiful. Soft and round and perfect. Her skin was creamy-white here, her nipples glowing a deep rose in the dense afternoon sunlight.

Slowly, carefully, he reached for her. Traced a finger over the blue veins that showed through the delicate skin. Circled her areola the way he knew she liked, savoring the softness of her as much as the thrill of finally having her in his arms again.

Unable to wait any longer, he leaned forward and took one of her nipples into his mouth. Sucked gently and reveled in her quiet gasp. In the trembling she couldn't hide and the fingers that clutched at his shoulders.

"You're so beautiful," he murmured as he kissed his way down her rib cage to her belly button. He paused to blow a stream of hot air directly against her navel, and she responded as he knew she would, with a giggle and an arch of her body that brought them into even closer contact.

"I love that you're still ticklish," he told her as his

fingers made quick work of the button and zipper on her jeans. Then he was moving lower, nuzzling the soft cotton fabric of her underwear out of the way as he ran his tongue along her bikini line.

She squirmed, bucked against him, but even as he tried to raise his head—to see if he'd gone too far—her fingers were tangling in his hair. Holding him in place as she moved restlessly beneath him.

He closed his eyes in relief, breathed in the sweet, sexy scent that was all Amanda. Then he slowly peeled off her jeans, so she was lying in front of him in nothing but a pair of black cotton hipsters that gaped at the waist.

He tried not to notice, tried not to concentrate on the weight she had lost because he knew he would lose it completely if he did. He'd start lecturing her for not taking better care of herself when the last thing he wanted between them right now was anger.

But it was hard to bite his tongue when she was so thin that her stomach was practically concave, her hip bones jutting out in stark relief. Hard to keep his mouth shut when he could span her waist with two hands, and his fingers overlapped.

"You have to take better care of yourself," he told her softly as he hooked his fingers on the waistband of her panties and pulled them down her legs.

She nodded. "I'm working on it."

"Good." He licked his way back up to her breasts, pulled one strawberry nipple into his mouth and started to suck.

She moaned, a breathless little sound that had him hardening to the point of pain. He moved to the other breast, gave it the same attention, then captured her lips in a kiss that broke the last ties of his control.

Sliding down her body, leaving kisses in his wake, he didn't stop until his shoulders were between her thighs and she was spread out before him, her sex soft and pink and beautiful. He slipped a finger inside of her, savoring the way she sighed and trembled. Then leaned forward and delivered a slow, lingering lick right up the heart of her.

AMANDA NEARLY SHOT OFF the bed as Simon's tongue circled her clit. The desire singing through her veins ratcheted up another notch. Instinctively, she clutched at his shoulders to hold him to her.

It felt so good to be with him like this, felt so good to touch him and let him touch her. It had been so long since she'd connected with another person in any way, let alone sexually, that she couldn't bring herself to stop this. No matter how sure she was that it was the wrong thing for them.

Orgasm loomed and she shuddered, tried to hold it off. She wanted this moment to last, if not forever then a little longer. She didn't want to go back to being angry with Simon or hating him or any of the other complicated emotions she felt for him. She wanted to stay right here—in the moment, in the pleasure—forever. Then she wouldn't have to think, wouldn't have to make a decision she knew was for the best, but would hurt them both.

Sensing her imminent release, Simon slipped his hand beneath her then slid one long finger inside of her sex. Amanda gasped, lifted her hips to meet him and shuddered as pleasure shook her to her very core.

He stroked her through her orgasm, stroking and licking and taking her higher until it was all she could do not to scream. When it was over, she collapsed on the bed and sucked in long gasps of air as Simon gently stroked her hair.

When she could breathe again, she turned to him. Held him against her as tightly as she could.

It felt so right to be here with him, to cradle his head against her breast as her body yearned for his, that it scared her. This wasn't how it was supposed to be. Not this comfortable. Not this good. "Simon, I don't think—"

He cut her words off with a kiss, so tender, so exquisite. "Don't think," he told her, and his green eyes were calmer than she'd ever seen them.

Leaning her head to one side, eyes still locked with his, she offered him her mouth again. He took it, and the sudden pressure of his lips on hers unleashed a maelstrom of confusion inside of her. Being with him was like finding herself again—sweet, warm and so familiar that it brought tears to her eyes—but it was also like losing herself. She wasn't sure which of the sensations was more frightening.

His hands weren't steady as they skimmed up her arms, but they felt good. So good. Everywhere he touched her came to life, every brush of his fingertips brought an extra zap of intensity to the emotions already riding her hard.

"It's my turn to touch you," she told him breathlessly. If this was it, she decided, if this was the only time they'd ever be able to put the past aside and love each other, she wanted to do it right.

She started to tell him how she felt, but he silenced the words with another kiss. And then he was rolling across the bed, spinning with her, lifting her above him as his mouth swept over the curve of her breast.

He settled her astride him gently, her knees on either side of his hips—and again it felt so right, so normal, so good, that she didn't know how to feel. "Take me, Amanda," he whispered. "Please. I don't want all this pain between us anymore."

She paused, savored Simon's words as much as the feel of him against her. He was right—the pain had gotten her nowhere. She had to let the past go, had to embrace the pleasure he offered her. It would be so much better than the agony that came before it.

With that thought in her head, she raised herself over him and slowly, carefully, took him inside her.

She rode him leisurely, sweetly, showing him with her body all the things she didn't want to say with words. Immersed in him, in everything that arced between them with each slow glide of her body, she kept the rhythm languid, steady.

The tension began to build in her, the ache between her thighs becoming more and more unbearable, and she could tell by his clenched fists and bowed body that Simon was feeling the same.

And still she kept moving, pushing both of them to the brink of release. Need was a living thing within her, but she forced it back again and again, unwilling to have this one perfect moment end. Unwilling to face the reality she knew was coming for both of them. She'd waited so long for this, to connect with the only man she'd ever really love, that she wanted it to last forever.

But the need continued to build until sweat poured from him, from her, then mingled as she leaned over him and slid soft kisses along his jaw and neck.

"Now, Amanda!" Simon's hands clamped on her ass like a vise. "Please, I need you. I need you now."

She needed him, too, needed this, and she was suddenly as desperate as he was. Giving in to the pleasure he gave her, she let Simon take control for the last frantic seconds. One powerful thrust, two, and they burned everything—past, present, future—to ash. When it was over, she scooted to the left side of the bed—Simon had always like the right—and rolled onto her side so that her back was to him. She needed a minute to think, to process, to figure out what she was going to do next.

Simon cuddled up behind her, his arm draped over her waist and his hand cupping her breast. He felt good, really good, and part of her wanted nothing more than to stay here with him all day. All night.

But that wasn't what this had been about, she reminded herself. Wasn't what she needed to be thinking about right now. Still, she gave herself a few minutes to lie there and soak up his warmth and the tenderness flowing from him to her. It had been so long since she'd been held like this that she wanted to keep it close to her heart for the weeks and months and years ahead.

She thought about changing her mind, holding off what she was about to say, but she didn't. Because no matter how good he felt, she knew he wasn't good for her. Just as she wasn't good for him. They'd had twelve years to get things right between them and they'd never been able to do it. Assuming that they could now was folly on both their parts. And she didn't have the time or the heart to make that kind of mistake again.

Though she had insisted to Jack she was fine, she'd known that she wasn't. Though she'd insisted to Simon that she could find her way home on her own, she knew she would have been lost without him.

But she was back home now—or as close to home as a woman who no longer had one could get—and it was time to face the truth. She had to get out now, while she still could. Because the longer she was around him, the more magnetic the draw between her and Simon became.

Smart, charismatic, sexy, he'd rung her bell from the first time she'd seen him. And even after she'd broken up with him—the hardest thing she'd ever done besides bury her little girl—she'd felt an unwitting attraction. Felt herself being pulled in by that sexual and intellectual magnetism.

Back then, she'd been strong enough to handle it. Strong enough to handle him. But now? Now she was so emotionally devastated that falling for him again would break her completely. It had been so much easier when she was angry at him for missing Gabby's death, when she could blame him for putting the news above their little girl.

But now that she'd seen him, now that she knew he was as broken up at losing Gabby as she was, it was a different story. Sure, he'd handled his fear of losing their little girl badly, but could she blame him when she'd fallen apart the second Gabby was gone? When eighteen months later, she still hadn't found a way to put herself back together?

No, she couldn't blame him, but neither could she risk her heart—and more important, her sanity—on a man she would never be able to count on. Right now, she needed stability more than anything else. More than sex or passion or love or even friendship. She needed to know that the status quo could be maintained.

For someone like Simon, that kind of stability was anathema. She'd been okay with that for a long time, content to simply be a blip on his radar whenever they were in the same general vicinity.

But not now, not ever again. She wouldn't survive losing him again, not while she was still so messed up over Gabby. Better to nip this thing in the bud than let it go any further. Better to get rid of him now, rather than spend the next few weeks waiting for the other shoe to drop.

She felt tears bloom in her eyes, but she blinked them away. She'd cried enough in the past few days to make up for a lifetime without tears. She was done with them. Done with Simon, as much as it hurt.

Right now her priority had to be getting well, putting her life back together. Inviting him in would do nothing but throw a huge wrench in her plans. Once she'd been willing to sacrifice anything for Simon, but no longer. She was smart enough to know that this time, both her sanity and her life were on the line.

Sitting up abruptly, she waited until his hand had dropped away before climbing out of bed.

"You okay?" he asked sleepily, raising his head to look at her.

"Fine." She headed for the bathroom, where she turned on the shower. She could smell him on her body, his scent seeping into her pores. And it was like it had been before, like it always was with them. Already, she could feel herself weakening, feel herself wanting to be with him. Just one more self-destructive impulse she wasn't going to give in to.

Simon opened the door just as she was ready to get in the shower, and he didn't look sleepy anymore. His green eyes were wary as they searched her face for some clue to what was going on in her head.

For long seconds, she stood there, completely vulnerable, as she watched him watch her. Then her common sense kicked in and she dived for the white hotel robe she'd left on the sink earlier, putting it on.

His eyes narrowed and he leaned back against the wall, arms crossed over his chest. He was completely naked, but that didn't seem to bother him—he obviously wasn't feeling half as vulnerable as she was. "What's wrong, Mandy?"

"I just need a shower."

"Yeah? Well, can I join you?" He moved forward, started to undo the sash on her robe as he skimmed his lips over her jawline. "I'll wash your back—"

"No." She jerked away, turned the shower off and went into the bedroom. If she was going to have this talk, it wasn't going to be in the smallest room.

He followed her, and this time when she looked at him, he was pale beneath his tan. "Did I hurt you?" he demanded. "Was I too rough?"

"No, it was fine."

"Fine?"

Now she'd offended him. "I didn't mean it like that."

"Well, how exactly did you mean it?" he demanded. "Because to be honest, I'm suddenly confused about what's going on here."

SIMON COUNTED THE SECONDS, a sinking feeling in his chest, as he waited for Amanda to answer his question. When he got to twenty-five and she still hadn't said a word, the worry coalesced into a ball of ice in the pit of his stomach.

"Amanda?" he prompted, determined to get her to talk to him.

"I'm tired, Simon."

He refrained from reminding her that they'd spent most of the day sleeping—but then again, she was so exhausted that probably hadn't made a dent. "Do you want to take that shower? And then go back to bed? You should eat something first."

"I will. But I need you to leave."

"Okay." He reached for his jeans, yanked them on. "I promise I won't bother you if you let me stay. I know how much you need to rest."

"It isn't that." Her tone was low, even a little apologetic, and every instinct in his body started screaming information at him that he didn't want to hear.

"Then what is it?"

"I don't— We can't—"

He started toward her, wanting to comfort her, to make whatever was going on in her head easier for her to talk about. But she turned away. Like she had when he'd offered to wash her back. Like she had when they'd finished making love and he'd wanted to hold her. When they'd been together before, she'd loved to lie in his arms for hours, talking about anything and everything that came into her mind.

That's when it hit him. He'd been making love to Amanda in an effort to reaffirm his feelings for her, to convince her to give the two of them another chance. She, however, had been doing the opposite. The tenderness he'd felt in her touch, the desire she'd given him like a gift, had been her way of saying goodbye.

He didn't want to accept it, didn't want to believe that he was right. He crossed to her, spun her to face him so he could look into her face. What he saw there had him fighting the urge to beg.

The truth of his realization was right there for him to see in her eyes. To feel in her body, which she held just a little apart from his despite his attempts to pull her into his arms.

Hurt swamped him and he eased back, letting his arms drop to his sides. Anger welled up, but he shoved it back down. He wasn't going to lose his control now, wasn't going to let her know how much she meant to him—or how much her rejection devastated him. Again.

He should have known better, should have realized that this was too good to be true. Amanda had done this to him before, gotten him completely wrapped up in her to the point where he wanted to confess his love for her, and then dropped him flat.

When it had happened last time, he'd been so unprepared that he hadn't been able to hide his shock—or his feelings for her. The humiliation had burned inside him for months. Years. This time, he wouldn't go through that again. He wasn't going to let her know how much she'd hurt him.

Instead, he cocked his head and forced the easy half smile that had gotten him out of sticky situations for most of his life. He only hoped it would work for this one, too.

"So, I guess this is it, then, huh?" Not knowing what to do with his hands, he ended up shoving them deep in his pockets so he didn't grab on to her and beg. The thought that he could behave so desperately, so pathetically, had him drawing back. The most vulnerable part of him—the side he'd only ever shown to her—was already buried.

"This is it," she agreed, and he should have taken satisfaction in the way her voice trembled. But her sorrow was another knife in his gut. She kissed her fingers, pressed them to his cheek. He wanted to hang here forever, wanted these last, bittersweet moments to go on and on and on, even if she had kicked him to the curb. He wasn't ready to let her go yet, wasn't ready to say goodbye to everything they'd once meant to each other. Everything he'd imagined they could mean again.

Not that he would ever admit that to her.

But then she was pulling away, crossing to the door. Opening it and waiting for him to walk out. A silent boot in the ass that got him moving like nothing else could. He put on his pants and slid his feet into his shoes, grabbed his shirt and pulled it over his head as he walked out the door without another word. He made it to the elevator at the end of the hall before he turned and looked back, expecting to see only the closed door of her hotel room.

Instead, she was standing in the doorway, watching him with bruised eyes as the too-big robe slipped off her shoulder. Worry welled up inside him—years of habit weren't going to be easy to break—and he waited a second for her to say or do something that would tell him she'd changed her mind. She never did and eventually the elevator doors opened. A room-service waiter got off, wheeling a cart loaded with dishes down the hall toward Amanda's room.

The last thing he saw before he got onto the elevator was Amanda stepping aside to let the waiter into her room and then closing the door firmly behind her.

CHAPTER TEN

AMANDA STAYED IN BED for a day and a half after she sent Simon away. She hadn't planned on it, hadn't planned on being flattened so completely by doing the right thing. The only thing. But every time she tried to get out of bed, every time she told herself she needed to be doing something—anything—she started to cry. Finally she gave up and just lay there, staring at the ceiling and wondering what was happening to her. Even in the worst months, right after Gabby's death, she hadn't felt so unmotivated.

So useless.

It was more than saying goodbye to the man who had been such a huge part of her life. After all, she'd done that twice before. Once, not long after Gabby was born and she'd known that his nomadic, breeze-into-town lifestyle could no longer be for her, not when she had a daughter to think of. At the time, it had been awful. She'd still been desperately in love with him and the idea of never holding him again, never getting the chance to show that love, was horrible.

She'd made it through, and they had forged a friendship during their daughter's lifetime that she had valued, even if she had never been able to depend on it, or him.

The last days of Gabby's life had proven how reliable

he wasn't. Which was why she'd walked away from him again directly after the funeral. That goodbye hadn't been hard—at the time, she was fueled by so much rage and sorrow that Simon had been nothing but a convenient outlet for her anger. He wasn't the only thing she'd been angry at, just the most tangible.

This time, though, letting him go felt different. Worse.

Maybe because she knew this was really it.

When Gabby was alive, she'd tied them together. While Amanda was working for For the Children, Simon had popped up in the same hot spot more than once. But now that Gabby was gone and Amanda had no plans to work in Africa or any other poverty-stricken part of the world, the connection between them had been completely severed.

When she got out of this bed, when she went about the process of putting her life together, that would be it. She would leave Atlanta and probably never see Simon again. It had seemed like a smart idea the other day, when she'd been kicking him out of her hotel room, but now it just seemed lonely. Miserable. A mistake.

Closing her eyes, she tried to wrap her mind around a world for her without her daughter or Simon in it. The mere thought had her breath hitching in her throat.

That was it, she decided, looking up at the rich, cream ceiling she'd been staring at for twenty-five hours straight. That was what hurt. Not only the knowledge that she was never going to see Simon again, but also the fact that, in saying goodbye to him, she'd said goodbye to that entire era of her life. Shut the door on everything that had happened during that time—

including, she was desperately afraid, her time with her daughter.

Turning her back on Simon felt like turning her back on everything he'd ever been to her, including the father of her child.

She didn't want to do that. Didn't want to let go of Gabby. Didn't want to say goodbye to the only person she'd ever loved unconditionally. But could she hold on to one without the other? And if she did hold on to Gabby, kept her memory close, would she ever get out of this bed again?

It didn't seem like such a terrible way to die. To just drift away slowly, silently.

T. S. Eliot was right, she thought randomly. This was how the world ended. How *her* world ended, at least. Not with a bang, but a whimper.

Oh, how the mighty had fallen. Hadn't it been a couple of days ago that she'd been determined to get her life back on track? Convinced she could do something that would make her matter to someone. Now she barely knew which way was up. Or even if there was an up.

Closing her eyes, Amanda tried to embrace the idea of just giving in. Of disappearing. She didn't want to do this anymore, didn't want to live this life she was trapped in. Working her way back seemed too hard...

Then again, as she stared at the back of her eyelids in this darkened room, she realized that giving up was just as bad. She'd expected it to be easy, to simply happen. Instead she was filled with a rage so deep, so intense, so fiery hot that she could barely breathe through it.

Was this really what she wanted? she asked herself, vaguely horrified by it all. To waste away?

And if she did, what the hell was wrong with her?

Who was this woman she was becoming, someone who would rather give up than fight? This wasn't the Amanda Jacobs she knew, the Amanda Jacobs who had worked so hard to be a good role model for her daughter.

That Amanda Jacobs had wanted to make a difference in the world, not die off with no more than a gasp.

This woman who hadn't gotten out of bed in close to two days—who had spent the past eighteen months being little help to anyone—was pathetic. Gabby would be so disappointed in her. The thought of her strong, determined daughter made Amanda want to kick her own ass.

The fury grew until it nearly consumed her—fury at the doctors who hadn't been able to save her daughter.

Fury at a fate that was so cruel as to gift the world with children like Gabby and Mabulu, only to take them away much too soon.

Fury at herself for withering up and trying to die when there were so many people left to help. So many people who lost children to ways other than cancer. So many children she might actually have a chance to save. Not in Africa, where the conditions were enough to bring her to her knees these days, but here, in Atlanta. Maybe she could make a real difference here.

Completely disgusted with herself and her pity party, Amanda threw back the covers and climbed out of bed. Then forced herself to make the walk to the bathroom despite her shaky legs.

Forced herself to step into the shower and stand there as warm water cascaded over her.

And when she got out, she actually made herself put a little effort into her hair and dress, to put on clothes that actually fit—in this case, the new pair of jeans and red blouse she'd bought the day after she arrived in Atlanta.

She'd have to see about getting more clothes if she was actually going to do this. One outfit did not a wardrobe make.

She filled a glass with water and choked down the vitamins she'd bought. Then she smoothed the only lip gloss she had—an old tube she'd found buried at the bottom of her backpack—over her lips and slipped into her favorite pair of walking shoes.

More than once, she started to give up, to let the depression and misery drag her to bed. But she didn't do it, some sixth sense inside of her knowing that if she gave in now, she'd never find her way to the surface again.

When she had done everything she could to get ready, when she could delay going into the real world no longer, Amanda grabbed her pack and—with a deep breath—walked back into the world.

It hadn't changed much in two days, and yet somehow, it felt as if everything had changed.

When she got down to the bustling street, she looked both ways, trying to decide which direction to go. Finally deciding that straight ahead was as good a direction as any, she started walking and, except for brief moments at traffic lights, didn't stop for three hours.

She walked the streets of downtown Atlanta, getting a feel for the city and its inhabitants. Traffic was terrible, the streets congested with cars and buses and more people than she had seen in one place in longer than she could remember.

She kind of liked it. The hustle and bustle of people who knew what they were doing and where they were going seemed to call to her, to tell her that everything would be okay.

Stopping for a pretzel and lemonade from a street vendor, she found herself charmed by his syrupy accent and friendly patter. She ate her treat as she wandered, a little shocked at how good the sweet, cold lemonade felt on her tongue.

As she walked, she exchanged pleasantries with people on street corners, asked directions of a couple of teenage boys hanging outside a coffee shop, and generally fell in love with the sweet rhythm of Atlanta. Before long, her cheek muscles were aching from all the unaccustomed smiling.

When she finally did stop, exhaustion suddenly overtaking her worn-down body, it was in front of a posh beauty salon called Charisma. She almost turned away, almost gave herself permission to hide in her hotel room again. Surely a three-hour walking tour of the city counted for something. She hadn't sulked, hadn't wallowed.

Maybe that was enough. Maybe she shouldn't try to push herself any more.

Still, something kept her from retreating. Maybe it was the little voice in her head that said she needed to push herself further. Maybe it was her fear of losing the modicum of control she'd managed to regain. Or maybe it was just the place she stood before, because if there was anyone in the world who needed a little charisma right now, it was her.

Pushing the door open, she stepped into the plush salon and looked around. It was decorated in lush golds and bronzes with smoky-blue accents. The furniture was ornate, the wall hangings quietly expensive and the people who worked there a little over the top. She fell in love at first glance.

A young girl, maybe eighteen or so, was standing behind the reception desk. Her eyes were heavily made up, her blond hair sticking out of her head in pointy blue-tipped spikes. Amanda wondered vaguely if she'd dyed it to match the interior of the shop.

"Do you have an appointment?" the girl asked in a chirpy yet somehow soothing voice.

Amanda shook her head. "I was hoping someone could fit me in."

"Oh, sweetie, we don't normally take walk-ins. But what do you want done? Maybe I can talk someone into staying late."

"I'm not sure what I want," Amanda answered, a little nonplussed at being called *sweetie* by someone who was half her age. Finally, she gestured to herself. "What do you think I need?"

The girl's eyes widened. "Oh, um…" She stumbled over her own tongue. "I'll be right back."

Right back actually ended up being more like ten minutes, and Amanda almost left twice, convinced the receptionist had forgotten all about her. But she forced herself to stay. She was tired of people looking at her with pity, tired of people not knowing what to say to her. It might be a long journey back to the land of the living, but she was going to take the first steps right now.

"Brick by brick, my citizens." Caesar's words, à la William Shakespeare, came to her, and she kept her feet planted firmly on the ground. She had to start laying the first bricks sometime. Why not now?

The receptionist came back with a gorgeous dark-haired man who had a heavy Southern accent and a flare for bright clothes. As he approached, Amanda blinked a little, wondering if it was possible to burn her eyes on the neon-yellow of his shirt.

"I am Marco. Fiona says you would like a make-over?" He eyed her with the same horrified fascination most people reserved for squashed bugs and traffic accidents.

Still, she liked the sound of that. A makeover. Yes, she would love one of those—it was the closest thing to a do-over this world could come up with. "Yes." She nodded. "A makeover would be wonderful."

"Of course." He reached for a limp strand of her hair. "What exactly would you like done?"

"You're the expert. What do you recommend?"

The look on his face was priceless and Amanda fought the urge to laugh. She knew she was in bad shape, but really, he almost seemed a little afraid of her.

"What's your name, sugar?"

"Amanda."

"Right. Amanda, can I be frank?"

"Of course." She bit her lip to keep from giggling. Which was strange, as she'd never been the giggling type.

He lowered his voice to a conspiratorial whisper. "Your hair is limper than overcooked spaghetti. Your skin is desert dry. You've got bags the size of Texas under your eyes and your nails... I don't even know what to say about your nails. No offense, sugar, but you look like you've spent the past year living under a hot rock. And not in a good way."

She did laugh then. She couldn't help it. He looked earnest and horrified at the same time. "Close. I've been in Africa. I'm a doctor and I was working in a clinic there."

"*Ooh,* well, in that case, everything makes so much more sense now." He shook his head. "Still, before you take off to be super-doc next time, you should really talk to me. We can find some products that won't let this—" he twirled his finger around to encompass all of her "—ever happen again."

She forced herself to nod seriously. "Thank you. I appreciate that. *So,* do you think you can fix me?"

He sighed hugely, but she would have to be blind to miss the gleam of excitement in his eyes. "Marco can fix anyone, sugar. Although, I admit, you might be a challenge. And I was supposed to get off early tonight." He sighed again. "But it's not like I can let you go around looking like that, now, can I?"

He turned to Fiona. "Get Lisa, Charles and Sabrina for me." Then he pointed at Amanda. "You, come with me."

She fought the urge to salute as she followed him.

"I'm going to be honest, sugar, Marco does not come cheap. But since you've been off doing charity work, I figure I can do no less. I'll give you fifteen percent off the works—provided you don't argue with me. All I want to hear from you is 'Yes, Marco.' Got it?"

She did salute this time. "Yes, Marco."

He grinned. "Gotta love doctors. They're such quick studies."

For the next four hours—well past Charisma's usual closing time—Amanda was scrubbed, buffed, dyed, polished and made up. She was also fed, twice, and plied with champagne. When she objected to the second plate of fruit and cheese Marco ordered for her, he simply glared and said, "What did I tell you you were allowed to say, Amanda?"

She sighed. "Yes, Marco."

"Sweet music to my ears, sugar." He handed her the plate. "Now eat, because you look a little like a famine victim yourself, and while it works for runway models, at your age, it's not such a good look."

"Hey! I'm only thirty-seven."

He quirked one dark eyebrow. "Seeing as how you looked a good seven years older than that when you walked in here, I rest my case."

Amanda blanched. She wasn't vain, but having close to a decade added to her age didn't exactly do wonders for her self-esteem. "You're going to help me with that, right?" She was a little surprised by the note of desperation in her voice.

Marco patted her cheek. "Sugar, I already have."

He spun her around so she could look in the mirror for the first time since she'd gotten there, and Amanda couldn't help gasping at the woman staring back at her. She was still too tired and too thin—Marco wasn't a total miracle worker, after all—but she looked about a million times better. He'd shortened her hair into a soft pixie cut that made her eyes look enormous. There had also been something in all the masks and treatments he'd used on her hair that brought the shine back.

And the scrubs and polishes he'd used on her skin had made it glow in a way it hadn't for far too long. With makeup covering her dark circles and an hour-long massage that relaxed her tense muscles, Amanda looked and felt like a new woman. Or at least, a much improved version of the old one.

Marco walked her to the front and handed her a bag full of makeup and hair products, along with a bill that rivaled one month of her normal salary. She was proud of the fact that she didn't flinch when she handed him her credit card, though at the same time she couldn't help figuring out how many children in Africa she could have fed with her evening's indulgence.

Still, when Marco handed her the credit-card slip, she tipped lavishly. And she didn't argue when he said, "I want to see you back here next Wednesday for another facial and body scrub. We'll also change your polish and I can work you in for a massage if you're willing to come in the morning."

She started to protest, but when he looked at her over the computer, one black eyebrow cocked warningly, she said the only thing she could in the situation. "Yes, Marco."

He grinned. "Music to my ears, sugar. Sweet music to my ears. Now get out of here and go do something fun. You look like two million bucks."

"Yes, but do I look thirty-seven? That's the real question."

He laughed and shooed her out the door. "Let's settle for the fact that you don't look forty anymore. Okay?"

She nodded as she walked out into the humid Atlanta night. Brick by brick, she reminded herself. Brick by brick.

THREE DAYS LATER, she stood outside a run-down wrought-iron fence and contemplated a different kind of makeover. The antebellum house in front of her was, cosmetically, in bad shape. But the bones were good, at least according to the inspection record the bank had given her. And if she closed her eyes, she could imagine what it would look like all fixed up.

She liked the soft brown of the bricks, but they were in desperate need of cleaning. Much of the trim paint had peeled off, which was just as well. She thought the black was too depressing. Maybe she'd have it painted a nice forest-green—the same shade as Gabby's eyes.

And Simon's, a little voice from deep inside of her said, but she ignored it. She'd done an admirable job of keeping herself busy these past few days, of not letting herself dwell on what had happened between them. It hadn't been easy, but she'd done it.

Beside her, Carol, the real-estate agent, cleared her throat, and Amanda jerked to the present. This was by far the most run-down of the places Carol had shown her, but it was also the one that spoke to Amanda the most.

Makeover. She held the word on her tongue, savored it. She had given herself a makeover—starting with that trip to Charisma and moving on to a shopping expedition of epic proportions, a regular eating schedule that she forced herself to stick to and even a couple of trips to the hotel gym. The result was she was sleeping better than she had in months, and if she still wasn't feeling like herself, then at least she was giving it her best shot.

But standing here, looking at this house that seemed to cry out for the same TLC she had desperately needed, she knew she'd found the next step on her journey. She turned to Carol. "I want this house."

The other woman didn't look surprised, but then, this was their third trip over here in the past two days. "Okay, then. Let's get started on the paperwork."

Amanda nodded, allowing the agent to lead her to her car. As she did, she was struck by an almost paralyzing fear. Was she really going to do this? Settle down here, in this strange city where she knew almost no one?

She thought of Boston again, of her daughter's bright eyes and pink cheeks as they wandered the streets together, before Gabby had gotten too sick. If she did this, if she bought this house, that time really would become a distant memory.

But it was only a memory, and so was her daughter. Gabby was gone, well and truly gone, and it didn't matter how much she cried or raged, screamed or bargained, nothing was going to bring her daughter back.

Though she'd known that intellectually all along, the emotional acceptance had been harder to come by. Was still hard to come by. She felt her resolve weaken, felt the words welling up on her tongue. It would be so easy to tell Carol to forget it, that she'd changed her mind.

But even as she started to do that, as she began to stumble backward from this step that suddenly seemed far too much, far too soon, the knowledge that it was now or never welled up inside her. She was at a crossroads. She could choose to wallow in the grief of the past or try to find a way around it to a better, happier future. One where she could once again be a productive member of society.

It wasn't about letting Gabby go, she realized, as she turned to look back at the house. Her daughter had already left long ago. This was about proving she was strong enough not to crawl into the grave with her little girl—which was a lot harder than it sounded.

But she was tougher than she looked, tougher than she'd ever been, Amanda reminded herself fiercely. And she could do this. Even more important, she would do this. She owed it to her daughter and…she owed it to herself. Better to be alive than the alternative, she told herself grimly. She would do well to remember that.

"I want to hire someone to do another inspection, to make sure that I'm aware of all the problems," she told Carol, more than a little surprised as the words tumbled off her lips. But she didn't want to take them back. Not this time. "The bank's inspection was done six months ago and I don't want any surprises."

Carol nodded. "I was going to recommend that. There are a couple of very reputable companies in town—I can text you their numbers when I'm at the office."

"Thank you."

The older woman smiled. "I'm glad you found a house that will work for you."

Amanda laughed. "Don't you mean a house I'm going to have to work for?"

Carol cast a last look at the dilapidated house. "Well, that, too. But I have a feeling you're going to enjoy every minute of it."

Amanda put a hand to her forehead to shield her eyes so that she could get one long, perfect look at the house she was going to try desperately to turn into a home. "Funny," she told Carol. "I have that exact feeling."

CHAPTER ELEVEN

S IMON FOLLOWED M ARK into The Chophouse, one of his friend's favorite restaurants in downtown Atlanta and one that just happened to be located in the Loews hotel. As they waited for a table, he couldn't help positioning himself so that he faced the lobby and could see anyone who happened to walk by.

Which was completely stupid.

It had been three weeks since they'd made love, twenty-two days since she'd kicked him out of her hotel room and her life, and as he stood here, desperate to catch sight of her, he felt like a junkie jonesing for a fix.

He wanted to make sure she was okay, he assured himself. That she was taking care of herself and not wasting away into nothingness. When he'd flown to Africa to get her, he'd promised Jack he would take care of her. It grated a little—okay, more than a little—that he hadn't been able to keep that promise. If he could see her…

The hostess walked them to the table and he practically dumped Mark on his ass in an effort to get the side of the booth that faced the lobby. His friend gave him a strange look, but he shrugged and slid onto the bench. Simon kept a sharp eye on the small section of the lobby he could still see. Thank God it was the part that led directly to the elevators.

Not that there was any guarantee that Amanda was still staying here, he told himself viciously. There was nothing to keep her here, after all, nothing even to keep her in Atlanta. She could be in Boston, for all he knew.

The thought gave him a hollow feeling in the pit of his stomach, one that underscored his lack of control in this situation and made him absolutely crazy. She'd been in rough shape when he'd left her—how was he supposed to live the rest of his life not knowing if she was okay?

"Hey, Simon, you all right?" Mark asked, eyeing him nervously.

"Yeah, fine." He yanked his focus to his friend with difficulty. "Why?"

The other man gave him a look that said he wasn't fooling him for a second. That was the problem hanging out with journalists—their bullshit detectors were so much better developed than most people's. Not, he supposed, that his friend actually needed that meter when Simon was acting like a total and complete maniac.

Forcing a calmness he was far from feeling, he spent the next few minutes acting as normal as possible—which meant he ordered a drink and food and only craned around his friend three times to get a better view of the lobby.

"So, are you serious about going to Yemen next week?" Mark asked him, once the waitress had brought their drinks.

"Yeah. Why wouldn't I be? The revolution's really heating up."

"I don't know. We just got back from covering the earthquake in Baja. I thought we were going to be in town for a couple of weeks, doing some local stuff. That's what we talked about."

It *was* what they'd talked about, when he had tried to arrange his schedule to spend as much time as possible with Amanda. Now that that option was off the table, he was almost desperate to get on location. Desperate to get away from the memories that seemed to haunt his every waking hour.

Still, he knew Mark had a family, unlike Simon and the other members of his crew, all of whom were young and anxious to see the world. "If you want to stay behind, I understand. I can call in a favor, get you assigned to someone local for a while. I'm sure the network would be okay with that."

"I thought you'd already used up all your favors with that overnight plane ride to Somalia."

Simon looked away. He so didn't want to go there. "I've still got a few up my sleeves."

Mark shook his head. "That's all right. I don't really want to work with anyone else."

"Yeah, but if you need to be at home—"

"It's fine. My wife knew what she was getting into when she signed on."

Yeah, but knowing what to expect wasn't the same as actually living it. Or at least, that seemed to be Amanda's complaint from the other night. The same complaint she'd used when she broke their relationship off almost eight years earlier. She wasn't willing to subject their daughter to his near-constant absences. He wondered if Mark was getting some variation of that talk at home these days.

"Look," he said, trying to be as honest as he could

without giving too much of his past away. He and Mark had been friends since he took this job, but that didn't mean he wore his baggage on his sleeve for the world to see. "You're a great cameraman, the best I've ever worked with. But your daughter is only going to be young once. You don't want to miss it all. I'll understand if you want to put in with a domestic crew, one that doesn't travel as much."

"I only have a few more years to do this before I promised my wife I'd give it up," Mark told him firmly. "I'm not going to cheat myself out of the career I want, the career I can have, just because she wants me home more. We had an agreement. So, Yemen, here we come."

He reached for his iced tea and took a long sip, making it clear that the conversation was over.

Simon let it go, and they spent the rest of lunch talking about the Yemen trip, other things going on at work and the Braves, who were having another crappy season. Yet even as he carried on his side of the conversation, Simon couldn't help thinking about what Mark had said.

It was like listening to himself eight years ago, and he wondered if he had sounded as put-upon, as aggrieved, as *selfish,* as Mark. Or was that his guilt putting a different perspective on the way he saw things now?

They were getting up from the table to head back to work when he saw Amanda, or a woman he thought was her, crossing the lobby at a quick clip. Not even bothering to make excuses to Mark, he took off after her, desperate to reach her before she stepped onto the elevator.

Except, as he got closer, he realized she couldn't be Amanda. This woman was wearing a flirty green dress and strappy, high-heeled sandals. She had an expensive haircut that showed only a hint of curl and glowed with vitality. He could see her only from the back as she waited for the elevator, but he must have been mistaken.

He was about to turn away when he caught her scent. Freesia. The fragrance went straight through him, had him hardening before he could even try to control his reaction to her. "Amanda?" It came out softer than he'd planned, but she must have heard him, because she glanced behind her with a questioning look.

One that turned into a genuine smile when she realized who it was. "Simon. What are you doing here?"

Waiting for a glimpse of you, like a lovesick idiot. He almost spit out the words, but bit his tongue at the last second. At least he hadn't lost all control of his vocal cords. "I was having lunch with a friend when I saw you walk by." No need to tell her he'd left Mark at the restaurant with his mouth open.

"You look great."

She flushed a little, as if she was embarrassed, and the color did amazing things for her face. It chased away the last of the shadows and made him remember, so clearly, the woman he had fallen in love with all those years before.

"Thanks. I've been…making an effort."

"It's paid off."

The elevator dinged and the doors slid silently open.

"Yeah, well. We'll see." She smiled at him again, then stepped into the empty car. "I guess I'll see you."

"Yeah, sure." He wanted to stop the elevator, wanted to climb in beside her and make her talk to him. But she'd made her position clear and he was going to respect that. Even if it killed him.

The elevator doors slid shut, and he turned away and walked back to Mark. The look on his colleague's face said he'd seen the whole thing.

"Old friend?" he asked.

"Something like that." Simon kept his expression neutral, even as he called himself every name in the book. He'd been a total idiot to run after her like that. What had he been thinking? That she would actually want to talk to him? After she'd kicked him to the curb almost before he'd gotten his pants back on?

What a joke. He had to get some control over himself. Of course, he had learned something from seeing her again. Amanda wasn't wasting away in her hotel room as he'd feared.

Mark was talking as they headed out onto the street, but Simon was too wrapped up in his own head to hear him, or much of anything else. It was obvious Amanda had moved on. Now he needed to do the—

"Simon! Simon!"

He kept walking, not even registering that someone was calling his name, until Mark grabbed his arm, stopping abruptly.

Ignoring the muttering of other pedestrians as they tried to get around him, Simon didn't have eyes for anyone but the woman in the emerald dress racing toward him.

"I'll meet you back at the office," Mark said drily, and Simon nodded, because it was expected of him, not because his brain had managed to interpret anything the other man had said.

"I didn't think I was going to get off that elevator in time. I swear, it hit every floor going down." Amanda stopped breathlessly in front of him.

He looked at her in confusion. "Why are you talking about the elevator?"

She shook her head, eyes sparkling. "I have no idea."

He waited, but she didn't say anything else, just stared at him for long seconds. Finally, when he couldn't take the silence any longer, he asked, "Did you want something?"

"Actually, yes. I know this is strange, since I'm the one who said goodbye, but I was wondering… I closed on a house today, over on Magnolia. Would you, maybe, like to come over for dinner and help me celebrate?"

He stared at her blankly as he tried to make sense of her words. "You bought a house? Here in Atlanta?"

She nodded. "I did. I know, it seems a little crazy, but I like this city. I can see myself trying to build a life here."

"Do you have a job?"

She shook her head. "Not yet. I'm trying to take things slow."

"Yet you bought a house?" He knew he sounded incredulous, but he couldn't help it. He was having a hard time wrapping his mind around the idea that Amanda was putting down roots in Atlanta. He'd lived here over a year and still hadn't even thought about moving out of his utilitarian apartment.

Her smile dimmed and her eyes lost a little of their sparkle. "Never mind," she told him. "It was a stupid idea—"

"No. I'd love to come." He reached for her hand, squeezed it tightly. "You know me, I was being an ass. But I would really like to see your house."

"Yeah?"

"Yeah."

She was smiling again, riffling through her purse until she came up with a pen and a scrap of paper. "Here's the address. And my new cell number in case something blows up somewhere in the world and you have to cancel."

He took the slip from her. "I won't cancel."

"Okay, then." She nodded, looking suddenly nervous. It was a good look for her. "I guess I'll see you around seven, then?"

"Seven, it is."

"Right. Well, then—" She took a deep breath. "Bye."

It was his turn to shake his head as he gently clasped her elbow, turning her around. "I'll walk you back to the hotel."

"You don't have to do that. Really, I—"

He placed a finger over her mouth and her eyes went wide and smoky. "I'll walk you back to the hotel," he told her firmly, and this time she didn't argue.

"So, tell me about the house," he said.

She laughed. "It's a wreck, kind of like me."

"You're not a wreck," he said, running his eyes over her from top to toes.

"Yeah, well, appearances can be deceiving. Anyway,

I fell in love with the house at first sight, if you can believe it."

Oh, he could believe it, all right. Twelve years wasn't long enough to forget what that first strike of lightning felt like. He cleared his throat. "I look forward to seeing it."

"Good." She glanced up. "Well, here we are."

"Yes. Here we are." Jesus. He was repeating every word she said like a damn parrot. He stepped away, let his fingers drop from her elbow. "I'll see you tonight."

Then he turned and walked away before he could do something stupid, like bend her over backward and kiss her the way he'd been dying to since the moment she turned to face him at the elevators.

Yemen trip to prepare for or not, he suddenly had the feeling that it was going to be a long, long, *long* afternoon.

WHAT HAD SHE BEEN THINKING? Amanda asked herself for the thousandth time as she looked around her decrepit kitchen. She'd invited Simon over for dinner when the house was a disaster, she had no furniture, and she didn't even have a kitchen to cook in. At least, not a functioning one. The remodeling company was due to come in tomorrow morning and start the process that would fix all that, but it definitely made it difficult to put dinner together tonight.

Oh, well, what was done was done. Out of desperation, she'd settled on picnic fare.

Not that this was any big deal, she reassured herself, as she spread out the quilt she'd bought that afternoon on the scarred wood of the dining-room floor. It was

sunny-yellow, with twists of lavender and green, and it
had made her happy to look at it. Which was why she'd
ended up buying it—she'd wanted to start out her new
life in this house with something sunny. Something that
made her smile.

She also wanted to start out with something meaningful, which was why she'd chased Simon down that
afternoon. Good or bad, their relationship carried more
meaning for her than anything else.

That was why she'd invited him, she reassured herself as she went back into the kitchen and gathered up
the things she'd bought for dinner. Not because she was
stupid enough to think anything could come of this
dinner. Not because she'd missed Simon these past few
weeks, though she'd tried her best not to. And certainly
not because she was planning on doing something so
stupid as falling for him. That ship had sailed long ago,
and she had no intention of ever making that mistake
again.

And even if she'd been crazy enough to imagine that
things might possibly work out between them, his reaction that afternoon, when she'd told him she'd bought
a house, would have cured her of the insanity. If she
hadn't known Simon better, she probably would have
been hurt by his reaction—he'd looked horrified at the
idea of her living so close to him. But she did know
him, certainly enough to understand that his horror
wasn't about her proximity, but about her rash decision
to put down roots. For Simon, signing a six-month lease
was a commitment of massive proportions. Buying a
house—even one she'd paid cash for—was way beyond
the limits of anything he could wrap his brain around.

Which was why she'd broken things off with him so many years before. She hadn't wanted—

Amanda cut her thoughts off before they could go any further. She wasn't going to think about that tonight. This was a celebration and she was going to treat it as such. Enjoy this new milestone in her life and let everything else fall by the wayside. At least for a little while. If she kept doing what she was doing, kept putting one foot in front of the other, then everything was going to be all right.

For the first time in her life, she had nowhere she had to be. Nothing she had to do. No one but herself to take care of. And if that last thought caused a little hitch in her chest—or a huge one, for that matter—then she was the only one who needed to know about it. She was going to put on a happy face and enjoy the hell out of her new life. Fake it till you make it. That was her new motto and she was sticking to it.

Dropping to her knees on the lush quilt, she spread out the food she'd bought. A crusty loaf of bread, some rich Brie that oozed warmly as she didn't have a refrigerator yet, green and black olives, pasta salad, fresh strawberries. And a bottle of champagne she'd been chilling in a small ice chest.

The plates were paper and the cups plastic, but somehow, she thought it would be a fitting celebration, anyway.

The doorbell rang just as she was popping a strawberry into her mouth. She glanced at her watch. Five minutes until seven—she was counting on at least fifteen more minutes before Simon showed up. But he'd obviously turned over a new leaf.

Or, in his way, he was trying as hard as she was to make this night special. Her stomach tightened a little at the thought, so she took a couple of deep breaths until it relaxed again. She could do this, she told herself, as she walked toward the entryway. It wasn't that difficult. Really, it wasn't.

By the time she'd reached the front door, she even believed what she was saying. Or at least she did until she opened the door and saw Simon standing there, a huge bouquet of flowers in one hand and a bottle of champagne in the other.

Her first thought was that he looked more handsome than any man had a right to. Her second was that she didn't stand a chance of keeping this simple. She tried to quash that thought as soon as it came to her, but it was difficult when Simon was giving her that half smile of his—the one that always made her a little giddy, even when she wished it wouldn't. Especially when she wished it wouldn't.

Damn it. She was doing okay. Making an effort. Yes, Gabby was still the first thing she thought of in the morning and the last thing she thought of at night, but it was getting better. She'd started to remember the good times with her daughter instead of only the bad. Had begun to allow herself to remember what it felt like to be hugged by Gabby—warm and sweet and slightly sticky—and the way her daughter's little hand had felt clasped in her own. It wasn't huge progress, but it was something. After all, she wanted to cry only five or six times a day now, instead of five or six hundred.

Which was why she needed to keep doing what she was doing. What she didn't need was to invite Simon in again, to leave herself vulnerable to him. Because no matter how many promises she made to herself about not making the same mistakes, the fact of the matter was, with Simon, she always did.

As she stared at him, Simon's smile faded, replaced by a look of uncertainty that was so unfamiliar she almost didn't recognize it. "Is something wrong, Mandy?" he asked.

His old nickname went through her like an electric current, delivering a pleasant warmth. And burning other parts of her to a crisp, she reminded herself viciously, because that's what electric shocks did.

"Mandy?" he asked again, and this time he reached for her. "What's wrong?"

Pulling back before he could touch her, she forced herself to snap out of whatever bizarre time warp her brain kept trying to slip into. Holding the door wide, she said, "Sorry about that. I'm still a little off sometimes. Come on in."

He crossed the threshold, handed her the flowers. They were freesia—her favorite.

"I thought you had changed your mind."

She smiled sadly. "Only about a dozen times or so since this afternoon."

He didn't laugh, as she'd intended. Only nodded as if he knew exactly how truthful she was being.

"When you said you'd bought a house, I didn't realize you meant one of these," he said, looking around the large antebellum house with interest. "I thought you went for more modern architecture."

"Usually, I do. But something about this place…"

She shrugged. "I fell in love with it the first time I saw it."

"I can see why." He said it with such a straight face that she cracked up.

"Use that face on someone who doesn't know you so well," she told him. "I am well aware that this place looks a disaster. But structurally, it's sound, and the rest is all cosmetic. All it will take is time and some TLC. Two things I happen to have a lot of right now."

His face softened, and for the second time that evening, he reached for her. She held up the flowers he had brought her, used them as a shield. "Thank you for the freesia by the way—and for the vase. I don't have one yet."

"I figured it might not be top of the list. And you're welcome."

"I have dinner laid out in the dining room, such as it is," she said, leading the way. "Or would you like a tour first?"

He glanced up at the peeling paint of the ceiling. "A tour would be fantastic."

"Really?" She glanced at him incredulously. "I don't have any furniture yet."

"That's the best way to see a house."

"Fine. Let me put these down." She dropped the flowers on the kitchen counter and then reached for the bottle of champagne he had in his other hand. "Would you like me to open this now? Or later?"

Simon's eyes darkened to a deep forest-green, and for a moment she was pulled into them, pulled into him. Taken back through time to the first bottle of champagne they'd ever shared—right after he had won his first Pulitzer for a series of articles he'd written about El Salvador. They'd killed the bottle, and he had drunk the last of it from her naked body.

It had been one of the best nights of her life. At least until she'd woken up and found herself alone, with nothing but a quick note from Simon telling her that duty called. She didn't see or hear from him until almost two months later.

Focusing on that fact, on the heartbreak she'd felt as days and then weeks had passed with no word from him, she yanked herself out of that small hotel room in Jamaica and back to the present.

"Later's fine," he said, his voice strained and eyes ablaze. "Unless you'd like some?"

"I can wait." She led him out the other side of the kitchen, trying to ignore the way her knees trembled. Or the way she felt his gaze burning straight through her back. She obviously wasn't the only one who remembered that night.

Despite the size of the house, the tour didn't last long, as there wasn't much to see—unless you were a contractor.

They ended the tour outside, in the gardens, just as sunset streaked across the sky. And even though the backyard was completely overgrown, it was still one of her favorite things about the house. In fact, she'd spent most of the afternoon messing around back here with her brand-new gardening tools, clearing a path through the weeds. She had visions of being able to sit out here on early-spring afternoons, before it got too hot, and sip lemonade as she watched the flowers grow.

It was a small dream, one as far removed from the

grand plans she'd once had to save the world as it could get. But it was hers. Something to hold on to, to focus on, when the dark days came. The image of her with the sun on her face and gardenias in her lap. Somehow she thought her beautiful, precocious, flower-loving daughter would approve.

"Gabby would have liked it out here," Simon said suddenly, his voice aching just enough that she wondered if he'd somehow read her thoughts. But a quick glance told her he'd taken one look at the wild tangle of flowers and his mind had immediately jumped to their daughter.

"I think so, too."

"I miss her."

"Simon—" *Don't,* she wanted to say. *Please, don't do this, not now. Not when I'm finally beginning to get my feet back under me. Please, don't drag me back down.*

But she'd been his daughter, too, and like Amanda, he'd been too busy trying to run away from the pain to grieve properly.

She lay a gentle hand on his shoulder and he grabbed on to it like a lifeline, holding so tight that she thought he might actually crack a bone.

"Right, sorry about that," he said, and he sounded so unbearably British that she wanted nothing more than to comfort him.

"You mentioned dinner," he said with a final squeeze of her hand before letting go.

"Of course, dinner. It's nothing fancy. I don't have a working kitchen yet."

"But it *would* be fancy if you had a stove to cook it on?" The blatant disbelief in his voice had her laughing.

"Hey, I've gotten better through the years."

"Well, you couldn't get worse, that's for sure."

She socked him gently in the arm. "I'll have you know, some people actually like my cooking."

"Let me let you in on a little secret," he said with a snort. "It doesn't count if they're starving."

She laughed despite herself. "Well, what does that say about you, then? You accepted my invitation to dinner even though you know I'm a terrible cook."

"It says I don't give a damn about the food. That I'm here because I want to spend time with you."

She stopped dead, right in the doorway to the dining room, and struggled to make sense of his words. To make them mean something less than they did.

He stood directly behind her, and then it was his turn to put his hands on her shoulders. She trembled a little at the delicate sweetness of his touch, and he pulled her against him, her back resting on his chest.

"Simon." She meant it to come out as a protest, but it ended up sounding more like a moan.

"I missed you," he said, brushing his lips over her temple.

She gave a slight shudder. "Don't say that."

"Why not?" His mouth skimmed across her cheek to a spot right beneath her ear. It was a spot he knew well, one that lit her up like the Fourth of July.

"Because I didn't invite you here for this." She tried to pull away, but she was too weak and he felt too good.

She waited for him to press his advantage, to turn

her in his arms and kiss her until she couldn't remember her name, let alone why sleeping with him was a bad idea. It was what the old Simon would have done. Enjoy the moment and to hell with the consequences. He'd burned her that way many times before, and deep inside she was deathly afraid—despite all the promises she'd made herself—that tonight wouldn't be any different.

But she wasn't counting on the new Simon. Because at the first hint of protest, he gave her a chaste kiss on the cheek. Then he released her.

"I think I could probably use that drink now," he told her as he walked through the dining room and into the kitchen.

For long seconds, she stood still as a statue, trying to figure out what had happened. Then, when it became apparent that no explanation would be forthcoming—either from him or from her own brain—she headed after him, trying desperately to convince herself that dinner was the only thing she wanted.

Unfortunately, it seemed her talent for lying to herself—especially about Simon—had disappeared along with everything else after Gabby's death.

Happy housewarming to her.

CHAPTER TWELVE

SIMON POPPED THE TOP off the champagne and resisted the urge to drink straight from the bottle. He felt as if he was going to explode, and if he couldn't have Amanda, then he definitely needed something to calm him down.

"I forgot to bring glasses," he told her as she entered the kitchen behind him.

"I got some." He heard her rummage around for a second, then she handed him two plastic champagne flutes.

He glanced at her in surprise.

She shrugged. "I bought champagne, too. Figured a celebration was in order."

"Absolutely." He handed her a glass.

"What should we toast to?" she asked.

He glanced around. "That the house doesn't fall down around your ears?"

"Excuse me. We're supposed to be celebrating my new home, not poking fun at it." She rolled her eyes, and it was such an un-Amanda-like thing to do that he stared at her. And then realized his mistake as he hardened to the point of pain. "Besides, it's not that bad."

"I know. I like it."

"Yeah, right."

"No, I do. It's got personality. I think it's a good start."

"Maybe. I hope so." She glanced around, and though her smile was a little tight, her eyes were clear. "So let's toast to that." She held up her glass. "To a new start."

They touched glasses, drank, and he never took his eyes off her. He couldn't. She really did look beautiful tonight, her skin glowing with a health and vitality that had been missing three weeks before. And though she was still too thin, it was obvious that she'd been making an effort to eat regularly. She filled out her jeans and scoop-necked T-shirt a little better than she had the last time he saw her.

He was glad she was doing well, thrilled that she was slowly moving past the nightmare of Gabby's death. But he wasn't sure what it said about him that, after everything that had passed between them, he still wanted her. Even when he knew that she didn't feel the same way about him.

"So, are you hungry?" she asked a little nervously, and he realized he'd been staring at her too long.

"Yeah, sure." As he followed her back to the dining room, the bottle of champagne still clutched in his hand, he didn't bother to tell her that food was the last thing he was hungry for.

He was supposed to be on his best behavior, after all, and accosting her the first time she let him back in was probably not the best way to convince her to continue whatever weird, twisting path their relationship was set to take next. He had no intention of doing anything to jeopardize this newfound truce between them. Even if it killed him.

And it just might, he thought, watching as she bent down to arrange something on the pretty yellow quilt she'd spread on the dining-room floor. He wanted nothing more than to reach out and trace the gorgeous curves of her ass. To run his lips down her belly and feast again on the sweet, syrupy warmth of her.

Putting on the best poker face of his life, he sat across the makeshift table and asked casually, "So, what do you have planned for the house? You said you were going to get the kitchen gutted?"

The look she gave him was half puzzled and half amused. "You don't really want to spend dinner talking about the house, do you?"

No, he wanted to spend dinner with her spread-eagled on the blanket as he trailed crushed strawberries over every inch of her before licking her clean. But since that option was obviously not available, he figured hearing about her plans was as good a way as any to try and dampen the raging erection he'd had since she opened the door.

Much to his surprise, dinner passed easily as she told him about the different phases of remodeling she wanted to do. The kitchen was first—she had hired a company to deal with it, and had already picked out appliances and cabinets. The other stuff—not including plumbing and electric—she planned on doing herself, one painstaking room at a time.

"I'm hoping it will be cathartic," she told him over another glass of champagne and the best Turtles brownies he'd ever eaten. "Working with my hands, fixing up the house. If I'm lucky, maybe for each room I put back together I'll get another piece of who I am back." She shrugged. "It's cheaper than therapy."

"I don't think you're missing that many pieces."

"You might be surprised. I'm pretty much a waffling ball of neuroses at the moment."

"I've seen my share of neurotics through the years, Amanda, and you do not fit that bill."

"No? Then how would you describe me?"

"My best guess? Someone who's down but not out. You've had it rough, no doubt, but you're making your way back—"

"Clawing my way back, don't you mean?"

"Whatever. As long as you finish the journey, how you do it doesn't matter to me."

She looked away. "I still don't know if…"

"If what?" he asked when it became obvious that she wasn't going to continue.

"If I can handle being with you again. I invited you here because I wanted you to know that I'm okay, that I'm putting my life back together. But I don't know how much more I'm ready for. If anything, I mean."

"Is being my friend really that stressful?"

She laughed, but the humor had drained from her beautiful face. "Yeah. It kind of is."

Well, wasn't that a kick in the teeth? And here he'd been on his best behavior all night. "I'm sorry. Do you want me to go?"

"I don't know what I want," she told him passionately. "That's the whole problem. I can't figure it out. I mean, I know I want the past two years to never have happened—to go back to a time when Gabby was alive and healthy and whole.

"But since I can't have that, I don't know what else there is to wish for. What else there is to want. And believe me, I don't expect you to stick around while I try to figure it out."

He stiffened before he could stop himself. "So, you don't want me to stick around?"

"That's not what I said. I don't know what I want right now and that's the truth. It's like I'm treading water, trying to keep from drowning. But no matter how hard I try to stay afloat, I keep getting pulled back under."

"And you don't think I can help with that?" He struggled to understand, but it was difficult when all he wanted to do was wrap her in cotton and keep her safe. Even if it meant she never got in the water again.

"I think you probably could. But I can't do that again. I can't put my emotional health and well-being in someone else's hands, because what do I do when it goes bad again, Simon? I don't know if I'd have the willpower to do all this again."

"You're so sure it will end?" He held his breath, waiting to hear what she would say. In his head, he knew she had reservations about him, about them, but he wanted the chance to prove her wrong. He wasn't the same man she remembered, wasn't the same man who was so caught up in his own control issues that he refused to believe his daughter was dying until it was too late.

Until she was already gone.

He'd learned his lesson and he wanted Amanda to know that. Didn't want to leave tonight until he'd gotten her to believe and accept that.

"I don't want to take the chance."

"Let me take the chance, Amanda. Let me take care

of you. I swear, I won't run out on you—" He broke off when he saw the look on her face. "I'm doing it again, aren't I? Trying to control everything?"

"A little bit." She scooted closer, until he could smell the sweet, spicy scent of her and it drove him crazy. He wanted to hold her, to kiss her, to make love to her until he chased the shadows from her eyes once and for all.

But then, that was a pipe dream, wasn't it? Life had given them both a lot of hard knocks until neither of them was the same person they'd once been. He needed to accept that he couldn't be everything to her this time around. She wouldn't let him.

He started to tell her he understood where she was coming from, but was stopped by the feel of her hand cupping his cheek. It felt so good to have her touch him again that he closed his eyes so he could savor every second of it.

A part of him wanted to reach up and capture her hand, to hold it right where it was until all of her warmth seeped into him. But he knew doing so would send the wrong message, so he kept his hands where they were—resting lightly on his knees—though it was damn hard.

"I know it's not fair to ask you to wait," she told him softly. "I thought we could let each other go and everything would be okay."

An instinctive protest rose inside him. "Amanda—"

"Shh." She moved her hand until her fingers covered his lips. "But that doesn't seem to be working out so well for either of us. I missed you these past few weeks, hated being this close to you and not having any contact with you."

Her words were exactly what he needed to hear and he nodded, encouraging her to continue as the beginnings of sweet relief started blossoming inside of him.

"At the same time, I don't know how much I have to give to anyone, Simon. Even you. Especially you. Every ounce of energy I have has to go toward making me well."

"I understand that," he murmured against her fingers, then insisted, "I do," when he saw her skeptical look. "But I was miserable without you these past weeks. Can't we just take things slow, try to be friends?"

"You really think we can do that? With everything between us?"

Hell, no. Not when he wanted her so much that every breath he took was an agony. But if it meant the difference between having her in his life or losing her forever, he'd wear the friend cap for a while. It wasn't as if he'd never had to do it before.

"Except for these past eighteen months, we've been friends all along, haven't we?" He did take her hand now, squeezed it. "That's a lot of history to just throw away."

"I feel closer to Gabby when I'm with you," she whispered.

They weren't quite the words he wanted to hear, but he knew what she meant. It was the same for him.

"I know," he told her.

"You don't mind?"

"She was my daughter, too." And her absence from the world was an arrow through his gut every single day of his life.

Understanding dawned and she scooted closer to him, until he could feel the warmth of her breath on his face. "I know. And I'm sorry for all the terrible things I said. At the funeral, when you came for me in Africa. I was in pain, but that's no excuse."

"Believe me, I'm not holding a grudge. I deserved everything you said, Mandy."

"No, you didn't. I was suffering and wanted you to suffer, too. I forgot that you already were."

He closed his eyes and lay his head on her shoulder as the old, familiar guilt overwhelmed him. Her arms came around him and she held him for long minutes, neither of them knowing what else to say but neither wanting to break the connection.

Finally, Amanda whispered, "Simon?"

He lifted his head reluctantly. "Yes?"

"I really want to kiss you right now."

"Thank God." The sharp blade of desire was slicing him from the inside out.

She laughed. "So, maybe, we can be friends that… kiss?"

He was so down with that. Would be even happier if they could be friends that touched and made love and— He cut off the train of thought before he ended up throwing her down on the quilt and trying to convince her, in the most pleasurable manner possible, to see things his way.

"Simon?" she prompted, her cheeks flushing a delicate pink color that only made him want her more.

"I thought you'd never ask."

He leaned in slowly, making sure to keep his eyes pinned on hers. He wanted to see her every reaction, to know if she was as into this as he was. Although if she wanted him half as much as he wanted her, they'd already be making love.

But this was a start, he told himself. More than he'd dared hope for when he showed up here this evening.

As he wrapped his arms around her slowly, he kept watching her, until she made a startled, needy sound that shot right through him and shattered his control. Lowering his mouth to hers, he took her lips in the gentlest kiss possible. A kiss that was twelve years in the making.

Her lips parted and he savored the sweet, sweet taste of her, though he didn't take the kiss any deeper. That's not what tonight was about, not what this new phase in their relationship was about.

As he kissed her, he repeated the words to himself like a mantra. Did his damnedest to keep his raging need under control. At least until she moaned and buried her hands in his hair, tugging him even closer.

His desire slipped the leash. Wrapping his arms around her, pulling her slender body against his, he prepared to devour her. At least until he heard the long, agonized squeal of brakes on the street beside her house, followed by the unmistakable sound of two cars crashing.

CHAPTER THIRTEEN

THE SOUND OF THE CRASH galvanized Amanda as nothing else could. Ripping out of Simon's delicious embrace, she ran to the front parlor. It was the room that gave her the best view of the street on that side of the house.

What she saw when she got there had her turning to Simon, who was right behind her, and barking, "Call 911 and get my bag. It's upstairs in the master bedroom."

Then she tore out of the house. When she got to the accident, for long, critical seconds she didn't know where to start. Everything looked bad.

But then the doctor in her kicked in and she started assessing damage. The first car had plowed straight into the front quarter panel of the second car, and from where she stood it didn't look as if either driver was moving.

Rushing around to the passenger side of the car that was hit, she opened the door and climbed in. The air bag had deployed and was slowly shrinking back, but she wasn't sure how much good it had done. The man was groggy, his face bloody. His left arm was obviously broken and a quick glance at the way the driver's side door molded around his leg told her they were going to need the Jaws of Life to get him out.

"Sir," she said in her most firm voice. "Can you look at me? Sir?"

He turned toward her voice, but his eyes were blank as they stared into hers.

"I'm a doctor. I'm going to try to help you, okay?"

No answer. Not even a flicker of acknowledgment that he understood the question. She leaned forward in the dim light of the car, saw that his pupils were different sizes.

"Shit," she muttered, looking over her shoulder for Simon. In the distance, she heard a siren kick on and then Simon appeared, her medical bag in his hand. "He has some kind of head injury," she told him. "Go check out the other driver."

As she took the man's pulse, she spoke soothingly to him, trying to keep him calm. He wasn't tracking very well, but she could tell he was in a lot of pain and the last thing she needed was for him to figure out that he was trapped in the car. He was already going into shock, despite the warm, humid night. She didn't need anything to make his condition worse.

She was in the middle of unwrapping a thin space blanket to cover him with—and keep him warm—when Simon's voice rang through the night. "Amanda, I need you over here."

Responding to the urgency, she covered the man quickly and then flung herself out of the car. Vaguely, she registered that there were other people on the street, but she didn't pay any attention to them. Certainly not after she saw the shape the other driver was in. Damn it, she'd picked the wrong car to go to first.

Simon was leaning over the driver, his hand clamped

to a wound on the man's thigh that was gushing dark, rich blood. It was hard to tell in the light from the car, but she was almost positive it was arterial blood. Which meant he wasn't going to last until the paramedics got here, not if she couldn't get the bleeding stopped.

"We've got to get him out of the car," she told Simon urgently. "He's bleeding out."

Simon responded instantly, and within seconds, the man was lying on the street, Simon on one side of him and she on the other, examining his wound. Something—a piece of glass or sharp metal—had sliced straight through his upper thigh to the bone, which meant the artery had definitely been hit.

Damn it.

"Give me your belt," she told Simon as she frantically sought to find the bleeder. It was almost impossible, though—there was too much blood and it was too dark for her to see.

Someone—one of her new neighbors, she assumed—rushed over with a flashlight. "Can I help?" he asked.

"Yes. Shine that directly over his leg, please." She took Simon's belt from him and wrapped it around the man's leg as tightly as she could. As far as tourniquets went, she'd seen better, but it stopped the bleeding enough that she could finally get her hands onto the artery.

She cursed as soon as she felt it. "Get two clamps out of my bag," she told Simon urgently. She had hoped it was only nicked, but it was actually sliced straight through. The man screamed and tried to knock her hand away as she pinched one side of the artery.

"I'm a doctor," she told him as she held on tight, her other hand searching for the second half. "I know this hurts and I'm sorry, but once it's done, you'll feel better."

"What—"

"Please, lie back down," she told him. "Let me get this done and then I'll explain what's going on." She breathed a sigh of relief as her fingers closed around the edge of the artery. She'd been terrified it had rolled up his leg and she was going to have to dig for it.

"I'm not sure what I'm looking for," Simon told her, his voice as low and calm as ever. Thank God. He held up two clamps. "Are these what you want?"

"Yes. But I can't let go," she answered. "You're going to have to put the first clamp on."

She wasn't sure who was paler—Simon or the man on the ground—but after a second, he shook off the horror and merely nodded. "Where do I put it?" he asked, leaning forward.

"Right above my fingers on the left." She shifted her hand as much as she could to make room for his larger one, but it was still a close fit. Simon fumbled the clip for a second, but finally managed to get it on the artery, right above where she pinched it closed.

"Give me the second clamp," she told him tersely, and within seconds she had the artery completely clamped off. "The paramedics better get here soon."

"Did you get it?" her patient asked, the words low and slurred. He was obviously in shock, and as she felt for his pulse, she experienced a second of panic. It was weak, thready and way too fast. He'd lost far too much blood.

"I did," she told him soothingly.

"Am I going to be okay?" he gasped.

"You're going to be fine." She didn't know if it was true or not, but she had no compunction about lying to the man. The last thing he needed right now was to freak out—more adrenaline would only make his heart beat faster and the situation worse.

"Thank you," he said, his hand groping for hers. She let him find it, and squeezed gently as his eyes slowly drifted shut.

"Hang on," she told him. "Just hang on."

The next few minutes passed in a blur as the paramedics finally showed up and she briefed them on what she'd done. It didn't take them long to get the arterial-bleed patient on a gurney in the back of the truck and speed away.

The second man was more difficult to free because of the way his leg was trapped. But the fire department had him out soon enough and then the only people left were the police, who took a brief statement from her, and the tow-truck drivers.

At that point, Simon slipped an arm around her waist. "You did good tonight."

She smiled a little. "I did, didn't I?"

"You're a fantastic doctor. No one has ever said differently."

"Yeah, but it's been a long time since my trauma rotation. I was a little freaked out at first."

"No one would have guessed." He turned her and slowly walked her up the sidewalk to her house. "But you need a shower. And those clothes are done for."

"I could say the same about you." She looked him

over, paused. Then added, "You can shower here, if you like." Even as she said the words, she couldn't believe they were coming out of her mouth. But she didn't take them back, despite the searing look Simon gave her.

"Much as I would like to take you up on that offer, I think I should probably head home. Based on the conversation we had earlier."

"Yeah, I guess." She fought not to show her disappointment, especially when he was only doing what she'd asked.

But she must not have done a very good job of it, because Simon groaned, his jaw tightly clenched. "Don't look at me like that," he told her. "Not tonight, when you've still got way too much adrenaline pumping through your system to make such an important decision."

She nodded. "You're right."

"Yeah. I am." He didn't move, though, just watched her carefully, his green eyes blazing.

Which meant he'd been pushed as far as he could go. She was going to have to be the one to do the right thing. The only thing. Being careful not to touch him, she took the front steps two at a time.

"Good night, Simon."

"Good night, Mandy."

The sound of her nickname on his lips weakened her knees and her resolve. But she forced herself to take the last few steps to the front door. She opened it, stepped inside, then waved before closing the door firmly behind her.

It was the right decision, even though it was harder than she'd expected it to be.

But it was the right one. She knew it was—if she started something with Simon again before she was ready, she was never going to heal. For most of their relationship, being with Simon had been all-consuming and she had easily lost herself in him. Now that she was finally on the road to recovery, she couldn't afford to do anything to jeopardize that. Not if she wanted to find her way back to where she once was.

When she was better, when she felt solid again, she and Simon could try to figure out the steps of their relationship. Until then, for the first time in her adult life, she was going to make herself a priority.

That was cold comfort as she peered through the window next to the door, watching him watch her. Waiting for him to get in his car. When he finally left, she leaned against the door. Her relationship with Simon was complicated, painful, but it had also been the most important relationship she'd ever had, excluding the one with Gabby. Simon had hurt her more than anyone else ever had, but he had also brought her more love, more joy. Had taught her what it meant to truly love someone else when she'd grown up isolated and alone, taken care of by her mother's relatives after her parents had died in a car crash, but never really loved. Never really wanted.

Simon had wanted her then and he wanted her still. And while she didn't want to forgive him for what he'd done, it was getting harder and harder to hold it against him. Not when she saw how severely he was punishing himself.

Confused, frightened, but also happier than she'd been in a very long time, Amanda slid silently to the floor. And wondered how on earth she was going to stop herself from falling for him. Again.

AFTER A NEAR-SLEEPLESS NIGHT, Amanda stood in her dining room, drinking convenience-store coffee and watching as her contractor systematically destroyed her kitchen, ripping it down to wall studs and subfloors.

There had been something cathartic in seeing the bare bones of the place, in knowing that very soon it would be whole and beautiful and, most important, *functional* again. In knowing that there was a timeline to completion.

If only her own life could be put back together as cleanly and quickly.

That wasn't going to happen, though. Not as long as she was in charge, bumbling her way along the road back toward sanity. It was a new path for her, one she didn't know well, and she figured she'd end up making a few mistakes along the way.

Brick by brick, she reminded herself as she took another sip of coffee. One thing at a time, and today that involved picking out paint for the master bedroom and bathroom, as well as buying a bunch of supplies to help her do the work.

After saying goodbye to the workmen, Amanda headed toward the closest home-repair store. She had a feeling she would know every inch of it before she was done with her house. It didn't take as long as she thought it would to pick out colors for her suite of rooms—cool, soothing blues that would complement each other and, she hoped, would have a calming effect on her.

She also stocked up on brushes, rollers, scrapers, paint trays, stir sticks and any and everything else she could think of. She also got a soft white paint for the ornate trim that lined the ceiling and floor of most of the rooms—the contractor had told her it was in decent shape, something she was grateful for as she'd fallen in love with it at first sight. She also bought a ladder, which she paid extra to have delivered since she didn't want to ruin the paint on her brand-new SUV by strapping it to the roof.

She left the store, loaded down with supplies and feeling more optimistic than she had in a long time. It felt good to have a project. As she put the supplies in the car, imagining the satisfaction of standing in her bedroom when the painting was completed, her mind drifted to Gabby and how much fun her daughter would have had directing the action as Amanda painted. Gabby had always been a bossy little thing and playing contractor on a job like this would have thrilled her to no end.

Amanda braced herself for the debilitating pain that thoughts of Gabby still brought. But they didn't come this time. Instead, a sweet warmth filled her, one that had her remembering again how good it had felt to be Gabby's mother.

Filled with purpose, and more than a little excited, Amanda slammed the tailgate shut and climbed behind the wheel of the SUV. Remodeling a house was such a contrast to practicing medicine in poverty-stricken nations. Still, she was chomping at the bit to try.

Thinking about Somalia made her think of Jack. He'd emailed her numerous times in the past couple of weeks and she hadn't bothered to respond. Maybe it was time to change that.

Pulling out her smartphone, she started to dial the number of his satellite phone, but in the end, couldn't do it. She wasn't ready to talk to him. Not yet. It was hard enough getting through the day when the only people she needed to talk to were the contractor and Simon. Adding someone else to the list—especially a friend like Jack, who had a tendency to get right to the heart of things—might upset the delicate tightrope she'd been walking.

Still, she couldn't totally ignore him. Instead, she dashed off a quick email telling him what she'd been up to and promising to call soon. Then she put the phone away and pulled out of the parking lot, determined to focus on the first project she had waiting for her at home.

Caught up in her thoughts, she made a wrong turn and ended up in a part of Atlanta she had never seen before. A quick glance around told her it wasn't an area she necessarily wanted to be in, even in the middle of the day. She locked her doors as she stopped at a red light, planning to make a quick U-turn the first chance she got. She froze when she saw a sad, decrepit-looking clinic at the corner on her left.

Unable to look away, she stared at it through the entire light, and when she finally ended up making that U-turn, instead of heading back to her house, she pulled into a small parking lot behind the clinic.

She sat in her car for a minute, debating whether or not she really wanted to do this. Whether or not she was ready for it. But then she remembered the night before, the pride and the exhilaration that had come when she'd stopped that man from bleeding out. And she knew, ready or not, she was going to take the next step forward on her journey.

She was at the door of the clinic before she realized she wasn't exactly dressed for a job interview in her jeans and white T-shirt. But she knew she was going in, anyway. If she walked away now, she wasn't sure she'd get the nerve to come back anytime soon.

Her first glimpse of the clinic might have shocked her if she hadn't spent more than a decade working under conditions in hard-hit developing nations. The walls were dingy and stained in numerous places with God only knew what. The chairs that lined the walls, crammed to capacity with tired, sick patients, were the folding kind, the paint peeling off many of them. And the small clinic staff that was trying to take care of everyone was obviously overwhelmed.

Amanda waited a moment, tried to decide how she felt about being here. Maybe it was too soon. But as an obviously sick baby began to wail in high-pitched distress, all she felt was a sense of homecoming. As if she was finally back where she belonged.

This wasn't Africa, wasn't For the Children, but she'd already figured out that she couldn't go back there. She looked at the waiting patients. Many of them seemed to have put off coming to the doctor until they had no choice, and Amanda suddenly realized that she *wanted* to do this.

Straightening her shoulders, feeling a professional determination that had been lacking in her for quite a while, she walked straight up to the desk and the woman she guessed to be in charge.

"The line starts over there," the woman said.

"I don't want—"

"Doesn't matter. If you want to talk to the doc, you need to stand over there."

"But I'm not here to see a doctor. I'd like—"

"You can't get a script without seeing the doctor."

"A script?"

"For pain medication or whatever it is you want. Lord deliver us from addicts looking for a fix."

"You think I'm a junkie?" Amanda asked incredulously. She thought she'd gained weight these past few weeks and lost that gaunt look.

"Darlin', I don't actually care what you are. If you want anything around here, you need to stand in that line over there and wait your turn." She tossed the last over her shoulder as she walked away, a stack of charts in her hands.

Amanda stood there for a moment, staring after the woman as she contemplated what she should do next. Finally, with a shrug, she got in line. If she wanted a job, she probably needed to talk to the doctor that ran this place, anyway.

It took her almost forty-five minutes to even make her way to the triage nurse, which bothered her a great deal. What if she was having a heart attack or a stroke? Or even a very high fever? Forty-five minutes to get an initial assessment was ridiculous. Urgent cases died in much less time.

When it was finally her turn, she said to the nurse, "I'm not here to be examined. I'm a doctor and I'd really like a chance to talk to someone about working here."

The nurse's mouth dropped open. "Are you kidding me?"

"Do I look like I'm kidding? I spent forty-five minutes in line to see you so I could get a job application."

The nurse smirked, as if she knew the punch line to an inside joke. "We don't take applications here."

"Oh." She glanced around. "You can't tell me it's because you have a full staff."

"No, it's because no reputable doctor actually wants to work here. Not for what the doc can pay."

"I do."

"Which immediately makes you suspicious in my mind, but what the hell. I'll take you back to meet Dr. C."

"I would appreciate that."

"Okay, then. Follow me."

There was a slight grumble from the people in line behind her as the nurse took her directly to the back. As she was led through the maze of exam rooms, Amanda noticed that despite the huge number of people being taken care of, the clinic was scrupulously clean. Old and worn, but definitely clean. She approved.

"You can wait in here. I'll send him back as soon as he finishes with his patient."

"Is Dr. C the only doctor who works here?" she asked.

"There are usually a couple of residents, but they pull night shift. And some local doctors volunteer a few hours here and there."

"But Dr. C. is the only full-time doctor?"

"It's his baby" came the cryptic reply. And with no further explanation, she was gone.

Amanda settled herself in one of the two chairs on the patient side of the desk and glanced around the cluttered office. It was small, with barely enough room for the battered furniture. Two bookshelves were crammed into the corner, every inch of them stuffed with medical texts and journals.

Dr. C's degree hung on the wall behind his desk. His full name was Lucas Carrington and he had graduated from Harvard Medical School a couple of years after she did.

Interesting.

After a few minutes, she grew bored with waiting and crossed to the shelves. She picked up one of the journals, dated the previous month. Not that it surprised her. The more she saw of this place, the more she was coming to realize that the elusive Dr. C didn't miss a trick. Flipping through the *Journal of Modern Medicine,* Amanda killed another twenty minutes before the office door flew open and Lucas Carrington—tall, dark and exceptionally handsome—came whirling in, chart in hand. "Latonya tells me you're looking for a job. I only have a minute—we're swamped today—but if you leave me your name and number I can get back to you at a more convenient—"

He broke off as he glanced at her. "You don't look desperate."

She raised an eyebrow. "I'm not."

"Hmm. It looks like I need to make time." He sank onto the corner of his desk, extending his hand. "I'm Lucas Carrington."

"Amanda Jacobs."

"Nice to meet you."

"Likewise."

"What kind of doctor are you, Amanda?"

"I'm an internist."

"And where'd you go to school?"

Her eyes flickered to the degree on the wall. "Harvard Med. A couple of years before you."

"Really? And you want to forsake all the glory that comes with being a Harvard grad to work here?" His voice was blatantly skeptical.

"I forsook it a long time ago. I've spent the past eleven years working in developing nations with For the Children."

"Really?" His interest sharpened and she got the feeling they were finally getting down to a real interview. "Tell me about it."

She did, relating as much of her story as she could in a few minutes—and leaving out the close call with a nervous breakdown that had been her real reason for leaving Somalia—before finishing with, "I've decided to make Atlanta my home. And while I could go into private practice or sign on with a hospital here, I was driving by your clinic a little while ago and figured working here would be more up my alley."

"I see. And all your credentials are in order, I assume."

She grinned. "Of course. I can have my transcripts faxed over."

"You do that." There was a knock on the door and he stood. "Coming, Latonya."

He turned to Amanda. "I have to go. But get those

transcripts to me. If you bring in a copy of your degree tomorrow, I'll let you work for a few hours. See how it goes."

"Tomorrow?"

"Too soon?"

"No, it's perfect."

"Good. I'll see you then." He started out the door, then turned at the last second. "The pay's terrible." He named a figure that was actually comparable to what she'd been making with For the Children.

"I can live with that," she told him.

"Something told me you could." He gave her a little salute that had her smiling all over again. "I'll see you tomorrow."

She nodded, following him out into hall. "Definitely."

"All right, then. Welcome aboard, Dr. Jacobs."

She practically skipped back down the hall to the waiting room. It looked as if she had a job. She couldn't wait to tell Simon.

CHAPTER FOURTEEN

SIMON STOOD ON Amanda's doorstep, waiting impatiently for her to answer. She'd slipped into his mind many times throughout the day—when he was working on the footage of the South American story and ran across an image of a doctor treating the sick and injured, when he was walking to work and smelled freesia. When he was sitting at lunch and Mark had ordered one of Amanda's favorite meals.

He'd tried to put her out of his mind, had reminded himself that they were just going to be friends, but it didn't matter. She crept back in, like she always did.

This time it was different, though. At least two or three times a day, he had to fight the urge to pick up the phone and tell her about some cool fact his research had uncovered or to ask her to go see a movie with him. They were both movie fiends, though their jobs had never allowed them to indulge in that pastime very often. And most telling of all, today he had put off his trip to Yemen, the first time he'd ever passed on a story, because he wanted to stay close to her. When he'd found himself rushing through a meeting on the state of the Middle East because he'd wanted to see her, he'd known he was sunk.

Which was why he was here, standing unannounced on her doorstep because she hadn't answered her brand-new cell phone all day. He hoped the Chinese takeout and latest DVD with her favorite actress would make up for the fact that he was stopping by unannounced. The last thing he needed was for her to decide he was trying to take care of her again. Even if he was, she didn't need to know. And if things went as planned, he'd get to spend some time with her, to see how she was doing. To hold her, and maybe even sneak in a kiss or two, if she'd let him.

When she didn't answer the door after a couple of minutes, he rang the bell again. And started to feel like an idiot—nothing like showing up at a woman's house, desperate to see her, only to find out that she had other plans.

He waited another minute, to be sure. Still nothing. Then he rang the doorbell one last time before heading back to his car, wondering what the hell he was going to do with all the food he'd bought.

Amanda's front door flew open when he was almost at his car. "Simon?" she called.

He turned, feeling pathetically grateful that she was home, after all. And burst out laughing when he saw her, dressed in paint-spattered clothes with a handkerchief wrapped around her hair and a long smear of blue paint on her cheek.

"I know, I know," she said with a grin. "It's a good look for me."

"No doubt. Painting, I assume?"

"The master bedroom, all the way at the back. I was in the middle of it when the doorbell rang." She smiled proudly. "I want to get it done first so that I can actually get a bed. My back is not as young as it used to be."

"Wait a minute. You're sleeping here already?"

"I know, it's crazy. But fun, too. Kind of like a prolonged camping trip, with running water, of course."

"Thank God for running water."

"My sentiments exactly."

"What about your stuff from Boston? You haven't had it shipped down yet?"

He felt like a jerk when her face closed up. "I decided I didn't want it. I'm going to have to arrange to sell it eventually, or donate it. This house is a fresh start for me and I think it'll be better if I don't weigh it down with stuff from before."

He nodded, thinking of her coffee table with the childish drawing of a flower in permanent marker in one corner. "That sounds like a pretty good idea, actually."

She smiled, held the door open. "You want to come in?"

"Absolutely." He held up the bag of takeout. "I come bearing food."

"Oh, thank God. I'm so hungry that I was contemplating gnawing my own arm off."

"Don't do that—I brought your favorite."

"Oh, yeah?" she asked, leading him into the dining room, where the yellow quilt was still spread on the floor. "What's that?"

"Kung Pao Chicken."

"Oh, right. Thanks." She didn't say anything else, just shook her head with a bemused grin, and his reporter radar went off.

"What's the matter?" he asked.

"Nothing. I appreciate the food, really."

"But?"

She went over to a cooler she had sitting in the corner. "Do you want water or a soda?"

"I'll take a Coke. And the truth, if you don't mind."

"It's nothing, Simon. Don't worry about it."

"Yeah, well, let me be the judge of that."

"It's stupid. I was amused because the truth is, I don't like Kung Pao Chicken."

"Since when?"

"Since forever."

"No way," he exclaimed. "I've gotten it for you a million times."

"I know. And I've never liked it."

"Why didn't you tell me?" He could feel color creeping up his cheeks, but he couldn't stop it. He felt like a total moron.

"I did tell you, a bunch of times. You kept forgetting, so I stopped mentioning it." She was spreading the food out on the blanket, but stopped when she got a good look at his face. "Don't worry about it, Simon. I'm sorry I said anything. Especially since I really appreciate you bringing dinner by."

But he barely heard her. He was too busy going over twelve years of shared past, trying to figure out what else he'd missed. If what she said was true, then he'd somehow been so self-centered, so wrapped up in himself, that he hadn't really listened to what she was saying. Which meant he was a complete asshole.

"Did I do that a lot?" he demanded. "Assume that I knew stuff about you? Not listen when you told me something I should know?"

"Come on, Simon. Let's not do this."

"Just tell me, Amanda. I want to do things right this time, and how can I do that if I don't know all the ways I screwed up?"

She sighed in exasperation. "It's chicken, Simon. Not the end of the world." She grabbed the container and took a large bite. "See, I haven't gone into convulsions yet. Now, come on, loosen up and let's eat. You brought enough food to feed an army."

"Yeah, but do you like any of it?"

"I like *all* of it, especially the hot-and-sour soup. Okay?"

It wasn't, really, but he didn't want to ruin her good mood. Already, he could see her wilting a little around the edges, the carefree smile she'd worn when he'd gotten there growing dim with annoyance.

"Yeah. And while we eat, you can tell me what your real favorites are. I promise, this time, I won't forget."

She laughed, and after a minute, so did he.

AFTER THEY'D FINISHED dinner and cleared up the trash, Amanda turned to Simon. "Do you want to see what I've done upstairs?"

"I'd love to. Have you been at it all day?"

"Well, except for this morning when I was dealing with the men ripping my kitchen to pieces." She led him up the stairs. "And my job interview."

"What job interview?"

"I'm going in tomorrow for a provisional first day at a low-income clinic over on Hyacinth. There are no guarantees, but I think I have a good shot at landing the job."

When he didn't say anything, she turned to look at him. "Simon? What's wrong?"

"You're really planning on staying."

"You're just now figuring that out? I sank three hundred thousand dollars into this place and you take it in stride. I interview for a job and suddenly you're shocked that I'm planning on making a life for myself in Atlanta?"

"I don't know. I guess I always thought you'd go back to For the Children. Back to Africa."

"I'm done with Africa, Simon. I just don't have it in me to watch any more children die. Not like that."

He didn't say anything, but then she didn't really expect him to. He'd left Africa nearly a decade ago because the famines had gotten to him, because he couldn't stand watching any more children slowly starve to death.

But before she could continue down the hall to the master bedroom, Simon swept her into a giant bear hug. She returned it with a laugh.

"Congrats on your new job! That's fantastic."

"I told you. It's not official yet."

"But it will be. That's what matters."

"Yeah, well. We'll see." She shrugged. "It's a beginning, anyway."

"It seems like you're saying that a lot lately."

"I like it better than the alternative."

He slung an arm over her shoulder and pulled her against him. "So do I."

"Good, because I want to finish this room today and I'm a little behind. So grab a roller and get started."

"It would be my pleasure."

Amanda crossed the room and turned the radio on, then reached for her own roller—and nearly painted the door frame blue as she caught sight of a shirtless Simon. He was already working, his muscles bunching and shifting as he covered the wall with long strokes.

He looked amazing.

Reminding herself that they were taking things slow this time around, she resisted—barely—the urge to run her hand down the smooth expanse of his back. Instead, she focused on applying the second coat to her own wall. They painted the room in companionable silence, talking randomly when the mood struck them. Amanda kept waiting for Simon to try to take over and start giving directions, but he never did. Instead, he seemed content to just relax and follow her lead.

It was a different dynamic than she was used to and one she had to admit she liked. Maybe he wasn't joking when he'd mentioned that he'd made some changes in his life. And if that was the case, so far she thoroughly approved.

Part of her wanted to go back to their discussion from the night before—the one about being friends, or maybe something more. The idea excited her, but at the same time, she was more nervous than she could ever remember being. They'd tried this whole thing before and both of them had ended up getting hurt. She wasn't sure if she had it in her to do that again—especially now that she wasn't only worried about herself getting hurt. The idea of hurting Simon was as painful.

At the same time, she obviously wasn't ready to say goodbye to him. She'd tried that a few weeks ago and here they were, sharing cozy dinners for two and painting her bedroom. She wished she knew what was happening between them, why she kept coming back to him. Was it because of her feelings for him—or because of his connection to Gabby? Until she figured that out, she'd be better off keeping her eyes, and her thoughts, to herself.

They finally finished the walls around ten-thirty, and she stepped back to peruse their handiwork. "Not bad," she told Simon with a smile. "For a jet-setting journalist, you're pretty good with your hands."

He smirked at her and she blushed as she realized how her words could be taken. Or at least how *he* was choosing to take them. But instead of rubbing it in—or offering to remind her how talented his hands were—he reached for a gallon of creamy-white paint.

"You want to knock the trim out tonight? It shouldn't take long to do the door wells and windowsills."

"Actually, I'm kind of tired. It's been a long day."

He immediately put the paint back down and crossed to her. "Turn around," he murmured, and when she did, he started kneading her neck and shoulder muscles. It felt so good that her eyes nearly crossed, though she didn't know what she appreciated more—the massage or the fact that Simon was the one giving it to her. She had a feeling it was the latter. So much for good intentions.

By the time he was done, she was a puddle on the ground—or pretty close to it. "Don't fall asleep," he told her as he pulled his shirt on. "You've got to lock the door behind me." He grabbed her hand and started down the stairway.

"You don't have to go so soon," she protested, even as she wondered what she was doing.

The look he gave her seared her all the way to the bone. "I think we both know if I don't go now, I won't go at all."

"Would that be so bad?"

Who was this woman and when had she completely lost her mind? Amanda wondered dazedly.

"Not from my point of view." Simon grabbed her and pulled her in for a smoldering kiss. "But then, I wasn't the one who, less than twenty-four hours ago, was saying that we needed to be friends. This is what friends do."

Another kiss that turned her brain to mush and he was gone, disappearing into the night with a click of her front door. As she turned the lock, she thought about what he'd said. And the fact that from the second he'd shown up in Africa, Simon had done nothing but what was best for her.

It was a whole different side of him, one she wasn't sure what to do with.

CHAPTER FIFTEEN

TWO WEEKS LATER, Amanda dragged herself determinedly out of bed. It was already seven forty-five and she was due to open the clinic at eight-thirty. Getting ready for work hadn't been a problem any other mornings so far, but today it seemed an insurmountable obstacle.

When Lucas had asked her what day she wanted off this week, she'd been an idiot not to say today. Though she'd been dreading it, somehow she'd thought that having something to do, someplace to go, would make things easier. After all, she loved working with these patients, loved being able to help in a way she hadn't been able to in Africa. But that wasn't enough. The idea of going into the clinic today made her want to slam her head into the nearest wall until she fell into blessed unconsciousness.

Unfortunately, that wasn't an option. Getting dressed was. Going to work was. Not sitting here, dwelling on the fact that today would have been Gabby's ninth birthday. That there should be chocolate-chip ice-cream cake and new art supplies instead of tears and recriminations.

She wanted that alternate reality, wanted her baby safe and whole and healthy, so bad that she could barely stand the torment of being in her own skin. She wanted to scream, wanted to smash things, wanted to burn her whole existence—including the new life she'd started working toward—straight to the ground.

She wanted her baby back.

Dear God, she wanted Gabby in her arms where she belonged.

The agony of it—the absolute, horrible unfairness of it—brought her to her knees, and for long seconds, she was unable to move. Unable to think. She could only kneel there, arms wrapped around herself, face buried in the sheets of her brand-new bed, slowly breathing as the pain rolled through her.

During the past nineteen months, she'd learned that if she could just wait it out, if she could just concentrate on inhaling and exhaling, the pain would become bearable. Not good, *never good,* but manageable—a dull ache that she could cope with. Today, the pain had become an excruciating wave, one that would easily drown her if she let it.

The abyss beckoned and Amanda felt herself sliding toward it, felt herself giving in. It would be so easy to crawl back into bed and pull the covers over her head. So easy to disappear. She'd done it before—literally and figuratively—and it had been so much better than this.

Then again, anything was better than this.

She'd actually pulled the covers back, had started to slide between them, before she regained control.

Withdrawing from the world wasn't going to solve anything, she told herself through the pain. Hiding wasn't going to bring her daughter back, and running away would only ensure that it hurt worse when the pain finally caught up with her. If she'd learned nothing else in those last, desperate months in Africa, she'd learned that.

Besides, if she gave in now, all the work she'd done since coming to Atlanta would come tumbling down around her like so many blocks, and she didn't think she had it in her to start all over again.

Doing her best to ignore the sadness crashing around her, Amanda forced herself to finish dressing. Then she dragged herself out of her bedroom and down the stairs, leaving her oh-so-tempting bed behind. She skipped the kitchen, with its brand-new flooring and paint, knowing there was no way she would be able to choke even a granola bar down, not the way her stomach was crazily churning.

Instead, she went straight to the garage and her SUV. The sooner she got to work, the sooner she could concentrate on something besides the fire in her gut and the flames that were slowly roasting her alive.

As she drove, she wondered how Simon was doing. Or if he even remembered what day it was. All week, she'd waited for him to mention something about Gabby, to suggest that they spend the day together, since they'd both be hurting, but he hadn't said a word. Then again, she hadn't been able to bring herself to say anything, either—somehow, in her head, vocalizing their loss just made it worse.

Maybe he felt the same way.

Or maybe he'd forgotten it was Gabby's birthday altogether. He'd been known to do that when she was alive. She'd wait to hear from him for hours—hoping for a phone call, an email, a present delivered via

Federal Express—but more often than not, she was disappointed.

Two days or two months later—or sometime in between—Simon would blow back into town, with an apology and a fantastic gift to smooth everything over. Sometimes it worked and sometimes it didn't—

She cut her thoughts off as anger welled inside her. The past was over. Yes, Simon had made some mistakes, but then, so had she. If they were really going to move on and give this friendship-and-maybe-something-more relationship of theirs a shot, she couldn't afford to dwell on what had happened in the past. She had to let it go.

She pulled up in front of the clinic, checked her cell phone for the tenth time. Still no text or call from Simon. She tried not to let it get to her.

Despite her best intentions, though, the day at the clinic started a little roughly. She was off her game and more than once found her mind wandering when she needed to be concentrating on her patients' symptoms. But as the day progressed, she managed to settle in, find her stride. That's when she knew she'd done the right thing. Better to be here, swamped with work, than at home, hiding, as the day crept slowly by. *Better to be living,* she repeated for what might have been the millionth time in the past few weeks, *than the alternative.*

And by the time six o'clock rolled around, she was functioning, which was more than she could say about this day last year. That was definitely progress, right? If you took enough baby steps, you could still cover the distance. It would take you longer than if you sprinted, but it didn't make crossing the finish line any less sweet.

Amanda washed up, took off her coat and stethoscope, then prepared to work her way through the last of her charts. Pulling out her cell phone, she checked her messages—again—but still nothing from Simon, which was weird. Very weird.

Usually, he called once or twice to check on her or ask her to lunch—or to firm up plans for dinner. They'd seen each other every day since he'd shown up on her doorstep with Chinese takeout, and so far, she hadn't regretted a minute of the time they'd spent together.

Despite their past relationship—or more likely, because of it—they were taking things slow. Concentrating on rediscovering what they liked about each other aside from the sexual chemistry that had always flared between them.

But as the sun prepared to set for the day, Amanda didn't know whether she should be hurt, angry or concerned. She ended up being a combination of all three and flipped on the television in the break room no one ever had time to use, just to see if all hell had broken loose somewhere in the world. It hadn't, at least no more than usual, which meant Simon hadn't had to drop everything and fly off to some hot spot.

So where was he? she wondered, stewing about the situation as she worked her way through the charts. Should she be worried that he hadn't called? Atlanta could be a dangerous place, after all. Or should she assume he was busy? Just because her life was beginning to revolve around him—

Amanda closed her eyes as she realized what she'd

admitted to herself. Her life was beginning to revolve around Simon? How was that even possible? And if it was true, how could she be so stupid? She knew better. Absolutely knew better.

Relying on him was like relying on the wind. He showed up when he was least expected, stuck around for a while, wreaking havoc, and then disappeared as quickly as he came. Sure, she was enjoying spending time with him, enjoying contemplating the possibilities of what could be, but that didn't mean she was starting to *rely* on him. She'd made that mistake once and it had nearly killed her. Doing it again was worse than stupid. It was emotional suicide, and now that she'd climbed out of that hole, she wasn't going there again.

"You look like someone shot your dog." She glanced up to see Lucas leaning against the door frame, his dark eyes curious and concerned.

"I'm just tired." She pushed away from the table. "I think I'm going to head home." *To my empty house.*

She didn't say the words aloud, but they echoed in her head. Normally, she didn't mind being alone, but tonight it seemed like the worst fate in the world. Way too much time to think.

"I'm off in half an hour. Can I buy a drink?"

She stiffened, a little surprised—and dismayed— by the suggestive warmth in his voice. "I probably wouldn't be very good company tonight."

"Hence the invitation. Come on, Amanda. I know this great little bar that makes incredible mojitos. Let me take you there, buy you a couple. It'll cheer you up, and I promise, I have no nefarious intentions whatso- ever."

"None at all?" She raised her eyebrow, pretended suspicion.

He laughed. "None at all. I swear. Come on. It'll be fun."

She was tempted to agree. The only plan she had for the night was going home, painting a room and brooding about her daughter. Having a drink with a friend would keep her from brooding about Gabby.

And she used to like mojitos. They were Simon's favorite drink, so she'd had more than her fair share, even if she had lost her taste for them after they'd broken up.

Going out with a friend, having fun. She added another X onto the checklist in her mind. Another solid step on her path to recovery.

"Fine. One drink," she told him with a smile.

"Excellent! Let me finish up the cases I have in the rooms, and then as soon as Mike and Priss show up, we're out of here." He sent her a wink as he backed out of the door.

Amanda finished her charts while she waited for him, figuring his half an hour would be more like an hour—at the earliest. Lucas had a difficult time letting go, and she had yet to see him leave the clinic even close to on time. Not that she could talk, since she rarely left right after shift herself.

But to her surprise, thirty-five minutes later he was standing in front of her, car keys in hand. "You ready?"

"Absolutely." She stowed her charts, said a quick goodbye to the two doctors who had just come in, and then they were off. She had a moment's surprise when she saw Lucas's car—a beat-up truck that was as far removed from the typical Harvard grad as he was himself.

"So, where's the bar located?" she asked as they pulled into traffic. "I'm still trying to learn my way around Atlanta."

"Not too far." He named two streets she recognized, largely because they weren't far from Simon's apartment. She'd been there three times over the past couple of weeks and it had saddened but not surprised her to see how barren the place was.

"Good. That's in my comfort zone, so I shouldn't have too much trouble finding my way back."

"Your comfort zone?"

"Yeah. I have about a ten-square-mile area that I'm familiar with. I've ventured outside it a few times, but I usually stay within it. Since everything I need is in those boundaries, it's not bad."

The look he shot her was rife with disbelief. "Aren't you the world traveler?"

"Are you kidding me? In most of the places I've worked, I've been stuck in about three square miles of desert or island or whatever. I may have traveled to a lot of countries, but believe me, I don't do many exciting things once I'm there."

"Too busy working?"

"Exactly."

He shook his head. "We make a great pair."

"I've noticed you practically live at the clinic."

"Yeah, well, I've noticed that you do, too. Maybe we should start planning to do things together—it will help get us outside our 'comfort zones.' Although, I admit, I'm willing to go more than ten miles in any direction."

A warning bell sounded distantly in her head, not because he was teasing her, but because he seemed to take it for granted that they'd be seeing each other outside work again. She'd like to make a friend or two here, but the last thing she wanted was for him to get the wrong idea. She could barely handle the friendship she had going with Simon right now. Anything else was completely out of the question.

Although, if she was honest, it was more likely that Lucas felt sorry for her. She'd been working hard to get more sleep and regain the fifteen pounds she'd lost, but to date, she'd only managed to put on three. Which meant she was still too thin, too drawn, too tired-looking.

It also meant she was being ridiculous. Shooting Lucas a grin, she finally let herself relax. They chatted casually the rest of the way to the bar.

She had a few seconds' hesitation when she walked into the place, largely because it was decorated in shades of Gabby's favorite color, green. For a second, she almost walked back out. How could she be here, having a drink, on Gabby's birthday? How could she be trying to have fun, when her daughter would never get to do any of this?

As if he could sense her hesitation, Lucas grabbed her elbow and propelled her to a table toward the back. As they slid into the booth, she was struck by how understated and comfortable the place was. She'd been imagining some chic downtown bar where people tried too hard to impress members of the opposite sex, and instead he'd brought her to a place that had a really nice neighborhood vibe. An upscale neighborhood, sure, but still a neighborhood and not a meat market.

They chatted over happy-hour snacks and what might have been the best mojito Amanda had ever had. Mostly they talked about the clinic, but occasionally the conversation got more personal. Lucas told her about growing up poor in Atlanta. His parents had worked overtime trying to feed their three kids and never gotten ahead. Many times they'd gone without the basics, like medical care, so that their kids could have a little more. That was why, when he'd gotten his Ivy League scholarships, he'd sworn to come back and help make life better for those who were struggling as his parents had.

She admired him for that. A lot of people would have taken their degrees and run, but Lucas had stuck it out. Had made something important in a community that had almost nothing.

Of course, he also got points for never prying—not once did he try to figure out why she was so sad. Instead, he simply tried to make her feel better. It had been a long time since she'd had such a nice, uncomplicated time with a man.

About twelve years or so, to be exact—unless she counted Jack.

As she was waiting for her second mojito to arrive, she got up to use the restroom. Raised voices were coming from a few of the stools positioned in front of the bar.

She paused and would have headed to her table to give whoever was so agitated time to cool off, except one of the voices, with its clipped British accent, sounded familiar. Pausing, she tried to get a good look in the dim interior.

She couldn't see much, but then it came again. A very annoyed, very male, very drunk voice demanding another drink in the most proper British accent she had ever heard.

What were the odds? she told herself, even as she inched closer. Of all the bars in Atlanta, it was ridiculous to think that Simon would show up in the one she was sitting in. Especially drunk. She had never once seen him even close to tipsy in the years she'd known him.

Still, now that the suspicion was planted, she wasn't going to be happy until she knew for sure that it wasn't him. Giving up on subtlety, she strode over to the men—and felt her mouth drop open at what she saw. Simon was propped on the bar, sheer will holding him on the bar stool. It was obvious he was too hammered to function. One wrong move and he was going to end up on his ass on the floor.

There was an empty mojito glass in front of him and he was in the middle of arguing belligerently with the bartender, telling the man that he was more than capable of holding his liquor. Which made her wonder how much alcohol he had imbibed.

A hell of a lot more than one mojito, that was for sure.

A few people had gathered behind Simon, whether to order drinks or watch the show, she didn't know. But as she wove her way through them, she got up close and personal with a man she was pretty sure was the club's bouncer. Terrific. Simon was famous enough that getting tossed out of a bar, totally drunk, was sure to raise eyebrows.

When she was finally close enough to touch him, she lay a hand on his elbow. "Simon?" she said. "You okay?"

When he turned to her, his eyes were bleary and unfocused, his face slack.

Shit. He was really gone.

"How many drinks has he had?" she demanded of the annoyed bartender, wondering if she needed to worry about alcohol poisoning.

"Six in the two hours since he's been here," he answered, as he shook a martini for another customer. "But if you ask me, he was drunk when he walked in."

"Terrific. Thanks." She turned back to Simon with a frown. "Did you drive here?"

"No. Walked. Best mojitos in the city." The words were slurred, his voice trailing off a little.

"So I've heard," she told him drily. "Now, we need to get you home."

"Not ready to go home yet."

"Yes, well, I think the nice gentleman behind you thinks differently about that."

"I want another drink." He spun the stool around to face the bartender, but he moved too fast and ended up sliding off and into Amanda. And though she was strong, she weighed about seventy pounds less than him and couldn't hold her ground. They both ended up on the floor.

"That's it, buddy," the bouncer said. "Time to close out your tab."

Amanda was pinned underneath Simon, and since

he was making no effort to try to get off her, she started to push at his chest. "Come on, Simon," she muttered in his ear. "Let's get out of here."

"Okay. Let's go." He didn't move.

Not even trying to disguise her eye roll, she shoved at him a little harder. "You need to get off me. I can't move."

"Oh. Sorry." He tried to push himself up, but ended up sprawling more fully on top of her.

"Seriously?" she demanded, not sure if she was talking to Simon, the bouncer or the universe itself. Pushing with all her might, she finally got him to roll onto his back. She started to scramble to her feet, and then Lucas appeared, extending his hand to help her up.

"Quite a trip to the bathroom," he told her, tongue firmly in cheek. "I thought maybe you'd run out on me."

"I got sidetracked."

"I see that." He glanced at Simon, sprawled on the floor. "Friend of yours?"

"Actually, yes." She bent and tried to tug Simon to his feet but didn't get very far.

With a grin, Lucas hauled Simon up. "Does he have a car here that you can drive home?"

"It turns out he walked. I'll have them call us a cab."

"Don't be ridiculous," her boss told her. "Let me close out our tab and I'll give him a ride home before taking you back to the office for your car."

She looked at Simon, bit her lip. "I think you should probably leave me at his place. I'm a little worried about alcohol poisoning."

Lucas's gaze sharpened. "Do we need to go to the E.R.?"

"I don't think so. I just want to watch him for a little while, make sure he's all right."

Lucas nodded, and thankfully didn't ask any more questions. He really was a nice guy—and an efficient one. Within five minutes, both tabs had been closed and they were pulling into the street.

Simon was stretched out in the backseat, so drunk that she didn't think he even realized they were in a vehicle.

"I really appreciate this," she told Lucas after giving him directions to Simon's apartment.

"No problem. Though you know I'm going to pepper you with a million questions when you get into work tomorrow."

"He's my ex," she told him.

"I figured. Better your ex than your current, if tonight's behavior is anything to go by."

"It isn't, actually. In the twelve years I've known him, I've never seen him like this." She couldn't help rushing to his defense, even though she had no desire to tell Lucas why today was such a rough one for Simon. If she did, she'd have to admit that it was an awful day for her, as well. And while she could see herself being friends with her boss, it was hard enough to live through today without actually having to talk about it.

Before she could say any more, they stopped in front of Simon's apartment complex. Lucas helped her wrestle him into the elevator. "You sure you're going to be okay?" he asked, before stepping into the lobby.

"Of course. I'm going to get him settled and then

watch him for a little while, make sure he's metaboliz-
ing everything okay."

Lucas nodded. "All right, then. I'll see you at work
tomorrow."

As the car quickly ascended the twenty-one floors,
Simon groaned and clutched at her. "Make it stop, for
the love of God."

"Are you going to be sick?" She tried to step away
from him.

"I don't know. Everything's spinning."

"Yeah, you're going to be sick." She fished in
his pockets for his keys, and as soon as the elevator
stopped, she hustled him out and down the hall. He was
so unsteady on his feet that she ended up half carrying
him to his apartment. As soon as she got the door un-
locked, he lurched toward the bathroom.

She made sure he got their safely, then turned around
and headed to his kitchen. If he had any hope of functioning in the morning, he needed to drink water—and
lots of it—before he went to bed.

After filling up a large glass and grabbing some ibu-
profen to go with it, she wandered back to the bathroom, where Simon was leaning weakly over the toilet.
"You doing okay?" she asked.

The sound of him getting sick again was her only
answer.

Leaving him to it, she went into the bedroom and
turned down his bed. A couple of minutes later, she
heard the water running in the bathroom down the hall
and went to help him.

She managed to get him into bed, but he turned his
head away when she gave him water.

"You need to drink," she told him in her best doctor's voice.

Finally, he did, draining the glass in one long gulp. Putting it on the nightstand, or trying to, he whispered, "Sorry about this, Mandy." His words were still slurred. "I didn't mean for you to see me like this."

She shook her head. "What were you thinking, Simon?"

"Didn't want to think," he mumbled. "Hurts too much."

Her heart broke a little for him, for this man who always, always, always stayed in control. For him to get this drunk—and in public—he had to be hurting as much as she was. She felt bad for all the terrible things she'd thought about him throughout the day. He hadn't forgotten Gabby's birthday. He'd been using it as another tool to torture himself.

She started to move away, but his hand snaked out, his fingers wrapping around her wrist. "Stay with me."

"I'm not going to leave you here alone," she assured him. "I'm just going to go in the other room. Let you sleep."

"Stay with me," he repeated, tugging at her until she gave in and sat by the side of the bed.

"Okay. I'll stay until you sleep."

He awkwardly maneuvered both of them until she was spread out on the bed next to him. "Sleep with me."

"Simon…"

He kissed her cheek so sweetly that she wondered if he had somehow sobered up, but a quick look in his eyes told her he was as intoxicated as ever. "Stay with me, Mandy." He rested his head in the curve of her neck. "Please. Don't leave me here alone."

She never had been able to resist him when he put his mind to it. Eventually, she nodded and he curled himself around her. "So cold," he whispered, shivering.

She pulled the comforter over him. She might die of heatstroke, but if it made him feel better—

He kicked the cover off. Then, with another long shudder, drifted off to sleep. As she lay there long into the night, listening to him breathe, it occurred to her that when he'd complained of the cold, he hadn't been talking about the temperature.

CHAPTER SIXTEEN

SIMON SURFACED SLOWLY from a sleep so deep it bordered on unconsciousness. His mind was sluggish, his body heavy, and he had no idea where he was. He remembered taking the day off work and drinking himself into oblivion, remembered walking down the street to the bar when he ran out of liquor in his apartment. But everything after his first mojito was a blur.

What had he done last night? he wondered a little frantically. And why wasn't his head throbbing the way it should be? It wasn't pleasant, but no one was wearing clogs and doing the cha-cha, either, which was probably more than he deserved.

Cracking his eyes open a little, he breathed a sigh of relief when he realized that he was in his own bed. So whatever he'd done, it couldn't have been that bad if he'd managed to find his way back to his apartment. He sat up slowly, and only years of controlling…everything…kept him from yelping in surprise.

He might be in his own place, but he was wrapped around Amanda. She was asleep, as dead to the world as he'd been moments before. But what was she doing here? In his bed? And how could he have been so drunk that he didn't remember?

A quick glance under the covers told him they were both fully dressed, which meant nothing had happened—thank God. He couldn't imagine not being able to remember making love to Amanda. But still, how had she gotten here? Why had she come?

Moving as quietly as he could, he slid out of bed and walked to the bathroom. It tasted as if something had crawled into his mouth and died overnight, and he was dying to brush his teeth. But the second he flipped on the light, his head exploded. Actually blew up at the same time that shards of glass stabbed into his brain. That had to be it—there was no other explanation for the pain.

Eyes closed, he fumbled the light off and immediately the pain got better. He brushed his teeth with his eyes half-closed, then went into the bedroom with the intent of crawling into bed with Amanda again.

He might not know what she was doing there, but that didn't mean he wasn't going to enjoy every second of it.

Except, when he glanced at the bed, she was sitting up and stretching, which did amazing things for her breasts. It was a view he took full advantage of, despite the headache brewing in the back of his brain. And as he walked closer, he wanted nothing more than to take one of her strawberry-red nipples in his mouth—through her blouse, if necessary.

He loved the little sound she made in her throat when he did that.

"You're awake," he said, parking himself on the mattress next to her.

"So I am." Her hand reached out and smoothed his hair back from his face. He figured he looked an awful lot like a wild man right now, but the tenderness in her eyes said that didn't matter.

"I'm sorry." At her inquiring look, he continued, "If I did anything last night to offend you. I don't remember what happened. I don't even know how I got here, let alone how you did."

She smiled. "Yeah, well, you were so drunk I'm shocked you remembered your own name for a while there. I found you in a bar, so wasted you could barely function. My friend and I brought you back here."

He groaned. "Oh, God, I'm sorry. Did I embarrass you?"

"I think he understood."

It took a second for what she'd said to register, but when it did, he felt his heart stop. "He?"

"Lucas. My boss. He took me out for a drink, since I looked so beat last night."

He didn't like the sound of that, didn't want her boss or any other man anywhere near her, but he knew better than to say anything. Yet. Besides, there were more important things for them to talk about.

"I should have called you. I meant to. I swear, I did. I just—" He sighed. "I couldn't. It was a bad day."

"Yeah." She nodded, reaching her hand out to squeeze his. "I know."

"I miss her, Amanda. I miss the way she used to tell those corny jokes. Remember? 'What did one bone say to the other bone?'"

The sound she made was half laughter, half sob. "'We have to stop meeting at this joint.'"

"Yeah." He shook his head. "I miss the way she was

always decorating something, making it prettier...and pinker."

"Including your favorite belt."

"Exactly. I yelled at her for that."

"Because she deserved to be yelled at." She scooted closer, until her head rested on his chest. "You can't second-guess every second of your time with her. For years, she was a typical, mischievous little girl—one who got in trouble sometimes. There's nothing wrong with that."

"There wasn't enough time. I didn't let there be enough time," he corrected himself. "I missed so much."

Amanda didn't say anything to that, but then, what could she? He had been an absentee father for Gabby's whole life. Wishing it was different wouldn't change anything. It wouldn't give him back all those birthdays he'd missed. Nor would it put him by Gabby's side the day she died.

Nausea welled up inside him, but it had nothing to do with the alcohol and everything to do with the many ways he'd failed his daughter—and her mother. He'd loved both of them more than anything, and he hadn't been able to handle that. Hadn't been able to tolerate the loss of control, and in the end, they'd all paid for his weakness. He'd lost both Gabby and Mandy.

Self-loathing overwhelmed him and he turned his head away from Amanda. God, some days he wished he could just shed this body of his. Slip out of his skin into nothingness. It would be better than spending his life trying not to see his own reflection in the mirror. Anything would.

Amanda reached up, turned his head to face her. "You have to let it go, Simon."

"I can't." He choked the words out.

"You have to. Or you're going to end up destroying yourself just as surely as I have. Isn't that why you came to Africa? To save me? Don't you think you deserve the same courtesy?"

"You didn't do anything wrong. You fought for her every day. All I did was run away."

"I failed."

"What?"

"I've spent my whole life making sure I never failed at anything. Even the patients I lost were ones who were so far gone when they got to me that I couldn't save them. Yet I couldn't save Gabby. No matter what I did, no matter what doctor I called or what treatment I tried, I couldn't make her better. I failed at the one thing I wasn't supposed to fail at."

Shock ricocheted through him. "Is that what you think? Mandy, you did everything you could."

"And it still wasn't enough. So, obviously, I missed something, let something slip. If I'd known sooner, if I'd tried a little harder, Gabby would still be—"

"No. That's not true. Sometimes people die, no matter what you do."

"Or what you don't." There were tears on her cheeks when she cupped his face in her hands. "She didn't die because you weren't there, Simon. In fact, I think she held on longer than she might have because of you."

"At her funeral, you said—"

She put her fingers over his mouth. "I said a lot of stupid things that day. I couldn't see past my own grief and pain to yours. Were you wrong to leave Gabby at the end? Yeah, I think you were. Do I understand why you did it? Yes. And I think, so did she. One of the last things she told me was not to be mad at you. That we were going to need each other.

"She's probably angry at me—I've done a lousy job of following her advice so far. God knows, she was full of instructions that last week."

He laughed. "That sounds like her. She was a bossy one."

"She took after her dad."

"Yeah, right. I'm the bossy one in the family." He sobered quickly as he realized what he'd said. He glanced at Amanda, tried to gauge if he should backtrack, but she was smiling.

"I'm glad you finally admit it."

"That's not quite what I meant."

"Yes, well, you said it. And I'm choosing to take you at face value."

"Amanda."

"Yes?" She looked at him, her face as serious as his tone had been. In that moment there was so much he wanted to say to her, so many feelings welling up inside of him, that he didn't know where to start. Didn't know how to tell her everything he felt.

In the end, he lowered his mouth to hers and kissed her with all of the rioting emotions inside of him, hoping like hell that she understood everything he was trying to say.

AMANDA MELTED AT THE FIRST touch of Simon's lips on her own. Rolling over for better access, she wrapped her arms and legs around him until she couldn't be certain where she stopped and he began. Exactly how she liked it.

She ran her fingers over the early-morning stubble on his jaw, smoothed them over his soft lips, then shifted so she could tangle them in the too-long hair at the base of his neck. Only then did she give herself over to the kiss, to him and the emotions that were ripping at every hidden scar she had.

This was a bad idea. She knew it. It was too much, too soon, too everything, and yet she was going to do it, anyway. Because Simon needed her and she needed him and there was no way she was going to walk away now. Not when she wanted this so bad.

Simon might have initiated the kiss, but she took over in the space of one heartbeat. He felt so good that she wanted nothing more than to lie here with him forever. Savoring him and this moment of absolute accord between them.

Her lips moved against his and she explored him, slowly, not like the other times when she tried to take as much of him as she could before she came to her senses. This time, she wasn't going to do that. She was going to savor every second of it.

Opening her mouth, she swept her tongue along his lower lip. Softly, sweetly, asking, not demanding. She felt the curve of his lips that told her he was smiling.

She toyed with the lush fullness of his lower lip before moving on to the sweet indention in the middle of his upper one. She felt him grow hard against her, reveled in the way every one of his muscles tightened as she teased the corners of his mouth.

He opened for her like he always did. She loved it, had always loved the way he responded to her. Just like she'd always loved him.

The realization swept through her and for a moment she wanted to run away, to hide. Being here with him, loving him again after all those months of pain and anger, made her feel naked, exposed in a way she couldn't stand.

At the same time, though, it felt good not to hide from him, or herself, anymore. And just because she loved him didn't mean she was expecting anything to come from this. She knew better. Simon would be with her until the next big story, and then he would be off again. Twelve years had taught her that much.

But that didn't mean that she couldn't enjoy what they had now, she told herself, sliding down his body to lick at his flat, muscular abs. He groaned, tangling his hands in her hair, and she grinned against his stomach. Lowered her mouth to skim his navel, then moved lower still, making sure not to touch where he wanted her most.

It was a game they'd played long ago, Amanda driving him as crazy as she could without actually taking him in her mouth, and it amazed her how quickly it came back to her, even after all this time. "Mandy, baby," he told her in a voice gone husky with desire, "please. Not now. I need you. I need this."

His plea shot straight to the heart of her, and she couldn't resist—she took him in her mouth, reveling in the way his hands clutched at her hair, his body moving restlessly against her.

She pulled him inside her mouth, sucked and

stroked, licked and laved, until he was pleading with every breath he took. Only then did she take him deep. He stiffened, groaned, then pushed her away.

"I CAN'T TAKE ANYMORE," he told her hoarsely.

"That's the point, isn't it?" She reached for him again.

It wasn't the point, not for him, not this time. It felt so good to have Amanda back in his arms that all he wanted was to hold her, love her. And when he came, he wanted to be deep inside of her. He was smart enough to know that after twelve years and a dozen countries, this was probably their last chance. Because of that, he wanted to brand her, mark her, hold her to him forever. He couldn't stand the idea of losing her, not again.

Leaning forward, he took her mouth with his own, using his lips and tongue to arouse her—to soothe her—in a way he never had before. He wanted her, God did he want her, but even more overwhelming than the desire blasting through him was the tenderness he felt for her.

He nipped at her lower lip, reveling in the sexy moan that followed, and sucked it into his mouth.

She went wild, her body bucking against him. Wrenching her mouth from his, she skimmed her lips down his neck and over his shoulder, and he shuddered with the effort it took to restrain himself when he wanted nothing more than to lose himself in her forever.

Reaching up, he cupped her face in one of his hands and just looked at her. From the little lines starting at the corner of her glorious eyes to the small scar that ran along the edge of her jaw to the random scattering of freckles that decorated her nose, he memorized her. Pulled her face, pulled *her,* deep inside him. Whenever reporting in some messed-up place got to him, whenever his guilt over Gabby threatened to overwhelm him, he would pull up this memory and remember that there was good in the world.

She'd always been a little shy, a little self-conscious, so he was afraid she'd pull away. Instead, she lay very still and let him look his fill. And, he realized with a little surprise, watched him as intently as he was watching her.

When his need to be inside her was nearly overwhelming, he moved over her so that every part of her body was covered by every part of his. He wanted to feel her everywhere.

Bending forward, he kissed the softness of her lips, the corners of her mouth. She was like the richest, smoothest velvet.

He wanted to be gentle, to give her the tenderness she both needed and deserved. But the moment her tongue tangled with his, he was lost. Lust rose, sharp and terrible and all-consuming. He ignored it, beat it down, kissed her some more. He was unwilling to give up her lips, unable to break the connection when everything inside of him clamored to be a part of her. To make her a part of him. He didn't lift his mouth until she whimpered, gasped for air.

Using his free hand, he pushed her shirt up, then slowly pulled the garment over her head so that he could see her small, round breasts and beautiful rose nipples. She was amazing, glorious, and as he ran his tongue around her areola, he had only one thought in his mind. To make her his, once and for all.

Then he forgot everything but the ecstasy of being with her as he licked and kissed his way over every inch of her body. He explored the curve of her shoulder, the bend in her elbow, the back of her knee. Then tickled her ribs with his tongue before moving between her legs and tasting her. Claiming her.

He slid his tongue over her sex, once, twice, loving the spicy scent and taste of her. Slipped inside of her and stroked her as her hands clutched at his hair, his shoulders. When he ran his tongue over the hard button of her clit, she sighed and moaned.

And then, with a quick flick of his tongue and a stroke of his fingers, he brought her to climax. Pulling back, desperate to see her, he worked his thumb over her, intensifying Amanda's orgasm even as he watched her take her pleasure. Her back bowed, her hips moved languorously against his hand, and her skin flushed a pretty pink that called to him, urging him to take all of her.

He was hard to the point of pain, but he wasn't ready to give up the view quite yet. Not when she was spread before him like a feast.

When she finally stilled, he spread her legs a little wider, then simply looked at her. Trailed a finger over the warm, slick folds, reveling in the feel of her desire for him.

"Simon!" It was a plea and they both knew it. "I want you."

"You have me," he murmured, sliding first one finger and then another into her, nearly losing it at the unbelievable perfection of her body. She was tight, hot, her muscles clenching his finger in a rhythm that resonated all the way to his erection.

Suddenly he knew he couldn't take any more. Rolling onto his back, he reached into the nightstand by his bed and pulled out a condom. After rolling it quickly down his cock, he pulled Amanda over him and, with his hands on her hips, gently guided her onto him.

She cried out as he sank into her, arched her back and clutched at his hands until he twined his fingers with hers. Something about that connection, that joining of Amanda's hands with his as she rode him, sent him right to the edge of his control.

Fighting to hang on, never wanting the feeling to end—never wanting the closeness between them to dissipate—he clung to sanity even as her breath grew quicker and her movements more frantic. He reveled in the feel of her around him, rejoiced in the slight pressure of her warm weight on his stomach as she slowly moved herself up and down him.

"Simon," she moaned breathlessly and he knew it was a plea, knew she was close to shattering again. And he loved it.

She gasped, arched, and he whispered, "Come for me, baby. Let me feel you."

And she did, her back arching as the waves exploded through her. Her sex clenched him again and again, pulling him deeper. Taking him home.

At the last minute, she leaned down and brushed her lips over his as her crazy, smoky eyes looked deep into his own. That was all it took, those moments of connection so deep and profound that he couldn't help feeling they would be tangled together forever.

With a moan, he let himself go and gave her everything he had inside of him. Everything he had to give.

CHAPTER SEVENTEEN

SEVERAL MINUTES LATER, Amanda stirred against him. "I've got to get up. I have to be at work by nine."

He wrapped his arms around her waist, held her long, lean body against his for a little longer. "Call in sick," he said. "We can stay in bed all day."

"It's only my second week. That doesn't seem like the most optimum way to keep my job."

"And that's what you want?" he asked, lifting his head to look at her. "To continue working at that clinic?"

She smiled at him, and in her face he saw shades of the old Amanda. The woman he had fallen in love with so long ago, and whom he'd thought was lost to him—and the world—forever.

"I really do. It's different than For the Children, but I think it was time for a change. Here, I can really help, you know? I can get to my patients before they're bloated from hunger or wasting away from an illness twenty dollars of antibiotics could cure. Here, I don't have to hold babies dying of AIDS, knowing there's nothing I can do for them.

"Besides, so many of the people I help don't have insurance or enough money to pay for a doctor in a regular office. They can't be seen anywhere else—and I like that I can help them."

It was the most passionate Amanda had sounded in a long time and it made him happy in a way he hadn't felt in years. He thought about what had just happened between them—not only the lovemaking but the conversation that had come before—and wondered if any of it would have been possible just a few weeks earlier. He doubted it, which meant he owed Lucas and his clinic big-time.

Which wasn't to say he wouldn't deck the bastard if he kept sniffing around Amanda. Gratitude only got a guy so far, after all.

Leaning forward, he brushed a kiss against her lips, then went back for a second and a third. It felt good to hold her again, without all the pain and angst between them. They'd always share Gabby's loss, always have that sorrow between them, but for the first time since Gabby's death, he felt hope.

Amanda's hands crept down his chest to his stomach, and he groaned as he caught them with his own. "We need to go. Since you're so fond of that job of yours, we have to get you there on time. I assume you don't have a car here?"

"You assume correctly."

"Then let's take a quick shower. I'll run you by your house so you can change before I take you to work." When she didn't move, he lifted an eyebrow. "Okay?"

She nodded and he got the feeling that he wasn't the only one having trouble talking. "More than okay."

"Good." Because he couldn't resist, he kissed her breathless one more time. Then pulled away with a satisfied grin and said, "Last one in the shower washes the other's back."

Amanda was off the bed in a flash, and in the bathroom before he was even halfway across the room.

Lucky him.

FOUR HOURS LATER, he wasn't feeling so lucky. In fact, as he pulled into the clinic's parking lot, he wondered if he'd even find Amanda here or if she'd gone out to lunch. He'd hoped to take her himself so that he could explain about the assignment that had just come up, but time had gotten away from him. That happened when you had to drop everything and prepare to leave the country with just a couple of hours' notice. Which normally he would have loved. But now, as things between him and Amanda were getting on track, not so much.

But when he walked in the clinic—a run-down building with a packed waiting room and nowhere near enough staff for the demand—he saw her right away. She was standing behind the front counter talking to an elderly African-American woman. About her medicine, he guessed, judging from the samples in the older woman's hands.

"You need to go to the window over there if you want to see the doctor," the woman behind the desk said, pointing to a long line at the other end of the counter.

"I just need to speak with Dr. Jacobs for a second—"

"Then you need to go get in that line over there." She turned away and began working on a file.

"But I'm not a patient. I wanted to—"

"Tell it to the nurse," she said, not bothering to look up.

"It's okay, Latonya." Amanda came up and rescued him. "He's my…"

Both Latonya and Simon looked at her, waiting to see how she was going to finish that sentence, though Simon figured he had a little more invested than the office manager.

"Friend," Amanda finally said, after a long pause. "He's my friend."

Friend? Simon scowled at the description, but didn't correct her.

Stepping around the counter, Amanda asked, "What are you doing here?"

"I had a little time this afternoon and thought I'd see if you were available for lunch."

"Lunch?" she asked, as if the concept was completely foreign to her.

"You know, that meal you eat around midday," he told her, exasperated. "Amanda, for someone who promised to take better care of her health, skipping lunch isn't exactly the best move."

"It's not that. I guess I'm used to meeting you somewhere instead of having you come here." She glanced at her watch. "I'm supposed to go to lunch in fifteen minutes. Do you mind hanging out for a little while?"

"Not at all."

"Great. I have two more patients to see and then we go."

It was closer to thirty minutes when she finally showed her face in the front again, but Simon didn't mind. The extra time had given him a chance to arrange the last of the details for the trip. After lunch, he'd stop by his apartment for the bag he always kept packed and then head straight to the airport. He shook his head. It was selfish of him, but he really couldn't help wishing the Middle East had waited a little longer before imploding.

"So, where do you want to go?" he asked Amanda as they walked outside.

"There's a good sandwich place a couple of blocks up," she answered. "You want to try it out?"

"Sure." He wanted to hold on to her hand, but didn't know how she'd feel about that—especially in her place of work. At the same time, he wanted her boss to know that the field was not clear. He might be disappearing for a couple of weeks, but he had no intention of giving Amanda up—not when he'd finally gotten her back again.

In the end, he didn't have to do anything, because Amanda looped her arm through his as they walked through the small parking lot to the street. "I'm glad you came by," she told him, resting her head on his shoulder for a brief second.

"Oh, yeah? Why is that?"

"Do I have to have a reason? Maybe I like spending time with you."

He liked that, a lot.

They chatted about random things for the rest of the walk—the humid weather, a movie they both wanted to see, places to go in the city. It wasn't until they were seated in the restaurant, and had placed their order, that he finally broached the subject of his trip.

"I need to tell you something." He watched with concern as her smile dimmed.

"When do you leave for the Middle East?" She made

a face at his confusion. "What? You think we don't have a TV at the clinic? I knew as soon as I saw the bombings that you'd be off to Lebanon before the day was over."

"I leave in two hours—charter flight."

She nodded. "Take care of yourself over there."

"That's it?" He knew he probably looked ridiculous the way he was staring at her, mouth open in astonishment.

"I'm not sure what you expect. A big-band send-off?"

"I thought you'd be…angry, I guess."

"Because you're doing your job?" she asked incredulously. "Come on, Simon. I'm not that kind of lover. You know that. I've never gotten angry at you for doing your job—"

"I remember differently."

"No. I got angry when you used your job to run away from a reality you didn't like. When you took on extra stories or special reports to get away from problems we were having, or Gabby's illness, or whatever it was you couldn't control. It's not the same thing."

He blanched to hear her speak so matter-of-factly about his biggest shame. "This isn't like that. I swear."

"I know." She leaned back to let the waitress put their food on the table. "Go do what you need to do, Simon. I'll be here when you get back. Just don't forget to call me this time—at least twice, so I know that you're okay."

"You could always watch my broadcasts," he said, tongue-in-cheek. He couldn't believe how happy her easy acceptance made him.

"I always do. Your broadcasts are what made me fall for you all those years ago. They show the best part of you, the one you try to keep hidden the rest of the time." She winked at him, then popped a potato chip in her mouth right before changing the subject.

THREE WEEKS LATER, Amanda wasn't feeling so accepting. Simon had been gone for twenty-two days—the Middle East kept getting hotter—and except for the first day, to tell her he'd gotten there safely, he hadn't called. That annoyed her, even as it worried her. If she hadn't been able to see his updates on television every night, she probably would have been beside herself.

As it was, every time she saw him she felt a rush of relief that he was safe, followed by an overwhelming surge of anger she couldn't ignore. Each night that passed without a phone call, a text, an email, made her just a little bit angrier—at Simon and herself.

She'd thought he—and their relationship—had changed. She knew they were at the beginning stages of learning how to be a couple again, but she'd thought she'd made her expectations clear. She expected to be kept in the loop this time, to be more than a convenience when he passed through town.

Her expectations had obviously been too high, and that was her fault. Completely.

But the fact that he was being an ass and not calling, that was all on Simon. It was hard to hide their true natures when they'd known each other so long. He knew that she was terrified of failing, and she knew that after sliding from foster home to foster home as a child, Simon was as terrified of growing attached to someone.

That didn't mean she was willing to put up with it. Not anymore. If they were going to form a lasting relationship, they would both have to learn to call each other on their shit. Otherwise, this would never work.

The fact that she was thinking of this thing between them as permanent—or even semipermanent—surprised her a lot. Two months ago, she would no more have considered getting serious about Simon than she would have dreamed about being happy again.

But sometimes, two months made a big difference in your life—and especially in how you viewed the world. She still missed Gabby terribly, still thought of her a million times every day, but she no longer wanted to climb into the grave beside her daughter.

And she no longer resented Simon. Oh, she was pissed as hell at him for not finding a way around his own neuroses and calling her, but she wasn't going to use it as an excuse to put distance between them. Not this time. She was going to hang tight—after she gave him a piece of her mind. But if he ever did this again, after she educated him, there would be hell to pay.

She was climbing into her car at the end of the day when her phone rang. Ignoring the stupid jump her heart gave every time she heard it go off, she almost let it go to voice mail. She just wasn't up for the whole charade of feeling her stomach quiver as she looked at the caller ID, hoping it was him and then being disappointed.

In the end, though, she reached for the phone and clicked it on right before it went to voice mail. She didn't bother to look at the screen and see who it was—if it was a telemarketer trying to sell her beachfront property in Arizona, then she so deserved it.

"Hello?" The line popped and crackled, and that's when she knew. It was no telemarketer.

"Mandy!" He laughed delightedly. "I didn't know if I was going to get you. I thought you might still be working."

"I just got off, actually."

"Excellent. So how are you? How's the clinic? How's the house?"

"Everything's good." She knew she sounded a little stilted, and forced herself to relax. He'd called, she reminded herself. That was what mattered.

Yes, but it took twenty-two days for him to do it, which wasn't exactly the stuff great love songs were made of.

"How are you?" she asked. "I watch you every night after I get home. How'd you get that black eye?"

He laughed exuberantly, and she could practically see him. Head thrown back, green eyes sparkling. "There was a mild disagreement over a taxi."

"I thought it looked like a fist had put it there." No way would she let him know how relieved she was that he was okay. He didn't need to know how much she worried when he was gone. It would only make things worse between them.

"Everything else okay?" she asked. "There's so much violence in your reports…"

"Everything's fine," he told her. "We're being careful." Then his voice dropped, got all husky, and it was the sexiest thing she had ever heard. "I miss you so much."

"I miss you, too." And then, because she couldn't not ask, she said, "I thought you'd call me more often."

"You told me to call you twice. That's what I'm doing. This is call number two."

"When I said that, I didn't realize you'd be gone for three weeks. I was thinking more like ten days or so."

"Oh." A pause. "I screwed up again, didn't I?"

Hearing the rueful note in his voice made the annoyance of the past couple of weeks disappear. And technically, he was right. "You did fine. I just miss you."

"That's what I like to hear. And that's why I'm calling, actually. We're flying out late tonight. I should be home by tomorrow evening, if all goes according to plan."

She grinned. She couldn't help herself. Simon was coming home. "Do you need me to pick you up from the airport?"

"Nah. Not unless you want to."

"I want to. What time?"

"I'll call you when we stop for fuel in Paris. Let you know what time to expect me."

"Wow. That will be three calls."

"Indeed it will. So, tell me, what have you been up to while I've been gone? What have you done with the house?"

"A lot, actually. Without you here to distract me, I was able to work every night."

"Sorry about being a distraction." Except, he didn't sound sorry. He sounded delighted.

"I can tell." She closed her eyes, pictured his piercing green eyes and wicked grin. Felt a tug of longing deep inside her. God, she missed him. And now that she knew when he was going to be home, the next twenty-four hours would drag on forever.

Since he seemed to really want to know about the house—and how cool was that?—she said, "I finished the master bathroom—I tiled it myself, ripped out the wallpaper and painted it a complementary blue to the bedroom. Had the mirrors replaced and repainted the cabinets. It looks good."

"Excellent," he repeated. "So, what's next?"

"I'm starting on the front parlor and guest bath downstairs. Then the dining room. I figure it will keep me busy for the rest of the month." And give her some-place to entertain. The fact that she could think about having people over showed how far she'd come in the past couple of weeks.

She smiled, proud of herself.

"And how's work?" he asked. "Still saving the world?"

"One patient at a time. How about you? When I see you on TV, you look tired."

He paused, and she knew him well enough to know he was running his hand over his face as he tried to choose the perfect words.

"Don't censor yourself," she told him. "Tell me."

"It's bad. It's really bad. They've bombed the shit out of this place and it had barely gotten back on its feet after the last peace talks broke down. The worst part is there's nowhere for the civilians to hide. Everything is fair game." She heard what he didn't say in the de-feated tone of his voice.

"I'm sorry."

"So am I. I swear, sometimes I think I'm getting too old for this shit."

Her heart stuttered a little, but she forced the relief down where it came from. One stray comment did not mean Simon and his wandering feet were planning on staying close to home. Only that he was tired of living in a war zone and needed a break for a little while.

Still, after they hung up, she couldn't help wondering if this was it. She was here in Atlanta, with no plans of moving anywhere else. Definitely not to go back to Africa. Simon was also here, and if he decided to settle down, take a job behind the news desk…things could really change for them.

The happiness that came with that realization gave her pause. Was she actually contemplating trying to forge a life with Simon? Again? Last time, it had blown up in their faces. Badly. Did she want to take that risk again?

Of course, it might be a little late to be asking herself that question, considering how excited she was about him returning home. What had started out in Africa all those weeks ago—a rescue mission on his part, a vendetta on hers—had somehow become so much more.

Panic welled up inside her at the thought, but she refused to give in to it. Besides, it wasn't as if her feelings for Simon were new. She'd loved him since those first weeks in Ethiopia all those years ago. Since then, she'd also hated him, been hurt by him, been furious with him.

But under it all, she'd known that her initial feelings had never really gone away. A small part of her still loved Simon. Now, though, she was discovering that it was much more than that. She was crazy about him, despite having enough baggage between them to fill the cargo hold of a 747.

The only question, then, was what was she planning to do about it? If she broke things off now, she knew she'd be all right. Could keep plodding her way back to mental health. But if she held on, if she kept going with this and it didn't work out, she'd be shattered and her battered heart broken into so many pieces she wasn't sure she'd find the strength to start over again.

The smart thing would be to cool things between them. To keep her emotions—and her recovery—on an even keel.

Yet even as she told herself what she needed to do, even as she understood the intelligence of what she was thinking, Amanda knew she wasn't going to take her own advice.

This relationship, this moment, had been twelve years in the making. There was no way she was going to back down now. And if, at the end, all the bricks she'd been so carefully laying ended up shattered around her, well, then, she would know that this time, she had no one but herself to blame.

CHAPTER EIGHTEEN

SIMON STRODE QUICKLY through the airport, leaving the rest of his crew behind—and he didn't even care. All he could think about was seeing Amanda again. Holding her. Making love to her. The past twenty-three days had seemed interminable. For the first time in his life, he hadn't wanted to be on location, doing the job he loved. He'd wanted to be home. With her.

It had taken every ounce of self-control he had not to call her on an hourly basis, just to check up on her. Just to hear her voice.

For a man who prided himself on his control, on his ability to live life on his own terms and no one else's, it was a humbling experience. Not to mention a terrifying one. Which was why he hadn't called her before yesterday. He had been so freaked out by how much he missed her that he'd forced himself to prove he could survive without her.

When she'd dumped him before, he'd had a rough time getting over her. And if he was being honest, he'd admit that he never really had gotten over her. Which was why he wanted to maintain some distance, hold a little bit of himself—of his heart—away from her.

But the second he'd heard her voice the night before, he'd known it was too late. And when she'd asked in that soft, quiet voice of hers why he hadn't called, he'd felt terrible and wonderful at the same time. He hadn't meant to hurt her with his silence—had only been trying to prove to himself that he could still live without her. But the fact that she'd missed him as much as he'd missed her was amazing.

He took the stairs down to baggage claim two at a time, his eyes constantly moving as he tried to spot her. He felt bad dragging her out to pick him up so late at night, but at the same time, he was thrilled that she was here.

He spotted her next to one of the baggage carousels, dressed in a pair of tight jeans and a black shirt that left one of her beautiful shoulders bare. She looked gorgeous and he had to fight the urge to vault over the side of the staircase in an effort to get to her more quickly.

She spotted him as he hit the last steps, and she gave him a shy smile. He leaped toward her, picking her up and spinning her around before claiming her mouth for a kiss.

She gasped in surprise and he took advantage, sliding his tongue deep inside her. She tasted just like he remembered, but better somehow. As if his memory hadn't been able to do justice to her.

When he finally lifted his head, he held her against him for long seconds. "You feel good," he whispered against her hair.

"So do you." Her arms were around his waist, holding him as tightly as he was holding her. "I missed you."

He grinned. "Let's go back to your place, so you can show me just how much."

"I'd like that."

He held her hand the entire way home because he couldn't stop touching her. Couldn't stop wanting her.

The drive was interminable, and by the time they made it into Amanda's driveway, he was wild to have her. Jumping out of the car, he left his suitcase in the trunk and all but dragged her up the stairs to the front door.

The second she opened it, he pounced on her.

Pushing her against the nearest wall, he slammed the door with his foot and then went about devouring her. He kissed her crazily, kissed her crazy, but it wasn't enough. He needed to see her, to touch her—everywhere. Needed to assure himself that she was still safe and whole and as desperate for him as he was for her.

He yanked her shirt over her head, nearly howled when he realized she wore no bra underneath. Bending, he took one small, gorgeous nipple in his mouth and began to suck. She cried out, and he might have thought he was too rough if her hands hadn't burrowed in his hair, holding him to her. Tugging him even closer, if that was possible.

"Simon!" It was a high, keening wail that shot straight through him. "I need you. I need—"

"I know, baby. I know." And then he was fumbling with her jeans, shoving them down her legs while she did the same to him.

By the time she freed him, need was a raging beast within him. His blood was roaring through his veins, demanding that he claim her, that he make her his in the most primitive way possible.

He licked his way up her body, took her mouth in

another kiss that had her moaning even as she tried to shake one leg free of her jeans so that she could mount him. Turning her around, he pressed her full-length against the cool, slick entryway wall. Then he slid his arm around her abdomen, cupped her stomach and canted her backward a little—so that her ass was lifted slightly.

Moving his other hand between her legs, he tested her readiness. She was wet, slick, and he nearly lost it. With a groan, he dipped one finger inside of her, pressed it against her most sensitive spot. She gasped his name, bucked against him, and he took a few seconds more to drive her all the way to the edge.

When she was panting and squirming against him, when she was begging him to take her, he bent his knees and slid slowly, determinedly, into her sex.

"Simon!" She screamed his name, convulsed around him, and he nearly came right there. Probably would have if he wasn't so desperate to give her more pleasure. To give her everything he could.

He was too far gone to take it slow, though, and he rode her hard. Through one climax and into a second. Over and over again, he thrust into her until her whole body was trembling and he was shaking from the strain of holding back.

"Simon, please," she said, her hands reaching back to grab on to his ass, to pull him forward into her with one powerful thrust. It was unexpected and shattered the last ounce of restraint he had. He came with a force that nearly brought him to his knees, pulse after pulse of bliss working its way through him while Amanda cried out, her tight, sweet body orgasming around him.

Suddenly exhausted, he let himself rest against her while he tried to get his breath back. After a minute, she started to laugh.

"You nearly killed me and you're laughing?" he asked, nuzzling her neck. He tried to sound offended, but couldn't do it with aftershocks of his orgasm still ripping through him.

"I was just thinking. Now that you've had dessert, would you like to have the dinner I made you?"

"You made dinner?" He tried to straighten up, but wasn't sure his legs would fully hold him.

"Mmm-hmm. Lasagna."

"I knew there was a reason I loved you," he said, dropping a kiss in the sensitive spot behind her ear.

And then froze as he realized that Amanda had stiffened against him.

EVERY MUSCLE IN AMANDA'S BODY seized up at Simon's words. Happiness bloomed inside her—it had been almost impossible to get him to admit his feelings for her in the old days, so she cherished the easy way he'd said he loved her.

The only problem was, he'd said it because she'd made him lasagna—and not because he was overwhelmed by his feelings for her. So what did that mean? Did he really love her or was he just using it as an expression, something along the ubiquitous "Love ya, babe" that guys uttered all the time without meaning it.

She tried to tell herself that was it, that he hadn't meant anything by the words, but suddenly they were all she could think of. Even as Simon eased out of her and she bent to pull her jeans up, the question reverberated in her head like a gong. Did he love her or didn't he?

And what was she going to do if he didn't, because as she'd waited for him at the airport, as anxious as a kid on Christmas morning, she'd known that her feelings for him weren't going away. They were the real deal and she was stuck with them, but that was no guarantee that he felt the same way.

"Well, that went over well," he said drily as he re-fastened his own jeans.

She didn't know how to answer. The words *I love you, too* trembled on her lips, but she didn't know if she should say them. Didn't know if he wanted to hear them.

Finally she said, "Did you…" She couldn't get anything else out, feeling tentative around him for the first time in many years.

He raised an eyebrow in that wicked, wonderful way of his. "Did I mean it? Absolutely, though I suppose saying it in reference to lasagna might not have been my smoothest move." His words were cool and confident, but she could see the uncertainty in his eyes. It felt strange to realize he was as confused and frightened as she was. But it felt empowering, as well.

Wrapping her arms around him as tightly as she could, Amanda said fiercely, "I love you, Simon."

When she tried to pull back, she couldn't. He was holding her so tightly she could barely breathe.

"I love you, Amanda. More every day I'm around you."

"Lasagna or no lasagna, that's good enough for me." She couldn't stop smiling.

He finally loosened his grip on her shoulders and stepped away. "Speaking of lasagna…"

She laughed. "Come on. I'll feed you."

THE NIGHT PASSED in such a blur that Amanda wondered if she'd be able to remember it all in the morning. Or believe it.

They ate lasagna sitting cross-legged on her kitchen counter, as she still hadn't found a table that she liked. Simon told her about his time in Lebanon, about the civilians who were displaced, injured or killed.

The children hit him hardest, and she thought back to his last two special reports—documentaries on the children of Afghanistan and the Colombian Andes. She'd watched them both and had been touched by his determination to get better conditions and more help for children who couldn't help themselves.

Simon had always been interested in stories about children, but since Gabby's death, it seemed to be his main focus. Another legacy their daughter had left behind.

By the end of dinner, Simon was drooping from jet lag, so she led him upstairs to bed. He drifted off before she did, and for the longest time, Amanda lay next to him and studied him in the dim light from the streetlamp.

He was still as beautiful as the day she'd met him. Time—and grief—had worn more lines in his face, but it looked as if he was going to be one of those men who got better with age. Lucky her.

She reached out a hand to trace his brow, still furrowed in sleep. It smoothed at her touch and she cuddled against him, relishing his warmth despite the steamy Georgia humidity.

She fell asleep like that, holding Simon in her arms, and woke a couple of hours later to find his mouth skimming down her stomach to her sex. He made love to her with a thoroughness that contrasted with his earlier haste and then fell back asleep. Over and over he reached for her through the long night, until she grew concerned that one more orgasm might kill her.

Exhausted, she finally fell into a deep sleep, only to be awakened forty-five minutes before she had to be at work by a steaming mug of coffee and a fresh croissant from the bakery down the street.

"You'll spoil me," she murmured sleepily, reaching up to give Simon a kiss.

"Better late than never," he said, his smile a little lopsided and sad.

Which she couldn't allow—there was no room for sadness or regret in bed with them—so she pulled him down to her and did a much more thorough job of kissing him this time around.

His groan was all the encouragement she needed as she slid slowly down his body to take him in her mouth. "Amanda. I—" Whatever else he was going to say was lost as his hands fiercely gripped her hair.

She stroked his chest, soothed him and then did her best to drive him out of his mind. And judging by his retaliation, she was pretty sure she'd done a good job.

An hour later, she strolled into work, late for the first time since she'd been hired. No one said a word, and she couldn't help wondering if it was because nothing short of Armageddon could wipe the smile off her face.

CHAPTER NINETEEN

AMANDA GLANCED AT THE CLOCK for the fourth time in as many minutes. One more hour. All this week, the days had seemed to drag. The clinic was as busy as usual, but somehow knowing that Simon was waiting for her made the time creep by.

It felt strange to feel like this at her age, especially with a man she'd been involved with in one way or another for the past twelve years. And yet, she wouldn't trade the feeling for the world.

"Seriously, Amanda, if your grin got any goofier, I'd swear you weren't in possession of all your faculties." Lucas shook his head in mock concern as he sat down at the break table to start his own charts. In the past few weeks, they'd fallen into a routine of hanging out together at the end of the day, talking about interesting cases or life or whatever else came to mind.

"Well, we can't all be dour stoics like yourself, Lucas. But if my happiness offends you, then I will do my best to keep it in check."

He laughed. "You know one of the things I most admire about you?"

"My incredible bedside manner?"

"Your ability to tell people to go to hell in the calmest, nicest way imaginable."

"Well, it's no 'bless your heart,' but I try."

"And you succeed." He waggled his eyebrows. "So, where's lover boy taking you tonight?"

"Nowhere."

"Hmm. He's cheap, is he?"

That startled a laugh out of her. "No. He promised to help me tile the guest bathroom. We can't really do that in a restaurant."

"Touché. How's your house coming, by the way?"

"Slowly. But it's coming."

"Well, if you and lover boy—"

"His name is Simon."

"Right. Simon. If you and Simon ever need a hand, let me know. Since I broke up with Stacy a few weeks ago, I seem to have an abundance of time on my hands. Especially since I have another doctor on staff who has considerably lightened my load."

"Yeah, well, it sounds like we need to get you a new girlfriend more than we need to give you a hammer."

"Um, no," he said drily. "There is no *we* involved in my search for lover girl. But thanks for being so concerned."

"You know, my neighbor—"

He put his hands over his ears with a laugh and started saying, "La, la, la, la, la, I can't hear you," as loud as he could.

"Okay, okay. I get the picture."

"I hope so." His eyes gleamed with interest. "That seems to be what people in love do. They try to set up others so that their whole world is bright and cheery."

She rolled her eyes. "Do I look like the bright-and-cheery type?"

"Six weeks ago, I would have said no. But lately, yeah. You kind of do. In fact—"

He broke off at the sound of shots being fired. They both leaped to their feet as screams echoed through the building. Amanda rushed to the door, but Lucas grabbed her and slammed her down onto the floor. He was already reaching for his cell phone.

"Stay down," he hissed at her as he dialed 911. "The shots came from our waiting room."

"We need to go see if everybody's okay," she told him fiercely.

"You need to stay right here until we know if the shooter is gone." Another shot echoed down the hallway. "There's no use in you getting killed, too."

"If someone's shot, they need a doctor!" He held up a hand to quiet her down. The 911 operator must have come on the line.

As he turned his attention to reporting the shooting spree, Amanda managed to get to the door without him noticing. Still on the floor, she peered down the hall, trying to figure out what was going on.

Latonya was on the floor behind the desk, hands covering her head. The cordless phone they used for the office was on the ground beside her, and Amanda could only hope she, too, had thought to dial 911. It was so much easier to get someone to your door quickly if you called from a landline.

Screams rose from the waiting room. There had been three babies under the age of one and a handful of toddlers, as well as older children and adults.

The only mass shooting she'd seen had happened when she was working in Sierra Leone. "Rebels" had come into the village near the hospital and fired on whoever happened to be standing around. By the time she and the other doctors had gotten to the scene, it was too late. Twenty-seven people were dead.

Please, God, don't let today be like that. Please, don't let me walk into that waiting room and see all those people... She couldn't even think the word. Instead, she started down the hallway, staying as close to the ground as possible. If she could see what was going on—

Another two shots rang through the clinic, followed by a bunch of vile words spoken in a rough voice. She heard the bells on the door of the clinic open and shut and then everyone started screaming and crying at once.

She was up and running and hit the waiting room to find three young men, dressed in gang colors, bleeding out on the clinic floor. For one second, she felt a blinding sense of relief—it was a gang thing, not indiscriminate shooting. The babies, the children, were okay.

And then, as she whirled into action, yelling for help, she got her first look at the boys on the floor—no way had the oldest seen his eighteenth birthday yet. Lucas came running, still on the phone with the police. Some patients rushed out of the clinic, while others gathered around to watch as she and Lucas assessed the victims. Two were dead, shot through the head, but one was still alive. He'd been shot twice in the chest and stomach and once in the head, but the last bullet had only grazed his temple.

"He's alive," she told Lucas, dropping to her knees

and trying to assess his wounds. The boy was a mess, the pool of blood growing beneath him.

"We're going to lose him if we don't move," Lucas said grimly, then called for a triage kit.

Lisa, one of the nurses, came running with one.

"Set up an IV," Amanda told her, yanking on gloves as fast as she could. "We need to find where he's bleeding from."

"Where isn't he bleeding from?" Lucas asked, but she was already probing the boy's chest, watching as he gasped and trembled. There was an odd hissing noise and she turned to Lucas. "We need to put in a chest tube—his lung's been punctured."

"How do you know?"

"Get your head down here and listen," she told him, even as she unwrapped the necessary equipment.

"You're going to be okay," she told the boy, who couldn't have been more than fifteen or sixteen. "I know it hurts, but hang in there. Let me do my thing. I'm going to take care of you."

Even as she said the words, she prayed she wasn't lying to him. Prayed that she would have the chance, the ability, to save him.

It had been a while since she'd had to insert a chest tube, but she managed to get it done pretty quickly. Within seconds, the boy was breathing easier, but it didn't seem to matter. Judging by the damage, the bullets had ricocheted inside of him, bouncing off organs as if they were bowling pins, causing massive amounts of bleeding.

She and Lucas managed to get some of the bleeders,

but by the time the paramedics arrived, the boy was in full-blown cardiac arrest. She started CPR, knowing as she did that it was too late. This boy, who hadn't even started shaving yet if his smooth chin was anything to go by, had died on the clinic floor. He'd died because she hadn't been strong enough, fast enough or good enough to save him.

She glanced at Lucas to be sure. He was already shaking his head. Taking off his gloves. She wasn't surprised. Lucas's practicality reminded her a lot of Jack, and she knew how willing Jack was to let a patient go when it was time. Just the idea of giving up hurt her, but the police were moving in, demanding to know if the boy was dead, grumbling about compromised evidence. Lucas helped her to her feet and she went, but she felt numb. Like Mabulu, this boy was one more child she hadn't been able to save.

It didn't seem fair. After eleven years as a doctor in out-of-the-way places, she had lost a lot of patients, sometimes as many as fifteen a day. But she'd never gotten used to it, had never been able to accept it the way other doctors could. She'd started practicing medicine in Atlanta because she'd wanted to work with people she could actually help.

Watching that boy die had brought her right back to where she'd been when she'd left Africa. Had brought home again just what a failure she really was. Right now, a policeman was probably telling his mother about his death.

She shuddered at the thought.

As Lucas led her away, she glanced down. Despite

the gloves, that boy's blood was on her hands. It took every ounce of self-control she had not to curl up and bawl like a baby.

SIMON WAITED IMPATIENTLY on the sidewalk in front of the clinic. He'd freaked out when it came over the wire that there had been a shooting in a low-income Atlanta clinic. When he'd found out that it was the one where Amanda worked, he'd jumped in his car and rushed over, calling her cell the whole way. She hadn't answered, which made the rush-hour drive interminable.

The only thing that had kept him sane was the news that no medical personnel had been injured. But until he saw her with his own eyes, he wasn't going to be satisfied. The cops weren't letting anyone into the building right now—it was a crime scene—and he was about ten seconds from losing his mind.

Where was she? What was she doing? Why wasn't she answering her phone? Desperate, he texted her again, and this time his phone buzzed within a few seconds.

I'm fine. Meet me around the back.

Relief flooded him. He sprinted around the corner and down the alleyway that ran behind the clinic. A cop was stationed outside, but before Simon could try to talk his way past him, Amanda opened the door.

His first sight of her nearly had his legs going out from under him. She was covered in blood—her shirt and pants soaked in some places and splattered in others. It looked as if she had been through a war.

"Simon?" She sounded uncertain, exhausted.

"I'm here, baby." He opened his arms and she walked right into them, burying her face against his neck. "You're not hurt?" He had to ask.

She mutely shook her head.

"Okay, then. Let's get you home. Are you done here?"

"Yeah. I just finished giving my statement."

"Good. I'm parked around the corner. Do you want to wait here while I get the car?"

"I can drive—"

"No, you can't." His tone brooked no argument. "I'm assuming the clinic will be closed for a few days?"

"I think so." Her arms tightened around him, as if she was afraid to let him go.

"You can come with me," he said. "The car's out front."

She glanced down at her clothes and moved away reluctantly. "No reason for me to cause a mass panic on the street when they see all this blood."

"I'll be right back," he promised. "Stay here."

She smiled wanly. "I'll be fine."

Despite her reassurances, Simon wasn't so sure. Her eyes were blank, her skin pale, and he wondered if she was going into shock. It was perfectly understandable if she was. His own heart rate still hadn't returned to normal after the horror of hearing she'd been involved in a shooting.

He sprinted all the way to the car, and was back in the alley no more than three minutes after he left her. Amanda was leaning heavily against the wall, as if it was the only thing holding her up.

She didn't say much more than the bare minimum

on the drive to her house. When he'd asked her what had happened, she'd shrugged, shaken her head. Then told him in very clinical terms everything that had happened. His heart had bled for her, even as he'd felt a sense of relief at finally knowing what had tripped Amanda out so bad.

She was mourning the boy she couldn't save. When a patient died, it always hit her hard, but when she thought she'd had a chance of saving him and he died anyway...she'd never found a way to cope. Some doctors drank, some had indiscriminate sex, some played basketball. Amanda brooded, going over everything she'd done again and again and again, looking for the one thing that might have changed the outcome.

Once he got her upstairs, he sent her into the shower and then went back down to make her some soup and a pot of the herbal tea she liked. He was done before she was, so he put the food on a makeshift tray and carried it upstairs to her.

The shower was still running.

Concerned, he went into the bathroom and found her on the shower floor, knees drawn up to her chest as the water pounded over her.

"Amanda!" He ran to her, yanked the glass door open with one hand while he turned the ice-cold water off with the other. The house's ancient water heater was obviously not up to marathon sessions.

"Come on, baby, let's get you out of there."

She didn't answer, so he pulled her to her feet and briskly dried her off before guiding her into the bedroom and sliding the worn T-shirt she liked to sleep in over her head.

"He was so scared when I got to him. I knew he was in bad shape, but I told him he was going to be okay."

"You did what anybody would do."

"Maybe I placed the chest tube wrong. Maybe I went for the wrong bleeder. I don't know."

"You didn't do anything wrong."

It was as if he hadn't spoken. "There was so much blood. I could have missed something—"

"You didn't do anything wrong."

"He was just a kid. I wanted to help him, but I didn't get to him fast enough. I stayed in the hallway, hiding. If I'd gotten to him sooner—"

"If you'd gotten there sooner, you might be dead. Amanda, I know it hurts, but you can't do this to yourself."

She stopped talking then, but he didn't know if he'd gotten through to her.

Sighing, he walked her over to the bed and got her under the covers, though it was only about nine o'clock.

"I was planning to work on the bathroom tonight," she said plaintively, and it was so off-topic, so unexpected, that he almost burst out laughing.

She was going to be okay. She might not be ready to let the boy go, but mentioning the remodeling was her way of saying that she knew life went on.

"The bathroom can wait until the weekend."

She sighed. "I guess."

He slid the tray over her lap. "Here. Eat your soup."

He wasn't asking and for once she didn't argue. Instead, she shrugged and lifted the spoon to her lips.

When she was finished, she slid down the pillows

and pulled the covers up to her chin. "Stay with me?" she asked.

"As long as you want."

Amanda smiled at that. "Don't make promises you can't keep, Simon."

He started to argue with her, but she turned the light off before he could even begin to mount a defense. "I'm not going anywhere, Amanda," he said fiercely, wrapping his arms around her and pulling her into his chest.

She didn't answer.

CHAPTER TWENTY

AMANDA WOKE ALONE, though when she rolled over she could still smell Simon on the sheets next to her.

Sitting up, she squinted against the bright sunlight and tried to figure out what time it was. The clinic was closed for the next three days at least, until the police finished their investigation, so she didn't have anywhere she needed to be. Which was a problem, because the desire to pull the covers over her head and burrow in was almost overwhelming.

She forced herself to get out of bed. She'd made a promise that she wasn't going to hide anymore, wasn't going to give in to the bad days, and she didn't intend to break it.

Slipping a robe over her nightshirt, she went in search of Simon. She hoped he hadn't left for work already. She wanted to talk to him, to thank him for taking care of her last night when she'd been so out of it.

She needed to do better. She knew that. But since Gabby, she'd had a horrible time dealing with her patients' deaths—especially the young ones. She knew their parents' grief, and it was hard for her to separate herself from it. She'd have to learn to cope or stop practicing medicine, but for now she was going to give herself a break. When she was better, when she'd healed some more, she would deal with it. Until then, she'd concentrate on doing what she'd been doing.

As she walked down the hall, she heard a noise coming from the bathroom below. A noise that sounded very much like a saw. She hotfooted it down there, then watched in disbelief as Simon nailed the baseboards into the wall opposite the sink.

He'd completed a large part of the bathroom while she'd slept. The cabinets were stained. The walls painted. The only thing left to do was to lay the tile and put on the baseboards.

It looked great, but she wasn't sure how she felt about him taking over like that. For her, it wasn't about how fast she got the remodeling done. It was about the process, the slow transformation. How was she supposed to heal herself if he kept stepping in and doing things for her?

"You've been busy," she told him when he stood.

He grinned. "You seemed concerned about the bathroom last night, so I thought I'd take care of it for you. Kind of a surprise."

"I'm surprised, all right."

His smile faded. "What's wrong?"

"Nothing." She shook off her mood. It was no big deal, right? He'd done the bathroom for her because he was being nice, not because he didn't think she could do it. He'd only wanted to help. Any problem stemming from this was *her* problem, not his.

"I'm hungry," she told him. "Are you ready for me to make breakfast?"

"Sure." He trailed her into the kitchen, wrapped his

arms around her waist from behind and placed a lingering kiss on her neck.

See, she reminded herself viciously. No problem at all. She was being overly sensitive. "What do you want?"

He laughed softly, and it sent warm air skimming across her ear. She shivered despite herself. "I have a few ideas."

"I bet you do. But I'm starving." She grabbed a pan and slammed it on the stove a little harder than she'd intended.

Simon let his arms drop, and when she turned to him, he had a strange expression on his face. It annoyed her, even though she was the one who put it there.

"You want French toast?" she asked, walking to the fridge to get eggs and milk.

"Fine with me." He reached into the cabinet above the sink, grabbed two mugs. She watched out of the corner of her eye as he filled them with coffee, then reached into the cabinet above him for the sugar bowl she kept there. Just when had he gotten so familiar with her house? And why hadn't she noticed it before now?

"Do you want strawberries?" she asked.

"Sure. You want me to wash them?"

He was being so agreeable it made her insane. How was she supposed to pick a fight with him if he wouldn't cooperate? Not that she wanted to pick a fight, she assured herself as she started cracking eggs. She hit one so hard that the shell shattered into the bowl.

As she fished around to get the pieces out, Simon came up to her and turned her to face him. "You want to tell me what's really going on instead of taking it out on everything in the kitchen?"

The small smile he gave her—as if he was trying to placate a patient at a mental hospital—only made her feel like a bigger idiot. "I'm being irrational," she said.

He nodded. "A little bit."

"Sorry. I just—I don't know. Everything feels off, since last night. Thanks for being there, by the way."

"I'll always take care of you, Amanda. I promise."

He meant the words to reassure her, but they got her back up all over again. Did he really have so little faith in her that he thought she needed to be taken care of? "That's just it, Simon. I don't want or need you to take care of me."

He reared back as if she'd slapped him. "What does that mean?"

"It means I'm a big girl. I can take care of myself."

"You know, I don't get you." For the first time, she saw a hint of anger slip through his calm facade. "When we were first together, you complained that I was never around. You ended things between us because you said you couldn't count on me—"

"That's not true. I ended things because it wasn't fair to Gabby—"

"Bullshit, Amanda. You ended things because you couldn't take me being gone so much, not because Gabby couldn't. So now that I'm here, trying to do my best to support you—"

"I don't want your help! I can do things on my own."

He laughed, but it wasn't a pleasant sound. "Yeah, right."

Ice slammed through her, made everything about her deadly cold. "Get out."

He stared at her. "What?"

"I said, get out. I don't need, or want, to be with anyone who thinks I'm not capable."

"I never said you weren't capable, Amanda. But everyone needs help sometimes."

"I don't need a part-time knight in shining armor, Simon."

"See. I told you it bothers you that I travel so much. You can never resist a dig."

She ignored him. "What I need is a man who believes I can manage by myself. I don't need one who gets up in the middle of the night to remodel a bathroom that I can do myself. That I wanted to do myself."

"I was trying to help." He stared at her, baffled. "I wanted to do something nice for you."

"Then buy me flowers. Don't undermine what I'm trying to do here, okay?"

"What are you trying to do? You're fixing up a monstrosity of a house that probably should have been razed to the ground. What's wrong with me helping with that?"

She reeled from the pain his words caused. Was that what he saw when he looked around this house, her house? A monstrosity? Something in terrible shape that needed all the help he could give it?

Even worse, was that what he saw when he looked at her? She didn't even know what to say to him.

Just then his cell phone rang. She waited for him to answer, and when he didn't, she whispered, "It could be work."

"It is work. But this is more important right now." Still, he glanced at the phone two or three times before sliding it into his pocket.

"Call them back, Simon. This can wait. I'm going to go get some clothes on."

She walked up the stairs slowly, hearing but not listening to the low murmur of Simon's voice. A trip would be good for him, for them. Give them some time to cool down and figure out what the hell they were doing together. Because there was something wrong here, something that went deeper than a bathroom or a business trip.

When he came into the bedroom a few minutes later, she was dressed in a pair of shorts and a tank top. Since the downstairs half bath was now pretty much done, she planned on tackling one of the others. She'd had all the supplies delivered the week before, so she could jump right in.

"Where are you going?" she asked, before she could stop herself. She'd told herself to play it cool, but it still bothered her when he went into war zones. So much could happen.

"I'm not going anywhere."

She whirled to face him. "What does that mean?"

"It means I think I need to be here right now, don't you? You had a hell of a scare yesterday, we both did, and I think I should stay with you for a while—"

"That's ridiculous, Simon. Go. Do your job."

"It's a job, Amanda. You're more important to me. I don't want to make the same mistakes I did before. If you need me, I want to be here."

All she heard was the doubt. "I don't need you.

That's what I keep trying to tell you." Yes, she'd fallen apart when Gabby died. Yes, she still had a long road back to being a whole person again. But she was going to get there. On her own. Why couldn't he see that? Why couldn't he understand that she needed to take care of herself? She couldn't fail again. She wouldn't fail.

"What's happened to you?" he demanded, stepping back from her.

"What is that supposed to mean? You know everything that's happened to me!"

"You never used to be like this, Amanda. You used to accept help—"

"How would you know? You weren't ever there to offer it. I did everything on my own and was good at it. Why you think you need to come along this time and be the big, strong man, I don't understand. Do you really think I'll ever let myself count on you? After what you did?"

The words were out before she could stop them. Immediately, she knew she'd gone too far. "Simon, I didn't mean—"

"Don't insult either one of us, Amanda. You meant it. Nothing I do is good enough. Everything I say is wrong." He shrugged. "Fine. But you're wrong, too."

He headed for the door.

"Where are you going?" she demanded.

"Afghanistan."

"Typical. The second you can't handle things, you're off and running." Even as she said it, she knew it was a cheap shot.

He was in her face in a second, his eyes absolutely

livid as he backed her against the wall. "Let's get one thing clear. I'm not walking. You're shoving me out the door—you don't get to have it both ways." He leaned down, gave her a brief but searing kiss that had her knees buckling and her brain cells imploding. "I love you, Amanda, but I'm not going to stay here and take this. Not even for you. Call me if you ever get your head on straight."

Then he was gone, stalking out the door without a backward glance. And she was alone, exactly as she'd wanted it.

CHAPTER TWENTY-ONE

IT HAD BEEN A REALLY crappy day. Laying her head down on the table in the break room, which still functioned as her desk since the second storage room had yet to be cleaned out to make her an office, Amanda admitted that every day had been crappy since Simon had left for Afghanistan.

And she had no one to blame but herself.

What had she been thinking, hurling those accusations at him? And why had she freaked out like that? It made absolutely no sense. Sure, she'd been distraught after the shooting but that was no reason for her to take it out on Simon. All he'd been doing was trying to help her.

But why hadn't he understood that that wasn't what she wanted from him, or their relationship? She'd dropped so low, had lost so much—including her faith in herself—she needed to find a way to get back to the capable person she'd been before. And she couldn't do that if he was always swooping in to rescue her. Couldn't fix herself if she always had someone around to fix everything for her.

Was that really so crazy? she wondered. Wasn't it a good thing that she'd finally healed enough to see where she'd gone wrong?

Maybe. But that was no excuse for the way she'd

treated Simon, no excuse for exploiting his weaknesses for her own selfish purposes.

God, when had she turned into such a bitch?

"Hey, whatever it is, it can't be that bad," Lucas said as he walked in. He crossed to her and rubbed a hand up and down her back.

"How would you know?" she mumbled, face still buried in her arms.

"Because nothing is." He tugged on a lock of her hair. "Come on, talk to me."

"You know, you're turning into the big brother I never had," she said, finally lifting her head. "I'm not sure if that's a good thing or not."

He snorted. "Especially since I'm three years younger than you."

"Thanks for pointing that out and making the day a little bit worse."

"Hey, honesty is always the best policy."

"Yeah, I'm not so sure about that."

He sighed. "Screwed it up with lover boy, did you?"

"I think so, yes."

"Call him up, tell him you're sorry. Trust me, guys like that stuff, since it happens so rarely."

"Yeah, well, it's a little difficult right now."

"Oh, yeah? Why is that?"

She reached for the remote control and turned the volume up on the TV as the anchor cut to Simon, live from Afghanistan. "That's why."

"Hmm, I see your point. When is he due back?"

"I don't know. We weren't exactly on good terms when he left."

"So email him. Surely they have the internet, even in Afghanistan."

"It's not that easy. We've been doing this same thing for twelve years now."

Lucas whistled. "Twelve years? And you're going to throw all that away because you can't admit when you're wrong? There's stubborn, Amanda, and then there's stupid."

"I know, I know. That's what I keep—"

She broke off at the sound of gunfire from the TV. Rushing over to it, she watched in horror as the camera fell, hit the ground. She expected it to go black, but it didn't. Instead, it showed Simon and two other Americans diving for cover as gunfire riddled the area. A huge explosion followed and the screen went black.

Seconds later, the regular anchor was back, ashen-faced and obviously shaken. "We apologize for that unexpected, and violent, end to the Afghanistan report. Please know we are monitoring the situation and will provide you with information regarding Simon Hart and his crew as soon as we find out anything." He cleared his throat. "In other news…"

Amanda didn't move as the man went on to talk about the huge dip in the American stock market that day. She just stood there, staring at the screen as every horrible thing that could have happened to Simon played through her head.

Please, don't let him be dead. Please, don't let him be dead. Those six words became her mantra as she watched the TV, waiting to hear something, anything, about the only man she'd ever loved.

"Amanda, sweetheart, why don't you sit down?"

Lucas took hold of her shoulders, steered her toward the table.

"I don't want to sit," she shrieked, shocked that the sound was coming from her. "I need to figure out if he's okay. I need to know—" Not Simon, she told herself. He always got out of these things okay. For years, people who worked with him had joked that he had nine lives. It wasn't possible that he'd used them all up. It wasn't possible.

"Of course you do. But I'm afraid you're going to fall down if I leave you there." He reached for his laptop. "Let's call the station. See what they say."

"I have the number." She crossed to her locker, pulled out her purse and reached for the card Simon had given her weeks before. It had both his cell number and the inside line for the news desk on it.

Lucas handed her the phone, and she dialed with shaky fingers. He couldn't be dead. He just couldn't be.

She all but leaped on the person who answered.

"I'm sorry. We're not at liberty to give out information about Mr. Hart over the phone."

"Please, just let me know if he's okay. That's all I need to know."

"Again, the policy states—"

"Screw the policy! Please, if he's hurt, I need to know."

"Who is this again?"

Amanda repeated her name. "I'm his—" What did she call herself? His girlfriend? His lover? The mother of his child?

"Actually, you're his emergency contact. I looked it up in the computer. I'm sorry, ma'am. We get all kinds calling in, trying to find out information about our reporters."

"Just tell me, is he okay?"

"I'm not sure we know anything yet, but let me put you through to his boss. Maybe John can help you."

Amanda nearly went crazy as she sat there, elevator music playing in her ear, waiting for Simon's boss to pick up. Finally, when she was going to try to get the operator again, a gruff voice came on the line. "John Bradford."

"My name is Amanda Jacobs and I'm a…friend of Simon Hart's. They transferred me to you. Is there any news? Is he—"

"He's alive, Ms. Jacobs."

Amanda sagged with relief. "Thank God."

"But he's been badly hurt. They're taking him to the American base for surgery, but right now I don't know anything more than that." His voice softened. "I'm sorry."

"It's—" She tried to speak, but her mouth was so dry it was impossible to form words.

"Ms. Jacobs?"

She swallowed convulsively. "I'm here. Please, can I leave my number? Will you call me as soon as you hear anything?"

"Of course." He copied down her number, repeated it back to her. "I promise I'll call you as soon as they tell me more about his condition."

"Thank you," she whispered before hanging up.

"He's hurt," Lucas said. It wasn't a question.

"Yes. Bad enough to need surgery, but his boss doesn't know anything more than that right now."

"So, we wait. Do you want me to take you home?"

She stared at him with unseeing eyes, trying to make sense of what he had said. Finally, the meaning sank in and she said, "No. I'm fine."

"You don't look fine." He crossed to the fridge, pulled out a cold soda. "Here, drink this."

"I'm not—"

"Amanda!" He got in her face and stared her down as he popped the top on the drink. "I'm being a doctor here, not your friend. Drink the damn soda. You look like you need the sugar."

She did as she was told, because she knew Lucas was right and it was easier than arguing with him. When she was done, he crouched down beside her, rubbed her back. "Now, do you want to stay here and wait or do you want to go home?"

"I don't know. I can't—" She. Damn it, she was not going to fall apart. Not now. Not ever again. She'd played the role of basket case long enough.

"Neither," she told Lucas. "I'm going down to the network's headquarters to hang out there. I want to know what's going on with Simon as soon as they do."

"They might not let you in," Lucas cautioned.

She grabbed her purse and keys from her locker. "Oh, they'll let me in."

And they did, after an initial argument. She sat in the back of a somber newsroom, and as the night progressed, other relatives of the Afghanistan crew joined her.

It was the reminder she needed—Simon wasn't the only one over there who might be fighting for his life. His cameraman, Mark Villanueva, had died from one of the first gunshots. His wife had left in hysterics, led away by her sister and father. Amanda felt terrible. She'd had dinner with the couple twice since she and Simon had started seeing each other again, and she had liked both of them immensely.

It was dawn before news came in about Simon's condition. He'd been shot in the shoulder, but after the explosion he ended up with shrapnel in his chest and abdomen as well as a concussion. The doctors had managed to remove the bullet and most of the shrapnel, but injuries from the flying debris were severe. It had required several hours of surgery to repair the damage, and though they thought he was going to make it, they were keeping him in ICU for a day before evacuating him via medical flight—at the network's expense— back to the States.

The doctor in her wanted details, but when it became obvious that she was not going to get them, she settled for rejoicing in the fact that Simon was alive. He was alive and he was coming home. For now, that was all that mattered.

SIMON AWOKE IN AN AMBULANCE. He was strapped in, an IV in one arm and a blood-pressure cuff on the other. "Where am I?" he asked in halting Dari, wondering where in Afghanistan he was being taken. He tried to lift his head to look around, but it took more strength than he had. Sinking onto the pillow, he closed his eyes and tried to ignore the pain ripping through his chest.

"Simon?" Strangely, that sounded like Amanda's voice. It couldn't be, but he opened his eyes at the feel of a soft, cool hand on his cheek. She was leaning over him, eyes wide and concerned. "Are you in pain? Do you need more morphine?"

He wanted to say yes, considering it felt as if an elephant was doing the rumba on his chest, but at the same time he wanted to know why Amanda was with him. "Where are we?" he asked, shocked at how hard it was to get those three words out.

"In Atlanta. We're on the way to the hospital. You were injured in Afghanistan—do you remember?"

"Yes." It wasn't something he was likely to forget, watching Mark die. Scrambling for cover himself. Hearing the bomb go off. He shuddered, then regretted the involuntary movement as it set off pain in new places in his body.

"Army doctors saved your life on base, and as soon as you were out of immediate danger, the network had you flown back here for treatment. You're going to be in the hospital for a while." She stroked his hair back from his face, and it felt so good to have her touch him again.

"You okay?" he asked, sure that the last—however the hell long it had been—had been terrible for her.

She laughed, and it sounded a little watery, but she was dry-eyed when she leaned down and kissed his cheek. "I'm going to be fine. And so are you."

"Yeah?"

"Yeah. I love you, too, and I'm sorry I was an idiot. I won't be that stupid again."

He stared at her in disbelief. "Now?"

"What do you mean? Yes, I love you now. I've always loved you."

"No. I mean, you're telling me this now? In an ambulance? When I can't do anything about it?" He winced at the pain caused by talking.

"You don't have to do anything about it." She brushed a kiss over his forehead, then leaned down and pressed the button on his morphine drip. "You just lie there and sleep. I promise I'll still be here when you wake up."

"For how long?" he asked. It was a challenge and both of them knew it.

"Forever, if you'll have me."

He smiled, a little. "I think I can pencil you in."

She laughed. "I was thinking more along the lines of indelible ink."

The morphine started kicking in, and he struggled not to float away. Not quite yet. "Be sure," he told her, though it didn't come out quite as strongly as he wanted it to. "Because this is it. I'm not letting you go this time. No matter how hard you try to push me away. I'm not going anywhere and neither are you."

"Twelve years and you haven't figured that out yet? Jeez, you're even slower than I am."

"I mean it, Mandy—" He was slurring his words, damn it. Hard to be taken seriously when he couldn't even form a sentence.

"Hush, and go to sleep. You can threaten me some more when you wake up."

"Not a threat."

"I know. A promise." She pressed a soft kiss to his lips. "Now hurry up and get well. I am more than ready to get started on our happily ever after."

He closed his eyes and did as the doctor ordered.

* * * * *

HEART & HOME

Heartwarming romances where love can
happen right when you least expect it.

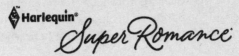

COMING NEXT MONTH
AVAILABLE MARCH 13, 2012

#1764 FROM FATHER TO SON
A Brother's Word
Janice Kay Johnson

#1765 MORE THAN ONE NIGHT
Sarah Mayberry

#1766 THE VINEYARD OF HOPES AND DREAMS
Together Again
Kathleen O'Brien

#1767 OUTSIDE THE LAW
Project Justice
Kara Lennox

#1768 A SAFE PLACE
Margaret Watson

#1769 CASSIE'S GRAND PLAN
Emmie Dark

HSRCNM0212

REQUEST YOUR FREE BOOKS!
2 FREE NOVELS PLUS 2 FREE GIFTS!

Harlequin®

Super Romance

Exciting, emotional, unexpected!

YES! Please send me 2 FREE Harlequin® Superromance® novels and my 2 FREE gifts (gifts are worth about $10). After receiving them, if I don't wish to receive any more books, I can return the shipping statement marked "cancel." If I don't cancel, I will receive 6 brand-new novels every month and be billed just $4.69 per book in the U.S. or $5.24 per book in Canada. That's a saving of at least 15% off the cover price! It's quite a bargain! Shipping and handling is just 50¢ per book in the U.S. and 75¢ per book in Canada.* I understand that accepting the 2 free books and gifts places me under no obligation to buy anything. I can always return a shipment and cancel at any time. Even if I never buy another book, the two free books and gifts are mine to keep forever.

135/336 HDN FC6T

Name _____
(PLEASE PRINT)

Address _____ Apt. # _____

City _____ State/Prov. _____ Zip/Postal Code _____

Signature (if under 18, a parent or guardian must sign)

Mail to the **Reader Service:**
IN U.S.A.: P.O. Box 1867, Buffalo, NY 14240-1867
IN CANADA: P.O. Box 609, Fort Erie, Ontario L2A 5X3

Not valid for current subscribers to Harlequin Superromance books.

**Are you a current subscriber to Harlequin Superromance books and want to receive the larger-print edition?
Call 1-800-873-8635 or visit www.ReaderService.com.**

* Terms and prices subject to change without notice. Prices do not include applicable taxes. Sales tax applicable in N.Y. Canadian residents will be charged applicable taxes. Offer not valid in Quebec. This offer is limited to one order per household. All orders subject to credit approval. Credit or debit balances in a customer's account(s) may be offset by any other outstanding balance owed by or to the customer. Please allow 4 to 6 weeks for delivery. Offer available while quantities last.

Your Privacy—The Reader Service is committed to protecting your privacy. Our Privacy Policy is available online at www.ReaderService.com or upon request from the Reader Service.

We make a portion of our mailing list available to reputable third parties that offer products we believe may interest you. If you prefer that we not exchange your name with third parties, or if you wish to clarify or modify your communication preferences, please visit us at www.ReaderService.com/consumerschoice or write to us at Reader Service Preference Service, P.O. Box 9062, Buffalo, NY 14269. Include your complete name and address.

HSR11

Get swept away with author

CATHY GILLEN THACKER

and her new miniseries

Legends of Laramie County

On the Cartwright ranch, it's the women
who endure and run the ranch—and it's time for
lawyer Liz Cartwright to take over. Needing some help
around the ranch, Liz hires Travis Anderson, a fellow
attorney, and Liz's high-school boyfriend. Travis says
he wants to get back to his ranch roots, but Liz knows
Travis is running from something. Old feelings emerge
as they work together, but Liz can't help but wonder
if Travis is home to stay.

Reluctant Texas Rancher

Available March
wherever books are sold.

New York Times *and* USA TODAY *bestselling author*
Maya Banks presents book three in her miniseries
PREGNANCY & PASSION.

TEMPTED BY HER INNOCENT KISS

Available March 2012 from Harlequin Desire!

There came a time in a man's life when he knew he was
well and truly caught. Devon Carter stared down at the dia-
mond ring nestled in velvet and acknowledged that this was
one such time. He snapped the lid closed and shoved the
box into the breast pocket of his suit.

He had two choices. He could marry Ashley Copeland
and fulfill his goal of merging his company with Copeland
Hotels, thus creating the largest, most exclusive line of re-
sorts in the world, or he could refuse and lose it all.

Put in that light, there wasn't much he could do except
pop the question.

The doorman to his Manhattan high-rise apartment hur-
ried to open the door as Devon strode toward the street.
He took a deep breath before ducking into his car, and the
driver pulled into traffic.

Tonight was the night. All of his careful wooing, the
countless dinners, kisses that started brief and casual and
became more breathless—all a lead-up to tonight. Tonight
his seduction of Ashley Copeland would be complete, and
then he'd ask her to marry him.

He shook his head as the absurdity of the situation hit
him for the hundredth time. Personally, he thought William
Copeland was crazy for forcing his daughter down Devon's
throat.

Ashley was a sweet enough girl, but Devon had no desire

HDEXP0312

to marry anyone.

William had other plans. He'd told Devon that Ashley had no head for the family business. She was too softhearted, too naive. So he'd made Ashley part of the deal. The catch? Ashley wasn't to know of it. Which meant Devon was stuck playing stupid games.

Ashley was supposed to think this was a grand love match. She was a starry-eyed woman who preferred her animal-rescue foundation over board meetings, charts and financials for Copeland Hotels.

If she ever found out the truth, she wouldn't take it well.

And hell, he couldn't blame her.

But no matter the reason for his proposal, before the night was over, she'd have no doubts that she belonged to him.

What will happen when Devon marries Ashley?
Find out in Maya Banks's passionate new novel
TEMPTED BY HER INNOCENT KISS
Available March 2012 from Harlequin Desire!

HDEXP0312